# NIGHTLAND

# NIGHTLAND

## LOUIS OWENS

A DUTTON BOOK

DUTTON

Published by the Penguin Group
Penguin Books USA Inc., 375 Hudson Street, New York, New York 10014, U.S.A.
Penguin Books Ltd, 27 Wrights Lane, London W8 5TZ, England
Penguin Books Australia Ltd, Ringwood, Victoria, Australia
Penguin Books Canada Ltd, 10 Alcorn Avenue, Toronto, Ontario, Canada M4V 3B2
Penguin Books (N.Z.) Ltd, 182–190 Wairau Road, Auckland 10, New Zealand

Penguin Books Ltd, Registered Offices:
Harmondsworth, Middlesex, England

First published by Dutton, an imprint of Dutton Signet,
a division of Penguin Books USA Inc.
Distributed in Canada by McClelland & Stewart Inc.

First Printing, August, 1996
1 3 5 7 9 10 8 6 4 2

 REGISTERED TRADEMARK—MARCA REGISTRADA

LIBRARY OF CONGRESS CATALOGING-IN-PUBLICATION DATA
Owens, Louis.
Nightland / Louis Owens.
p.   cm.
ISBN 0-525-94073-1
1. Racially mixed people—New Mexico—Fiction.   2. Drug traffic—
New Mexico—Fiction.   3. Ranch life—New Mexico—Fiction.
4. Cherokee Indians—Fiction.   I. Title.
PS3565.W567N54   1996
813'.54—dc20                                                96-10405
                                                              CIP

Printed in the United States of America
Set in Bembo
Designed by Jesse Cohen

PUBLISHER'S NOTE
This is a work of fiction. Names, characters, places, and incidents either are the products of the author's imagination or are used fictitiously, and any resemblance to actual persons, living or dead, events, or locales is entirely coincidental.

This book is printed on acid-free paper. ∞

*This book is dedicated to my Aunt Betty, who asked the right questions at the right time, and to my mother and all those Cherokee Baileys who gave her life and stories.*

# 1

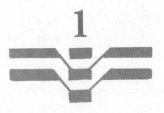

It looked like a black buzzard creased against the western horizon and angling toward him. But then the body twisted and he saw that it was a man, the black form of a man floating from the heavens with outstretched arms. The great arch of New Mexico sky, piled high in all directions with blue-gray thunderheads, held the dark shape, cupping it so that to Billy Keene's eyes the man hung almost suspended between sky and earth. Then an object separated from the body and drifted like a leaf off toward the wooded ridge, and Billy saw the dead spire of the juniper at the same instant the body struck and was impaled, the silvered shaft through belly and back so that the man flailed for a moment and then hung limply, black-suited fish bait against the heavy sky. A snake's tongue forked deep into the mountains, fire leaping from sky to earth and back again.

For long minutes Billy stared at the body, the deer rifle dangling in his right hand and his hat pushed back over his brown ponytail. Below, directly behind the snag of the juniper, the Plains of San Agustin were a wide swath rising up in the blue north to the Bear Mountains and the Gallinas and Datils with their crests drowned in cloud. Against the darkening plain, he could see the twenty-seven massive white dishes of the Very Large Array, and as he watched, the two-and-a-half ton antennas, with a single, painfully slow movement, began to turn their concave faces in his direction.

The body tree stood stark against the land below, its lower branches—like bare, twisted bone—lifted as though offering man to sky and cloud. Blood coursed through cracks in the old wood to darken the central spire, and blood ran from the chest down across the face and onto a gray branch two feet below. Blood made a black line down the branch, pooling against the trunk of the ancient cedar. Lightning flashed behind the first layer of cloud, a wink of light like a switch thrown quickly on and off, followed by a muttering of thunder deep in the sky's throat. The body tree pulsed, and the white faces of the Array leapt from the earth.

Billy pursed his lips and whistled two shrill, hawklike notes. He rested the rifle butt on the toe of his boot and watched the body. After a moment, he whistled again. In the foothills of the Magdalenas, a coyote barked.

"Will!" he shouted. "Goddammit, Will!"

The answer came from directly behind him, scarcely more than a whisper. "It's okay, Billy. I'm right here."

Billy spun to face the big man who had walked out of the sparse piñon and juniper forest at his back. They were identical in height, but the other man was much thicker and heavier through the shoulders and chest, his movements slow and determined. Both wore stained, sand-colored cattleman's hats, faded and ragged Levi's jackets, and blue jeans that fell to the heels of their western boots. Billy's clean-shaven face held thin blades of shadow angling down from narrow green eyes, an inch-long zigzag scar marking one cheek. The other's face was broad and flat-planed, weathered, and dominated by dark brown eyes. Black hair flecked with gray fell straight from beneath the hat to the edge of the turned-up corduroy jacket collar.

"Holy mother of God." Will Striker pushed his hat back, cupped a hand across his forehead, and looked at the tree. His other hand held a scoped rifle with its barrel tilted toward the dry and rocky earth.

"You see him fall?" Billy asked.

Will shook his head. "Didn't see anything at all." In the west a wire-thin band of sun cut across the cloud base and turned the pines of the Magdalena crest into black arrows pointed at the sky.

"All of a sudden he was just up there," Billy said. "Like he was dropped by the Creator himself."

"You didn't see or hear a plane?"

"You think he fell out of a plane?"

Will looked toward the northern horizon. Down on the flat, the dishes of the Array were fully turned, and their white faces held deepening pools. He thought of the pronghorns that would be grazing in the shadows of the radio telescopes. "Probably couldn't have seen a plane in those clouds," he said. "Or heard one, maybe, with that thunder."

"You're saying he fell out of an airplane." Billy frowned and studied his friend.

"Or got thrown out, I guess. We better tell the sheriff."

"That should be good," Billy said, "explaining this one to Nate."

"Christ-all-mighty." Will looked at the body and then down at the ground. "That's a hell of a thing, Billy."

Billy began walking up the slope, entering the squat juniper and piñon forest through one of many wide clearings. "Something else fell up here," he yelled over his shoulder.

"What?" As Will began to follow, a current of light eddied through the clouds directly overhead and a deep, conversational rumbling shook the sky. At once, as if in reply, a gust of thunder rattled across the western horizon.

Billy stopped and looked back. "I don't know," he half shouted. "Something sort of floated down over here somewhere. A kind of square thing."

Will moved to his left, taking a different path into the low, twisted trees, and saw at once a juniper that looked like it had been stomped on. The sweet smell of bruised cedar filled the air, and the center of the bushy tree seemed to have imploded, with the brittle, gnarled branches smashed and drawn into a rough circle. In the middle of the circle was a gray rectangle.

"I think I found it," he yelled. He pushed his way through the rubble and dragged out a large, odd-looking object partially covered with webbing and tangled, shredded white material. The gray cover was torn and gouged, with jagged bits of branch sticking out of the surface. The raw, powerful smell of cedar swarmed in the clearing.

"What do you think it is?" Billy said, materializing suddenly.

Will knelt awkwardly, one stiff knee only half bent, and turned the object over before reaching for the sheath knife on his hip. A drop of rain thudded against the back of his hand as he cut the harness away and tossed the torn parachute to one side. He began to hear and feel other fat, isolated drops striking his hat, and above his head the sky split and snapped like a doubled belt, the sound gone as soon as he heard it, leaving a wounded feeling in the air.

Billy squatted and looked closely at it. "Duct tape," he said as he watched Will insert the knife tip and make a shallow cut across the top. The gray tape parted to reveal a hard Styrofoam surface.

Will made a second cut around the perimeter of the rectangle and slipped the knife back into its sheath. Using both hands, he tore the thick covering off and stood up, holding a large rectangle of tape and Styrofoam in each hand.

"That poor bastard must have slipped when he was throwing it out," he said, nodding toward the lower slope.

"It's a suitcase," Billy replied. He moved closer, unfolding a heavy Buck knife, which he jammed beneath each of the clasps on the aluminum suitcase. When both clasps were pried loose, he put the knife away and lifted the lid.

"Holy shit."

"What is it?" Will dropped the scraps and squatted.

Billy lifted a small bundle from the case. He held the bundle close to his face and then handed it to Will.

Will turned the thing over, examining both sides and running his finger along the edges. Finally he said, "There must be a hundred twenties here, Billy."

"This bunch is fifties." Billy handed a second packet of bills to Will and began rifling through the stacks of bills inside the suitcase.

Will dropped both bundles and stood up.

"There's thousands in here," Billy said, looking down at the suitcase where a few desultory raindrops were splattering.

"A hell of a lot of thousands," Will answered. "A goddamned hell of a lot."

"Think it's counterfeit?" Still kneeling, Billy picked up a packet and examined it closely. He reached into his jacket pocket and brought out a small box of wooden matches. He set the money down, struck a match, and held it close to the packet of bills.

"They look real as hell to me, Will. Most of them look used."

"I guess we got something else to tell the sheriff, now that we've done what Jace would call tampering with the evidence." Will picked up his rifle, pulled a bandanna out of his hip pocket, and began to wipe the gun.

Billy stood up slowly and adjusted his hat more squarely on his head, keeping his eyes on the still-open suitcase. "Wait just a minute," he said. "Think about it, Will. We're out here chasing deer and a suitcase full of money falls out of the sky. You think this is going to happen again? It's a gift from the Great Spirit, Will."

Will pushed the wadded bandanna back into his pocket and held the rifle in the crook of his arm. The sliver of sun had dropped behind the Magdalenas, and the flat bases of the thunderheads formed a close ceiling. The whole sky rumbled, and diffuse lightning forked tentatively over mountains and plains.

Will took a deep breath and let it out slowly, feeling the electricity crawl up his spine and tingle across the breadth of his back. He looked up, pushing his hat back a little as he did so. "Looks like those monsoons finally got here. It's fixing to rain like hell."

Billy cast a disinterested glance upward before focusing again on the suitcase. "It doesn't rain around here anymore. But think about this, Will; just concentrate your mind for a minute. With a little bit of what's in this suitcase you could put in a new well and invest in breeding stock again. You could stop busting your ass for Ruiz and all the rest. And I could pay off the loan on our place. I could take a fistful of this and tell the bank to shove it up its fat goddamned ass, maybe even rebuild. Hell, Will, we could both have real ranches again."

Will looked down toward where the body tree was hidden in growing darkness. "It's corpse money. Money a man got a tree through his guts for. We both know where money like this comes from."

"Money don't know where it came from." Billy shoved both hands in his jeans pockets and touched the suitcase with the toe of his boot. "There's only one kind of money, and that's the spending kind. Goddammit, Will, think about it. Like you say, it must've come from a plane. I mean it couldn't have come from anyplace else, right? Well, whoever was in that plane probably don't know his ass from a hole in the ground about these mountains. And if he does, he sure don't know a couple of guys like us just happened to be here. We're way the hell and gone out here in the middle of the Cibola National Forest. Unless we take a shortcut across that government radar shit, the nearest spur road's a two-mile walk, and then it's ten miles of four-wheel drive to pavement. How the hell is anybody going to know where this damned thing fell or who found it?"

"Think what Grampa Siquani would say about this, and about that body down there. Besides, people don't go to this much trouble just to throw away a suitcase full of cash, Billy."

They both looked toward the sky, balanced tenuously upon the highest pines. A few drops of rain swept across the little clearing, and they hunched their shoulders against it.

"Grampa lives in a different world, Will. And they wouldn't drop it so damned far out in the mountains, where it'd take them all day to get to it. That doesn't make any sense. It has to be some kind of freak accident, and we're the lucky ones who happened to be here."

Will shrugged. "Maybe they had to drop it early, or maybe they couldn't see where they were because of the clouds. Or maybe they have their own shortcut in mind." He rubbed his chin. "Who knows? But we both know it's drug money. They fly up from

Mexico all the time, right through these mountains." He looked southward, as though imagining the whole complex story that had led to the man in the tree.

"Then to hell with them," Billy said. "They don't deserve this money."

Will shook his head once more and let out a long breath. "There's a man dead down there. We can't just leave a man like that."

Billy settled his hat more firmly on his head and stared off into the trees for a moment, chewing the inside of one cheek. He turned back and looked at the ground near Will's boots. "This money came from assholes and it was going to assholes. And if we turn it over to the sheriff it'll go to more assholes. The same government assholes that want to take the ranch my family put fifty years into, the same ones that'll be foreclosing on your place someday if you can't get water."

He raised his eyes to meet Will's. "We can't make that fellow down there any less dead. What we can do is not be fools. If it was me down there, I'd want to be left just where I was."

"If it was you."

"Nothing we do'll make any difference to that fellow now, Will. I'll bet he'd want us to take this money so those sonsabitches that threw him out couldn't come back and find it. I'll bet he's watching us right now and saying, 'Do it, goddammit.' "

Will looked at the suitcase. "So now you think somebody threw him out?" He adjusted his hat with a thumb and forefinger on the brim and seemed to be studying the suitcase. "If we had any brains we'd toss that thing back in the bushes and run like hell." Letting go of the hat brim, he rubbed the stubble under his chin with the back of his fist. Finally he said, "But we never had any brains, so I guess we'd better get out of here before they figure out where it fell."

Billy grinned. Removing his belt, he closed the suitcase, wrapped the belt around it, and then looked up at his friend. "Better give me yours, too."

Will removed his own belt and held it out toward Billy. Before he released it he said, "You remember Grampa Siquani when we were kids talking about a spell for stuff you find, like buried treasure? Something about smoking it with rabbit weed to keep off evil?"

"I can't remember all that stuff, Will. Grampa Siquani told us a thousand stories. Besides, does this look like buried treasure to you?"

Will let go of the belt. "I guess not, but we're in damned deep shit if we do this," he said.

Billy tore off the remainder of the duct tape and padding and wrapped the coupled belts around the suitcase. When he was finished he stood up and wiped his forehead on his jacket sleeve. "We've been in damned deep shit all our lives. We're just going to be in deep shit and rich now. Can you get my gun?" He nodded toward the rifle.

Will picked up the other deer rifle. "You said it came from the west?"

"West? Now don't start in with Cherokee superstition. I get enough of that from Grampa." Billy started down the hill, saying over his shoulder, "It's funny. I was following the biggest damn buck I've ever seen, six or eight points. Every time I'd lift my gun, the thing would disappear. It was like it led me to that spot and just vanished. Then when I looked up, I thought at first I was seeing one of those buzzards, the ones that fly down from the Rio Salado." He stopped and turned to face his friend. "Nothing we do is going to make that fellow any less dead, Will."

Will looked close into Billy's eyes. "It came from the west, and you say you thought it looked like a buzzard? Doesn't this feel funny to you? Didn't Grampa Siquani talk to you about such things?"

"Can't see the moon tonight," Billy replied, starting down the slope once more. "I hope we don't break a leg before we hit the Land Cruiser. Sure I've heard the stories, but in case you haven't noticed, it's damned near the twenty-first century. I don't pay a lot of attention to superstition and fairy tales."

As they passed the tree, Will went to the twisted base and looked up. The body was folded over the spire, the face bent so that it stared in toward the tree trunk, and Will circled the tree for a better look. In the poor light, the face was strangely white and detailed, almost luminescent, the eyes black and shining and the blue lips set in what looked like a tight, sad smile. It was nothing like the face of a dead man. A line of blood had run down across the face, and the long black hair was sharpened into points where the blood had dripped. The hands and bony wrists hung straight from white shirt cuffs and black suit coat, the fingers spread as if grasping at the earth. On the middle finger of the right hand blood swelled from the face of a large turquoise ring, as if gathered from the stone itself. Will shivered. It looked like the face of an Indian, with broad forehead and nose and thin-set lips, but it was white, pure white.

When they reached the ancient Toyota Land Cruiser hidden in a clump of piñons, Billy opened up the back and pushed the suitcase inside. They climbed in, Billy behind the wheel and Will on the passenger's side, with both rifles held in front of him against the dashboard. Billy pulled out the choke and turned the key, and the beat-up vehicle roared. Close in front of them, lightning flashed toward the earth, the fire hanging in the air as the sky snapped and then exploded like two blocks of wood smashed together. As the rattling Land Cruiser began to move on the Forest Service fire road, the scattered drops of rain became a cloudburst, hammering on the roof and erupting from the windshield.

"It's always the second one you see," Billy shouted above the roar of rain as he pushed the choke halfway in. "The one that jumps from the earth back to the clouds. You never see the first one."

Will watched a spindly thread of lightning touch the silhouette of a mesa several miles to the east. "You believe that?" he shouted back.

Ahead of them the land dipped into a shallow, brushy valley and then rose again to a sharp ridge. Darkness lay like a river in the bottom of the valley, and as they watched, the dark rose toward the ridge top, the rain-filled sky dipping to meet it and seal the whole world in slate.

Billy turned the headlights on, and the lights tunneled a few feet and were thrown back at them by the rain, so that they crept ahead in darkness that was almost complete. Unaffected by the slow wipers, the rain flooded on the windshield, distorting even the dark outside.

"Looks like we finally got some real rain," Billy said.

"We'd better think carefully about this," Will responded. "Somebody's going to be mad as hell."

Billy eased the Land Cruiser onto the crest of the ridge and stopped for a moment, letting the motor idle as he pushed the choke button the rest of the way in. Everything before them was black.

"Can't see much of diddly-squat," Billy said. "We sure don't want to get stuck out here. Since when did Will Striker worry about somebody being pissed off?"

"Since the somebody turned out to probably be a bunch of guys with machine guns. Just take—" Before he could finish, the air in front of them erupted with light and the howling of hammered wind. Out of the clouds a machine loomed, the bulbous glass front slanted toward them, the lighted interior warped and driven by the rain. The machine seemed to concentrate the screaming storm in one monstrous vortex as the blades pounded the air and beat on the cab of the Land Cruiser.

Billy's foot slipped off the clutch, and the vehicle lurched and died. Then the windshield exploded in an incoming shower of light and sound.

In a single motion, Will grabbed one of the rifles and shouldered the door open. He fell out of the door and rolled until he lodged against the thick trunk of a juniper. He'd fired the first round at the hovering copter and was working the bolt for a second shot before he was conscious of acting. He could see the outline of a man leaning from the side of the machine, and he heard the slugs striking the heavy body of the Land Cruiser with strangely soft, breathless sounds. He pointed the ought-six toward the man, ignoring the useless scope, and squeezed off a shot, levering the rifle bolt for a second and third shot while his ears rang.

The dark figure with the gun tumbled back into the helicopter, and just as suddenly as it had appeared the machine lifted backward and was gone as though sucked into the night sky by the storm. Its lights hung in the clouds and rain for an instant and then vanished, and the night seemed abruptly emptied of sound.

Through the heavy rain, Will watched the place where the helicopter had been. The hair on the back of his neck rose, and the air around him tightened. A blade of lightning slashed across the sky, and in the distant belly of the clouds there was an explosion. Branches of flame leapt outward from a dense core and vanished as they fell, leaving only the rain and the weak lights of the Land Cruiser angling into the night.

He waited a few seconds and then rose to his feet in a crouch, the bad knee aching.

"Billy," he said softly, and then, "Billy!"

"Over here."

The lights of the Land Cruiser went out, and Will moved toward the vehicle.

"You okay?" Billy was crouched with the other rifle behind the open door.

"Yeah," Will replied, dropping to a squat beside his friend. "Couple of scratches maybe."

"Me, too."

"That was their shortcut," Will said.

"Jesus." Billy's voice was almost a whisper. "Was that what I thought it was?"

Will nodded in the dark. "It must have been the lightning. Maybe one of our shots hit a gas tank or something, and the lightning set it off. That's the only thing it could've been."

"Looked like it exploded down toward the Array. How the hell could they find us in all of this?"

Will rose to his feet. "Good question," he replied. They stood silently for a moment, both staring up in the direction of the explosion, and suddenly Will said, "Shit!"

He went to the back of the Land Cruiser and jerked the door open, dragging the suitcase out onto the fire road. When he had the belts loose, he pried the suitcase open and began rifling through the bundles of bills, plowing furrows through the money and shoving it into the open top.

"What are you doing? That money's going to be wet as hell." Billy leaned over his shoulder to watch. "I can't see a thing."

"Goddammit!" Will held up a small black object, no bigger than a deck of cards. "A radio transmitter. A goddamned tracking device." Dropping the device onto the ground, he stomped with the heel of his boot and then stomped again.

"Nobody else better be homing in on that sonofabitch." He pried the smashed fragments out of the mud and hurled them into the brush. "Let's get out of here. We're in this thing now."

Billy threw the suitcase back inside the Land Cruiser, slammed the door, and trotted around to slide behind the steering wheel. He pushed a rifle toward Will. "I guess I grabbed your gun when I jumped," he said. "Maybe you should reload both of them."

"Yeah. We'd better hope those guys didn't radio somebody else."

The rain swept through the empty frame of the windshield as Billy eased out the clutch and let the vehicle slip forward. "Christ," he whispered, "I can't see squat."

When he had both rifles reloaded, Will rested them side by side through the windshield frame. "You get any of that glass in your eyes?" he asked.

He saw Billy's head move in negation. "I'm okay. How about you?"

"No."

"The lightning must've blown that chopper all to hell."

Will watched a candelabra of fire dance out of the clouds several miles away and instinctively counted the seconds before the thunder came rumbling across the sky.

"We're in this thing, now, Billy. Right in the goddamned middle of it."

The Toyota slid sideways, and Billy cut the wheel against the slide until they were straight again in the rutted tracks. The road flattened out, and he shifted into second.

"We better clean those rifles real good when we get home," Billy said. "Sticking out like that they're going to be piss-full of rain."

Twenty minutes later, they came to a post-and-wire gate, and Billy stopped. When the Land Cruiser was on the other side, Will closed the gate, slipping the barbed-wire loop over the gatepost.

Billy leaned out the window. "How about releasing the hubs while you're out there?"

Will unlocked the four-wheel-drive hubs and climbed back inside. Crossing the headlights, he looked ghostlike and menacing.

Billy turned onto a two-lane asphalt road, and they headed east. The dark land on either side of the road broke in ragged black canyons, dropping toward the valley of the Rio Grande twenty miles to the east. The rain had moved on, and only a few orphaned drops came through the windshield.

"Those Apaches used to ambush people right here," Billy said. "Geronimo himself used to hide out in this country. You know, he had an Apache baseball team in prison down there in Florida that beat the pants off the army team."

When Will didn't answer, they drove in silence for several minutes, the only sound the whine of the transfer case and the rattling of the '77 Land Cruiser's joints.

Finally, Will said, "We've got to think this thing out, Billy, if we're going to do it." As he spoke, headlights appeared over a rise ahead of them and they began to hear the sound of a low-geared vehicle. A dark rectangle shrieked past, the tires and drive train screaming.

In the mirror, Billy watched the taillights disappear with astonishing speed. When he took his eyes off the mirror, he saw that Will was watching through the rear window.

The Toyota groaned and the groan rose to a scream as Billy pushed the accelerator to the floor. They bucked out of a dip in the road and were hurled violently over the far side. There was a crash and the sound of metal being ground away followed by a clatter.

"Damn. That fender's been loose for ten years," Billy yelled into the rush of wind. "I guess it's gone now."

Will pulled the bandanna out of his hip pocket and folded it into a triangle, which he tied across his nose and mouth. He tugged the hat tightly over his forehead and squinted at the night that hurled itself toward them. "Don't roll this sonofabitch," he shouted through the bandanna.

Billy rubbed a fist across first one eye and then the other and glanced sideways at Will. When he shouted back, his words picked up the shrill of the hurricane swirling inside the Land Cruiser. "You look like a man, Mr. William Striker"—he sucked a deep breath and his voice rose to match the storm—"who just stole a million dollars."

## 2

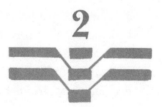

The ranch was black. The headlights glinted across two small, silver trailers set a hundred feet apart and a high-clearance pickup before Billy stopped in front of the bent outline of a barn. Will got out and rolled the door open, and Billy drove the Land Cruiser into the barn and killed the engine.

Will slid the trollied door closed and felt for a switch beside the door. A pair of floodlights, mounted on overhead beams, illuminated the Land Cruiser and the tall stack of rotting, gray hay bales it nosed against. Will looked around the crowded barn, at the decaying seeder and the harrow with its tines like spindly teeth, the broken and cracked harnesses and rusting troughs. The shadows of long-dead and abandoned machinery reached spidery arms toward Billy's crouched form. Laid down over the composting smell of old hay was the sharp odor of grease and oil. Will shivered, feeling ghosts in the old barn.

"Let's see just how deep the shit really is," Billy said as he turned the suitcase over and dumped the bundles onto the hay.

Will paused to wipe one eye with a corner of the bandanna that now hung around his neck. Then he folded his arms and watched Billy shove the money into two roughly even piles.

"How's Grampa Siquani? I didn't see a light in his trailer. Carla must be asleep, huh?"

Billy glanced up and then looked back at the money. "Yeah. They're both probably sleeping. Grampa's fine. Jesus Christ, look at this." For a moment he stared in silence at the money and then he said, "You have any paper?" Before Will could answer Billy pulled a piece of paper out of his shirt pocket, unfolded it, and tore it in half. "You got a pencil?" he asked as he shoved the paper toward Will.

When Will shook his head Billy got up and reached into the Land Cruiser, returning with a pencil that he snapped in half. Taking out the Buck knife, he sharpened a broken half and handed it to Will.

"Better keep track," he said. He picked up a bundle and began thumbing the bills.

Will shifted a decaying hay bale and sat down so that his hands were at the same level as the money. He counted two damp bundles of a hundred twenties each and then began to sort out the other bundles of twenties, checking to be sure that all were the same thickness. When the twenties were neatly stacked, he counted the fifties and then the hundreds. When he looked up, Billy was watching him with an expression that merged joy and terror.

"Four hundred and fifty," Will said, watching his friend's eyes.

"Four hundred," Billy said at last. He reached out to touch Will's shoulder with the fingers of one hand, the touch tentative, as though he were afraid electricity might leap between them. "Almost a million dollars."

Will removed his hat and set it on top of the money. He used both hands to unknot the red bandanna and then rub the bandanna over his face. Folding it neatly, he stuffed it back into his pants pocket and then ran the fingers of his right hand through his hair. Billy watched his friend's movements with fascination, a smile playing at the corners of his mouth.

Will set the hat back on his head. "You can't tell anybody about this, Billy. Not even your grampa." He watched the money as if it might coil and strike. "Not a word or a hint." A spattering of rain swept over the barn, dancing briefly on the tin roof.

"Those kinds of people know what to do with money like this," Will went on. "We don't."

"What are you talking about?" Billy's smile grew thinner. "Since when did you forget what to do with hard cash? First thing I'll do is pay off the bank."

Will nodded. "We start spending this kind of cash, people are going to get curious."

"To hell with people."

"Right, to hell with everybody. But let's see, some land-poor half-breed who hasn't had a goat on his ranch in ten years goes into a bank with thirty thousand bucks in a sack. 'I'm here to pay off my mortgage,' he says. Am I being paranoid when I suggest the FBI will be knocking on his door within twenty-four hours? But it's okay, because he can just tell them a man fell out of the sky with a suitcase full of money. Oh, and by the way, the guy's still out there with a tree through his guts. And then there's the people who might still think this money belongs to them."

"They're dead. Nobody could've survived an explosion like that."

"You really think he came out of that helicopter?"

Billy looked at the empty suitcase. "You're right. We would've heard it, so it had to be a plane, didn't it, up above the cloud cover?"

Will nodded. "We don't know how many there are."

"Jesus H. Christ."

They stared at the twin stacks of bills for a moment. "Those drug dealers launder it," Will said finally. "They invent some kind of fake business, a front like a pizza parlor or something, and funnel the cash through the business."

"I thought that was the Mafia. I saw it on *60 Minutes*." Billy stared at the stacks of bills.

"Damn!" Will shook his head.

"What?"

Will smiled softly. "We don't have to invent a fake business. We've got the ranches."

Billy rubbed the bridge of his nose and looked at Will with half-closed eyes. "And you're the one always telling me to be realistic. They're fake all right. You think anybody'll believe you and me are making money all of a sudden, when neither one of us has seen a cash dollar from our places in twenty years?"

"It could work if we're careful. If we don't get greedy. Let's say, for example, I pretend to sell old Satellite for five thousand. I make up a bill of sale, put five grand in the bank and hide Satellite in the barn."

Billy shook his head. "That bull must be twenty years old. He's deaf and blind as a bat, and he hasn't been able to get it up in ten years. On top of that he always was retarded. I've seen those wild-ass heifers of yours push that old fart around with him bellowing like a baby for you to come and save him. Face it, you don't have a cattle ranch. You've got a retirement home for old cows." He picked up a packet of hundred-dollar bills and slapped it against his leg.

"Satellite took a ribbon at the state fair."

Billy grinned openly. "Ten years ago. And that other runt bull of yours wouldn't get five bucks neither. Hell, I'll bet your heifers got so desperate waiting for those bulls to get a hard-on they went out and bred with elk. You're going to have a herd of whiteface herfelk come spring."

"Look, it's just the principle that counts. I could say some rich wacko like Jane Fonda and that guy she's married to wanted my bull for some reason. Maybe they wanted a pet bull. Five thousand or ten thousand bucks to them is like fifty cents to anybody else."

Billy lifted one of the bundles in each hand, seeming to weigh one against the other. "Like that fat-bellied pig Jace left you."

"It's potbellied, but yeah, that's what I mean."

"It sure as hell is."

"I mean that's what they call them. Potbellied pigs."

"You ever think of eating that pig?"

"It's Jace's pig. Besides, nobody eats potbellied pigs. It'd be like eating a dog."

"People do. You ever think it'd serve her right for sticking you with a pig like that? Not to mention that horse-sized dog." Billy stacked the bundles on top of one another. "I always thought some people must eat those pigs when they get tired of them." He looked up. "The *Albuquerque Journal* said Jane Fonda and that guy are raising buffalo. They're buying up half this state to raise buffalo, so what would they want with a Hereford bull so old he can't chew grass? Besides, you tell anybody you got five thousand bucks for one of those bulls, even from Jane 'I love Vietnam' Fonda, and they'll lock you up somewhere."

Will shrugged. "That's not the point, Billy. It doesn't have to be Satellite; it could be anything. We just have to figure out the details. Meanwhile we have to hide this stuff. And we can't start flashing money around. People have already died for this money; we don't even know how many. We have to let it cool off for a while."

Billy looked at him and grinned. "You sound like one of those cop shows on TV."

Will looked at the Land Cruiser. One wheel gaped where the

fender had been, and a line of bullet holes marched across the hood to the missing windshield. "You'd better keep the Toyota in the barn. We don't want anybody seeing that."

Billy looked sadly at the bullet holes. "You know how many seventy-seven Cruisers are left in as good a condition, not even a spot of rust? It's a classic, but I guess I'm grounded. Let's split this and each hide half of it. There's a duffel bag in the tack room we can use. That way—"

They both jumped as, with an implosion of feathers, a barn owl plunged out of the rafters. The pale bird dipped and fluttered in a circle, the soft wings whispering, before it rose back into the dark.

## 3

When Will got home, the rain had stopped, and the buzzards were on the fence again. In the periphery of the headlights, he could see their half-dozen humped forms against the lighter backdrop of the barn. He cursed and pulled his pickup to a stop in front of the barn. Lifting the rifle from its rack behind the seat, he pushed the door open with his shoulder and worked a shell into the rifle's chamber. Once out of the truck, he swung the rifle toward the air above the birds and fired from the hip. The shot echoed up and down the canyon, deafeningly loud. The buzzards tumbled backward into the sky like the shadows of drowning men, beating one another with ragged wings as they fought for air. Behind and below them the big barn stood awkwardly, the outline seeming to tilt against the night and the roof deeply swaybacked. The shadowy bulk of an equally swaybacked horse nosed the top board of the barn corral, apparently unfazed by buzzards or rifle shots.

The shot continued to echo across the bottom of the canyon and then bounced back at him. "Next time," he muttered.

"Who ever heard of buzzards killing anything?" he said as he turned around. "Goddamned *zopilote* carrion eaters."

As he spoke a huge, curly-haired dog and a short, fat pig strolled around the side of the house, walking side by side in the corridor of the headlights and pausing once to shake in unison as if they had just awakened. Nearly as big as a Shetland pony, the dog ambled up to push its nose into his crotch and snort loudly. Will shoved the enormous head away, ruffling one ear as he did so, and at the same time felt a blunt pig muzzle snuffling at his knee.

"Evening, ladies," he said, and he reached down to scratch the top of the pig's head. Instantly, the dog's muzzle was buried in his side.

"You're jealous of a pig, Maggie," he said to the dog. "Have a little self-respect."

In the previous week, the buzzards had killed three chickens, collapsing on the hens like ugly death dropped from the sky. Alerted by the chicken's shrieks, he'd seen one of them from his bedroom window. A Plymouth Rock had wandered into the corral, and huge wings were engulfing the squawking hen. A couple of sledgehammer blows from the buzzard's beak and it was over. The other buzzards had watched with interest from the fence, one of them shifting from foot to foot with excitement. When the chicken was still, they lunged from the fence to dance like thin old men around the kill.

He'd looked them up in his father's bird book. They were black buzzards, not the turkey vultures he'd always seen around the ranch. The book said vultures didn't have any feathers on their heads so they could stick their heads inside carrion without getting messy, but it didn't say buzzards killed livestock. Vultures, or buzzards, weren't birds of prey, but since they had sailed in on one of the fronts out of the west, these carrion-eaters had been hunting his chickens. He'd locked up the chicken run, but the ingenious hens kept finding leaks in the old wire and squirming out to their deaths until there were only a half-dozen left. Twice he'd seen Molly slinking along the fenceline, her porcine silhouette stealthy and low to the ground as she inched toward the buzzards. But each time just as the pig gathered her muscles to spring, the buzzards had risen awkwardly into the air, easily escaping the sow's snapping jaws.

"At least Molly tries to catch those bastards, but what's wrong with you, Maggie?" He scratched the massive dog between the ears. "You're a cow dog who's afraid of cows; that's what's wrong with you. I've got a useless Belgian cattle dog and a fat-bellied house pig too slow to catch buzzards and carrion-eaters playing falcon with my feathered livestock. I own two senile, impotent bulls I couldn't get five bucks for and a dozen cows somewhere out in the hills that think they're antelope. Some big-time rancher." The dog shook its whole body as though it had just climbed out of a bath, and he noticed light-colored grains in the dark around its furry mouth. "Birdseed again? Jesus Christ, you two." The piñon jays knocked the seed to the ground and the dog and pig competed with the coyotes to lick it up. Dog turds, pig droppings, and coyote scat, all heavy with birdseed, littered the ranch. Despite the self-feeders he'd built in the barn for dog and pig, both animals seemed addicted to the seed. "Maybe I ought to take you out with me to find those heifers," he said, "jump-start that genetic memory so you don't think you're a bird dog. Maybe Molly here could herd cattle, too." He bent down to slap the pig on her wide, flat rump. Molly scampered in a gleeful half-circle and then snuffled up to his leg again as if nosing his jeans for buried truffles. He shook his head at the animals and made a mental note to refill the bird feeder the next day. This time of year there were grosbeaks, juncos, towhees, chickadees, and little white-breasted nuthatches, plus the jays. He could sit for an hour at a time watching the feeder through the window of his bedroom. In the mornings sometimes tassel-eared squirrels and fat cottontails showed up to spook the quail and glean beneath the feeder, and he'd seen sharp-shinned and Cooper's hawks haunting the piñons around the feeder waiting for an absentminded bird. Like the hawks, he had watched the quail and cottontails with dark thoughts. The only thing better than a fat cottontail sizzling in a frying pan was quail breast fried in butter. But he couldn't bring himself to violate the bird feeder.

He reached into the pickup and shut off the headlights, jerking the duffel out before he kicked the door closed. With the rifle in one hand and the duffel bag in the other, he turned toward the house and abruptly stopped. Without the illumination of the pickup lights, the home he'd been born and grown up in seemed suddenly distant and strange, a dark stone set down in the night. In the daylight the house showed the patterns of its adobe bricks where the plaster had been lost to wind and snow and driven sand. But on such a moonless night it became an upthrust of the earth itself, the windows a deeper black in the yard-thick walls. Behind the house he could sense in the differing textures of blackness the way the landscape climbed in a narrowing vee toward the mountains, ending where the mountains ended in a dull saw's edge against the sky. He began walking, forcing his will toward where he knew the front door to be, hearing the dog and pig scuffling along at his back. The thunder had moved to the east, but the air remained slick with electricity.

He pushed the heavy door open and reached for a light switch before tossing the duffel in ahead of himself. With lowered head, Maggie lunged past and collapsed on a woven rug in the center of the wood floor. He started to yell at the dog but suddenly Molly shoved her broad belly between his legs and the door frame, rushing to settle beside Maggie on the rug. Both looked up at him with questioning faces, two lines of muddy prints leading to where they lay. "Cow dogs and pigs belong in the barn," he muttered unconvincingly. But the dog and pig had both been slipping past him frequently in the last few months, and most of the time he'd let them stay all night on the rug.

"To hell with it," he said. "I guess I'm an eccentric rich man now. You want the spare bedroom, ladies?"

The animals raised their heads in one motion, Maggie's curly hair spiraling up from her forehead to give her an expression of great innocence.

He nudged the dog with the toe of his boot, saying, "You, Maggie, are a damp dog of very little brain—as dumb as a mud brick and just as worthless. But you are a ferocious guard dog, aren't you?" He curled his lips back in a snarl, and the dog watched him quizzically. "And you, Miss Piggy, are a walking pork chop, and not a damned thing more. Remember that.

"Come on," he said, patting his thigh for encouragement as he leaned the rifle against the wall beside a glass-fronted gun cabinet. "Let me show you to your new quarters."

He headed down a hallway and the animals rose and followed in single file, Molly bringing up the rear. At the far end of the hall, he opened a door and turned on the light. A big double bed with an elaborately carved oak headboard stood at one end of the room, a rich-looking burgundy comforter spread across it. Gray Navajo rugs hung on two walls of the white-plastered room, and a floor-to-ceiling pine bookcase hid the third wall, crammed with books both vertical and horizontal, books his mother, who had trained to be a country schoolteacher but taught only a single year in Oklahoma, had spent half a lifetime collecting and teasing him into reading. *Robinson Crusoe*, *Treasure Island*, *Huckleberry Finn*, *Little Women*, a volume of English poetry, the Bible, and countless more; he'd read them all equally, carrying the pain of Buck's sordid death with him for months while yearning for Twain's great river as though it were a place he'd once known and lost. He'd lain in bed listening to his mother intone the bell-like sorrow of *Dover Beach*, seeing with dark clarity the vast edges drear and naked shingles of the world while imagining sad foreign rooftops. His eight-year-old mind knew the man was talking about loss, but of what? The poem's darkling plain and ignorant armies clashing by night reminded him of Grampa Siquani's stories of the darkening land and the black path of the west, but for his mother the words seemed to call up other memories, or half-remembered stories of another life and world. Her green, glistening eyes had taken on mysterious depths when she read such things, the music of her voice deepening and measuring a life he couldn't fathom. All around him, beginning with his earliest memory, had been a Cherokee world in which the earth and sky were densely inhabited and one need only recall the right story to know how to act. But his mother had not been Cherokee, or even Indian. Like his father and Billy's grampa, Siquani, his mother had stories of little people, but Irish little people were different. They were irrevocably strange and foreign. Raised by parents who had sent her to school and then died, leaving her nothing but a love of words and a belief that words might be enough, his mother seemed a permanent visitor in the Indian world of her own house, pleasantly surprised by its strangeness and reconciled without resistance to her exile, giving in to loneliness only enough to wall herself in with books. He came very early in his life to believe that the Cherokee world was made of spoken words, told into being with living breath, while the white world had been formed and imagined on pages that then waited patiently to be spoken into life. To his young mind, it was as if the Indian world was always new, made again and again when his father or Billy's grampa told the stories, but that the white world had been formed long ago and lay there in books ready to assume the same form each and every time the pages were opened. Like the Bible.

He'd been denied only one book from his mother's shelves, a novel called *The Last of the Mohicans*, which Caleb Striker had read half of before hurling it into the fireplace that dominated the fourth wall of the bedroom. It was his father, then, who'd begun to make trips to the library in Socorro to bring back books on the Cherokees, Mooney's collection of stories, a novel about Tsalie, the Cherokee hero, books about the Trail of Tears, life before the Removal and life in Indian Territory. Between them, his parents had sent him from high school to the University of New Mexico with a scholarship and a hunger for stories. And then at the beginning of his second year he'd met Jace, fallen in love, and received the phone call that brought him home. Stuffed everywhere into the shelves were books Jace had added while she'd been making the hundred-mile drive twice a week for seven years to attend classes at the university, mostly books by women he'd never heard of.

He ran a finger along a row of book spines, his fingertip coming away thick with dust, and thought about that previous life when he'd read books, had lost himself in books. When he turned around, the dog and pig sat together just inside the doorway, each on her haunches, watching him intently. Because the door had been closed for so long, he thought, maybe they were shocked to find this new part of their world, or maybe they'd expected to find Jace still in the room, waiting all that time.

With the toe of his boot he straightened a woven rug beside the bed, and then he looked up to see a large web filling one ceiling corner above the cherry chest that had been his mother's. The web, with its heavy, dust-coated filaments, caught the light, and he had the sudden impression that without the spider's work the room might collapse. The air felt as dry as old bone. Dust covered everything, and scraps of moths and other dried insects littered the floor. In the few spaces left between books and bookshelves, smaller webs had become cluttered with dryness and death, and the big, curtainless side window seemed to suck light from the room into its black plane. A full-length mirror beside the chest gave him back a reflection of himself that was heavy and dark, a block of shadow rather than a man.

He'd moved out of the room the day his wife announced she'd been offered a position in an Albuquerque law firm and was leaving. Carrying his clothes in three armfuls into the back room that had been his as a boy and then his son's until he, too, left for college, he'd traded the big double bed for the cot his father had made out of hand-split cedar, traded the down comforter for Pendleton blankets, the rugs and bookcase and chest for the cluttered fly-tying table he'd built and the mess of hats, chaps, gloves, ropes, boots, mink oil, and boot grease that he thought couldn't be trusted to the barn tack room. He'd pulled the room over himself like a blanket of sorrow, of self-pity, fully conscious of the childish sullenness of his act but incapable of doing otherwise.

He couldn't remember the last time he'd been inside the bedroom he'd shared with his wife, the room where he'd been born and where one of his own children had been conceived. Looking around the room now, he felt like a man who'd gone back to the country of his birth from long exile and found the familiar world shrunken and strange.

He walked to the bed and patted the dusty comforter as he looked back at the two animals. "From now on you sleep right here, ladies—rain, sleet, mud, ticks, foxtails, skunk, or whatever. Jace made your bed, now you get to lie in it. It's only fitting." He patted the bed again, and Maggie walked cautiously to the bedside, looked at him probingly, and then, with a strenuous push-off, hoisted her hundred and forty pounds onto the comforter, where she collapsed with a long expulsion of breath and cloud of dust, her great head sinking deeply into the down pillow.

"What about you, Molly?" He walked over to where Molly still sat on her broad haunches, looking with porcine amazement at bed and dog. "It's really okay. Honest." He scratched the top of her head, patted his thigh, and walked sideways toward the bed, and Molly waddled slowly after him. At the bedside, he touched the comforter beside Maggie and said, "Come on, girl. You can do it."

Molly looked up at him, her little eyes suspicious. For a moment she hesitated, and then she hurled herself suddenly onto the bed, bolting from floor to comforter with astonishing agility. In one motion, she had lain her plump black body alongside Maggie, her dark, doubting eyes never leaving Will's face.

He went to the door and turned the light off. *"Buenas noches, hermositas,"* he said as he went out.

In the living room he noticed that the house had the warm, musty smell of lightning season at high elevations. He scanned the room. After forty-six years, the house he'd known all his life had changed, and it wasn't just the gut-shot television. He revolved slowly in a three-hundred-and-sixty-degree turn.

The brown Mexican blanket had slipped off the leather couch and lay piled on the floor, and he paused for a moment, wondering if he'd left it that way. He remembered it lying neatly across the back and cushions of the old, cracked couch. The stone fireplace had a cold, evil cast to it. The imploded television was animated with hatred since he'd put a thirty-ought-six slug through the next-to-last president of the United States right in the center of the screen. For a reason he hadn't bothered to explain to himself, he liked having the shattered television in the room. "Don't feel so goddamned special," he said. "I shot the radio first." The radio had been in the bedroom and had perished from a single pistol shot in the dim light of dawn. For a moment, looking at the television, he tried unsuccessfully to remember who the current president was, but he'd decided a long time before that it wasn't his country. The country that had a president on television was somebody else's and he wanted no part of it. He let the thought go and picked up the duffel and rifle.

In the kitchen he dropped the bag on the linoleum and laid the rifle across a heavily scarred pine table. Raising the lid on an enamel pot on the gas range, he looked inside before striking a match and lighting the burner under the pot. While the coffee heated, he went down a short hallway to the room he slept in and returned with a metal rod, pieces of rag, and a can of gun oil. When he got back, the dog and pig were in the kitchen, lying side by side between table and stove, each eyeing him as he walked in.

He sat at the table, and, ejecting the remaining shells, he cleaned the rifle, ramming the oiled rag through the barrel and then running it over the whole exterior. When he was finished, he reloaded the gun and leaned it in the corner across from the stove. Then he went to the gun cabinet in the living room and took out the twelve-gauge and a box of double-ought shells. He loaded the shotgun, pumping a shell into the chamber with the safety locked on. Working the action on the shotgun, he felt a thin edge of excitement crowding into his senses, a sharp feeling like waking up. It had been a long time, he realized, since anything had happened, since anything mattered. Now life was different. People with guns were seeking him at that very moment, gathering their resources in the darkness, ready to balance their favorable odds against his. Of that he had not the slightest doubt. And there was money on his kitchen floor. He took the shotgun into his bedroom, placing it against the wall at the head of the bed.

When he returned, he opened the duffel bag and poured the money into a heap on the floor. He sat in the uncomfortable kitchen chair and looked down at the bundles. In the weak kitchen light the money had a dirty, grayish sheen to it, and after several minutes he shoved it back into the duffel bag and hooked the bag closed.

He went to the sink and washed his hands, using liquid dish soap and rinsing carefully in the thin stream from the spigot. After drying his hands, he poured a cup of the foul coffee and sat down at the table once more, rubbing Maggie's chest with the toe of his boot and seeing as if for the first time the scars of fifty years in the soft pine of the table. He felt under the table's edge for the marks of his father's name, running the tips of his fingers over the deep cuts, to spell out the Cherokee letters of *asgaya* and *uhni*, the name of a warrior, Manstriker. Somewhere in the dry, mirage-weighted air between Oklahoma and New Mexico, where imagined rivers rode upon the asphalt to spill into sand breasted by the family's old truck, his father had softened his Cherokee name, becoming Cal Striker the way his best friend, Ross Kaneequayokee, had become Ross Keene. But when he made the kitchen table, splitting and planing the pine by hand, it was the Cherokee that he carved on the underside, the ancient warrior's name. Will ran his hand across the open-grained wood of the tabletop, feeling the oily residue of his life and his parents' lives. The leftovers of his own son and daughter, and a wife now a hundred miles away in an Albuquerque town house with Formica and microwave, *saltillo* tile, Jacuzzi, and career.

He looked at the sink discolored by years of tainted water, the wood countertop with its thick layers of chipping green paint, the window above the sink that had never let in sufficient light, the groaning and chattering refrigerator he'd bought the year Holly was born. Twenty-five years ago. He remembered not being tall enough to turn on the tap at the sink back when the water had run clear and plentiful, and his father lifting him so he could hold a tin dipper under the faucet. And he remembered holding his own daughter up so she could catch the slow, stale water in the same dipper that still hung on a nail above the sink. He ran a hand through his thick hair, plagued by a feeling that he'd left something undone, something crucial that hovered just outside his consciousness. Something deadly.

When the phone rang he jumped and then almost ran to grab the receiver. The voice he heard was familiar and warm. "Will?"

"Hello, Jace." He took a deep breath.

"Is everything okay, Will? You sound funny."

He looked at the duffel bag and nodded. How the hell did she know? "Fine, Jace. Everything's fine."

"I just called to see how you are," she went on. "I called yesterday and the day before, and you didn't answer. I was worried."

"I know," he said. "How's the law business?"

"Why do you do that, Will? Why don't you answer the god-damned phone? You know I worry about you. I mean, what if something had happened to you? How would anybody know?"

"Nothing could happen to me, Jace. I'm safe and boring, re-member? Nothing could ever happen down here. Somebody told me that once."

"Don't do that, Will. Are you okay?"

He heard the tremble start in her voice. "Sometimes I just don't want to talk," he said. "I vant to be alone."

"Very funny. What if something happened to Si or Holly and I had to reach you?"

"Okay, Jace." She'd used her ace in the hole too quickly, he thought, bringing up the kids like that as if they weren't both grown and living their own lives. She must be tired, or maybe she was in a hurry. "From now on I'll answer the damned phone every time it rings."

"Don't get mad, Will. You know I worry."

"Yeah." He reminded himself that the voice on the phone belonged to his wife of twenty-five years, but when he tried to summon her image he saw the other woman in the Albuquerque town house, the one in a blue suit who claimed she still loved him but couldn't live with him. Who hadn't been back to the ranch in months.

"So who are you screwing now, Jace?"

There was a long silence before she said, "Goddamn you, Will Striker. You answer the fucking phone from now on." Then she hung up.

"Nothing to worry about," he said, regretting his anger and meanness as he did every time and wondering why she never reminded him that it was her ranch, too, if it came to a divorce, though neither of them had ever mentioned the word. It was a community property state, so he'd have to sell and give her half the value, which was nothing. The land that had been worth three dollars an acre in the thirties was virtually worthless sixty years later—too far from civilization to be developed, too dried-up and dead for ranching or farming. And it wasn't just the water. It was as though a force had gone out of the very earth. The scrubby prickly pear, piñon, and juniper hung on, scorched and brittle with a kind of resignation he felt in the dry air, but about their roots the earth turned gray and hard, showing ribs of hot granite. Other ranchers and the people of small towns in the region had grown tight-mouthed and bitter, the neighboring county a few miles away even passing an ordinance requiring its citizens to bear arms. The same county's board of supervisors had issued an official warning that environmentalists might be shot. The land was dying and the people were beginning to turn on one another like grim survivors. Hell, he thought, I might as well be on a reservation, but reservation life was long over for Cherokees. Compared to the Indians of New Mexico, Cherokees might as well be Norwegians. That's how a lot of other Indians thought of Cherokees anyway.

Fortunately, the ranch was paid for, and his parents hadn't succumbed to the temptation of a second mortgage the way Billy's had. But only the scrawny piñon and juniper could bring in cash, and he'd have to cut every tree on the ranch for firewood to buy his wife out. He could sell the big Caterpillar, the last thing of real value on the place, but the D-6 had been some kind of dream for his father, as though if he, an Indian, could possess the power to move mountains, something would change. Now the machine sat under its shed roof like a great riddle. Besides, it brought in occasional government contract work and a job now and then from another rancher with real work to do, enough to justify its existence maybe.

Sometimes, usually in the dark hours of morning, he'd lie in bed and wonder at the incredible fact of his life with the woman he'd married. Two people met and made children and a life. It all seemed crucial at the time it was happening, like destiny or fate, but when you looked back it was a joke and an accident. It could have been anybody each one of them married, any of millions of people out there, and they would have called it love and been just as happy or unhappy. Just accidents that put people in certain places at certain times. And when he lay there missing the touch of his wife, the deep, warm smell of her sleeping breath and the curve of her back, feeling as though half of himself had fallen away in the night leaving a dull and bottomless pain, he told himself it wasn't love and it wasn't her but something else. That somehow he had driven her away was a thought that crept up from the dark to gnaw at him. As the ranch dried up more and more with each rainless year, he felt himself dry up with it. "You don't care about anything," she'd accused him finally. "You act like you're asleep all the time." After the children went off to college and marriage and their own lives, he yearned for the sounds and smells of them, the feel of small arms around his neck and the clutter of random, young lives in the old house. He found himself sleepwalking through his days, working on other men's ranches when work was offered, hunting or fishing with Billy, but feeling less and less.

He and Jace had used up a good portion of the only lives they would ever have. That's what they had given each other. And maybe it was worth it. One of his first memories of Jace showed her to him alone against the horizon of his parents' mounded graves, her face etched with a sorrow for people she had never known. He remembered at that moment a love that left no room for doubt. And then other things happened, and they ended up in different lives a hundred miles apart. He suspected that his wife had started seeing other men almost as soon as she moved north; he had felt it in his gut. But maybe he was wrong, and perhaps it didn't matter anyway. Maybe four years of solitude, broken by occasional visits from grown children and brief, formal encounters with a woman who was still his wife, were necessary for a man. Maybe walking out at daylight to scatter cracked corn to half a dozen chickens and stroke the neck of a gray-muzzled mare was enough. But then the buzzards had come, darkening the very air of the ranch.

He felt a tingling in his blood, like a limb waking up from sleep. "I lead the safest life in the world," he said to the dead telephone receiver. "Except that sometimes a corpse falls out of the sky with a suitcase full of money and a helicopter tries to blow my head off." He looked at the duffel bag. "Jesus Christ," he whispered. "That's it."

He realized all at once that the man from the sky had changed everything. The helicopter that burst from the storm to kill them had changed everything. The too-late monsoon season rolling in from Arizona had brought a different life, and that life sat on the floor close to the table. In his mind he saw the body out there, poised in a kind of isolation he had never even imagined. What, he wondered, would Jace think about it? Being a professional person now, a lawyer, maybe she would be on the other side. It struck him that finally, in midlife, he and Billy had stepped outside the law, like the famous outlaw Billy Pigeon, who could turn himself invisible with Cherokee magic. With their decision, they'd positioned themselves irretrievably. Or maybe like their Indian ancestors they'd been positioned by events they could have neither foretold nor resisted. Perhaps an amalgamation of bloods had flowed together through time to place them outside of everything. Mixed-breeds. Breeds. Outlaws. Positioned by events such as the drunk driver who'd appeared one clear morning on an empty road to cross the line and kill his parents, and like Jace getting pregnant with Holly. So that within a month both his parents were dead and he, a college dropout who'd barely gotten started, had brought home from the university a wife with already the stirrings of a new family and, maybe, a long resentment.

He considered places to hide the money, and the answer came to him at once. Taking the big flashlight from the top of the refrigerator, he picked up the duffel and went toward the back door.

He angled across the yard past the abandoned playhouse and the pump shed. No water had passed through the gas-powered pump in more than five years, and it was undoubtedly froze up by now. To the right of the pump shed was the big steel tank he filled with water from town. Twenty feet past the water tank, he stopped at what looked like a hatch-cover in the earth. A few yards away, their hunched shadows dark against the backdrop of the barn, the two bulls stood shoulder to shoulder, either asleep or watching him. The dozen whiteface heifers he still ran just for sentimental reasons would be out somewhere in the scrub, maybe hanging around near the muddy pool where sulfur-tasting water trickled out of a rock wall, the last water anywhere on the ranch. But Satellite and Trinity were spoiled. They'd been weaned on sweet water, and now in old age they hovered close to the barn and the trough he kept filled with the tank-truck. In youth they'd squared off many times over bragging rights to the range, blustering and threatening to put one another in early graves, but in old age they'd come together to stand in shelter and shade. Watching them, Will imagined that the old warriors with their bowed heads were reminiscing about the high grass and sleek heifers of years gone by, probably boasting about how low their scrotums had hung when they were young.

He set the duffel on the ground and went toward the barn, returning moments later with a short length of rope, a hammer, and a pick. With the pick he pried the wooden hatch up and pushed it backward, uncovering a large hole in the earth. He put the pick down and grabbed the flashlight, shining it across the underside of the wood and around the perimeter and finally into the hole itself. Everywhere in the light, things moved. Spiders seemed to freeze in confusion, and a six-inch centipede flowed smoothly over the lip of the hole and down into darkness. With a small stick, Will flipped a black scorpion several feet from the hole.

When he was certain no rattlers were hiding around the old well, he propped the light carefully, fished several large nails out of his pocket, and nailed the knotted end of the rope securely to the underside of the well cover. He tied the duffel to the rope and lowered it into the dark. Using the pick once more, he lifted the wood and pushed it so that it fell into place over the hole. In the morning he'd make it look like no one had touched the old well in twenty years.

When the children were little, he'd thought often about filling in the old Spanish well, but he'd never gotten around to it and the kids hadn't thought to pry up the heavy lid and fall in. Walking back toward the barn, he realized for the first time that he'd been reluctant to fill in the old well simply because he liked having it there. He liked knowing that at least a hundred years ago men had dug into the earth and found water. As a boy he'd tried to imagine it. How had they kept digging once they found the water? Did a man stand down there up to his knees, waist, or neck in water still digging and sending buckets of rock and dirt up by rope? He'd imagined how that would have felt, standing in earth-cold water and staring up at a square of blue sky thirty feet above. The image had touched a deep feeling in him, like a dim memory he couldn't bring into focus.

By the twenties and early thirties, when everyone was in flight from what they called the Dust Bowl to the east, the old well was already dry and the adobe house had begun to fall in upon itself and the surface of the land was burnt-over and lifeless. Except for the few that watered at the pool on the far boundary of the ranch, even most of the pronghorns had scattered westward onto the damper plains along the White Mountains. Like the antelope, the heirs of the original land grant had drifted away to hire out on Mormon cattle ranches in Arizona. Only one of the original Meléndezes still lived close by, and Will occasionally wondered if Mouse Meléndez, who'd been in California most of the last twenty years, even remembered or cared that the thousand acres and a lot more had once belonged to his family. Cal Striker and Ross Keene, two full-blood Cherokees, had seen an article in a newspaper. Carefully pressed in the family album, the article from the *Corona Maverick* advertised that "land can be bought as cheap as $2.50 per acre." With their wives, white women who had given up a great deal to marry Indian men, with a pittance of oil money from Sequoyah County, Oklahoma, and accompanied by an old man named Siquani, the two men had glanced at the dried-up one-horse town of Corona, New Mexico, and continued up onto the Continental Divide, where they'd bought the thousand acres for almost nothing, which was precisely what the acres were felt to be worth.

What the cattlemen and miners of Magdalena didn't know was that the old man named Siquani had already walked the land with a forked willow branch and the branch had tugged toward the earth. What the others hadn't understood was the steady, muted voice of thunder that rose and began to hover conversationally over the western mountains almost as soon as the ranch changed hands. Camped beside the spring, the two couples listened as Siquani, already so old that no one remembered whose grandfather he really was, knowing only that Ross Keene bore his name and so called him Grampa, talked of bones in the dry earth beneath them.

"I thought it might be different, but the earth is full of death here, too. In this land they have stopped the water. I would say we should move on, but I think the whole world is the same, and besides, the Thunders promise that someday the bones in this land will let go. In the meantime I think the dead will relent a little, so we should stay."

So the two men bought the thousand acres, divided it into two equal parcels, and had wells drilled. Thunder called, mild rains swept in long gray lines from the west, and windmills tugged cool, sweet water from beneath their feet. Water ran in a thin, spring-fed stream through the center of the thousand, passing not far from the old Meléndez adobe, and grass grew. With their wives they rebuilt or built houses and barns, made distinct and separate access roads from the highway, put up fences of wire and twisted juniper posts, grew stunted hay and cattle, produced each a single son given identical names, and then, in different ways and with their wives, died violent and sudden deaths.

On both ranches then the rains stopped, and the voices of thunder fell silent. The sparse stream vanished and the wells slowly dried up. Wind drove down out of the west and spun the blades of the Aeromotor mills, but the pumps found no water and the bearings grew thin and froze tight. Old Siquani walked the land once more, knowing beforehand the futility of his search, and his forked willow stick neither dipped nor trembled. He searched without success for a salamander and finally went to the rock spring with only a cedar branch, submerging himself for four consecutive dawns, but if there was water left, the dead had drawn it so deeply into the earth that the old Cherokee magic couldn't reach it. "The dead have the water," he said, shrugging.

Will Striker and Billy Keene drilled deeper wells and replaced windmills with gas-powered pumps, and for a brief time the earth gave up water until the gas pumps failed, too. The vegetation took on a dull, blue-green gloss, and the grasses grew squat and thin and headed out before they would be scorched seedless from the earth. The stream that divided the ranches became a ditch of gray rocks and struggling weeds. Lizards and dull brown squirrels scurried amidst the brush, leaving distinct trails in the dusty streambed, and coyotes traveled there by night between the mountains and the broken lands below. For several years the sky grew increasingly remote, sending black cloud shadows across the earth without rain, and Will remembered his parents' stories of the thirties and that flight from the ovens of hell they called the Nation, or Indian Territory, or Oklahoma, the home of red people.

Leaving the hammer and pick inside the barn, he walked back to the house, thinking again of the body tree, of the white face and dark eyes. He couldn't shake off a feeling that the dead man had known of his presence and expected something from him, that something or someone was waiting for him to act. But the something was only guilt, he told himself as he entered the house. And the someone was Will Striker. The man from the sky was dead.

## 4

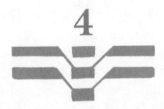

Billy Keene rose when the sun began to light the sink full of dirty dishes. In a dream he'd been walking in a forest where crows fluttered like black leaves, cawing and croaking at him, when suddenly the shadow of an owl had plunged through the canopy of trees, causing the birds to vanish and his eyes to open to sunlight.

Rubbing both hands over his face, he rolled from the twin bed and headed for the toilet, but his right foot caught and he fell headlong, breaking his fall with a hand on the edge of the bed.

He pushed himself to a sitting position and turned to see the silver suitcase, open and filled with money, wet Levi's, socks, and shirt beside it.

"Oh shit," he said.

He stood up and closed the lid, shoving the suitcase beneath the bed and tugging a blanket so that it hung down to the floor. A pair of red panties fell onto the floor, and he picked them up between thumb and forefinger and examined them.

"So she forgot one thing at least," he said aloud as he dropped them into a garbage bag that stood, overflowing with coffee grounds and cans, by the table. Then he went to the tiny window over the sink and looked out. His grandfather was already on the little wooden deck in front of the other trailer, standing straight and still in his canvas tennis shoes and looking toward the east, his mouth moving without sound.

Abruptly the old man's face turned to the trailer window. Billy waved a hand and the old man waved back, his braids jerking as he raised his arm, and the shiny black leather vest flapping like a crow's wings. Billy waved again and headed for the trailer's minuscule bathroom.

When the coffee was ready, Billy pulled on a clean pair of jeans, filled two cups with black coffee, and left the trailer, balancing the overfilled cups delicately as he felt his way barefoot across the fifty feet of hard-packed dirt between the two trailers. The old man had sat down in a straight-backed chair and seemed to be studying the eastern sky, where a bright red blanket lay over the far mountains. Billy handed him one of the cups, and he smiled toothlessly. "Thanks, Grandson," he said. "I think my blood needs some of your strong coffee this morning. It feels sort of stuck." He rolled his shoulders slightly, holding the cup at arm's length, and nodded toward the sunrise. "The red one's coming."

Billy sat down with his legs dangling off the deck, shivering a little in the cool summer morning, and followed his grandfather's gaze to where the sunrise had now begun to ripple across brilliant rags of cloud. He had years before given up trying to follow the old man's thoughts, but as he watched, a raven flapped out of one of the thin cirrus clouds and banked into the sunrise. The black bird seemed to burst into flame, its heavy body and broad, fringed wings turning a violent red. For an instant the red raven hovered against the cloud, and then it soared out of sight.

"That thunderstorm's probably all the way to the Staked Plains by now," Billy said, thinking about how unpredictable New Mexico weather was. In Albuquerque they gave weather reports by neighborhood. He sipped the black coffee, imagining the bundles of money in the silver suitcase.

"I guess your new girlfriend left while you was out hunting yesterday. This fellow in a rattly old truck come out, and she put her suitcase in the back of that truck and left."

Billy snorted. "Was it a big guy with long hair and a beard?"

The old man nodded.

"That's Mouse Meléndez. You didn't recognize him?"

"That one that got his name from tanning mouse skins when he was a boy? He used to come out here to play when you was little. He was a good boy."

"He moved back from California with a bunch of his friends from out there," Billy said. "Maybe him and Carla will make each other happy. Carla wasn't comfortable here on the ranch." Billy sipped the coffee and studied the red clouds. "That's sure a pretty sky," he added.

"Red sky," the old man replied. "That girl was only here two weeks. She was a good girl, but how come you always choose them real young ones, Grandson? You bring 'em out here and they're happy for a little while, winking at me and bringing me coffee, and then pretty soon they take off. It's because they're so young. You ought to find a grown-up woman. A woman needs to be seasoned, to put up with the likes of you."

"Maybe you're right, Grampa. But I'm beginning to suspect that my girlfriends always leave because they can't get into your pants. I'm getting a little jealous. I think they're just using me to get close to you, and then you don't oblige."

The old man chuckled. "Maybe I do oblige. Maybe this old man's too much for them."

Billy examined a callus on the side of his big toe. "Carla and me were just too different, I guess."

"Everybody's too different, maybe. Them crows was talking this morning." The old man looked away from the sunrise toward the dilapidated barn. Along the sinking ridge pole of the barn a dozen glossy black crows were perched, preening and pecking absentmindedly at one another. They spread their wings and danced along the roof, one or two occasionally fluttering into the air a couple of feet before dropping back down. "Crows ain't always reliable, but they say something's going on. Something rode in on that big storm, they say. From the west."

Billy glanced toward the barn crows. For as long as he could remember there had been a flock of crows perched along the barn, whitening the corrugated tin roof with their shit, diving to steal scraps from the outraged chickens that had long since vanished, and quarreling with each other about everything that happened on the ranch. He knew crows didn't live that long, but the flock never seemed to change, as if it wasn't crows but some kind of crowness that inhabited the ranch. All of his life he'd watched the man he called Grandfather and his father had called Grandfather scatter treats for the loud, ungrateful birds, everything from apple cores to leftover meatloaf or pan-fried bluegills. The old man and the birds seemed to have a kind of grudging relationship with one another, not respect or even fondness exactly but something more like an ancient kinship. Watching the crows, he recalled the dream and felt a sudden urgency to do something with the suitcase beneath his bed, but he didn't dare move it out of the trailer while the old man was watching.

"It's funny, Grampa. I was dreaming about crows last night."

Siquani looked hard at him. "A man dreams about crows, it means folks is talking about him, jumping on him somewheres."

Billy shrugged, the scar on his cheek seeming to redden with the growing sunlight. "It was just a dream, I guess."

"You didn't get no deer, huh?" the old man said.

Billy held the cup close to his mouth as he shook his head, thinking that the old man was looking at him strangely. "It's too damned dry. The deer all went over to that Black River country where it still rains."

"Will didn't get none neither?"

"Nope. Maybe we'll go out again next week," Billy replied, seeing the body again free-floating toward him. He knew he wouldn't go there again, not next week or ever.

"You didn't speak with the Little Deer. You got to ask permission. A man that forgets to do those things right can get himself pretty crippled up. Awi Usdi can make a man's legs crooked and shrivel up his arms so he can't hunt no more."

Billy shrugged. "That was the old days, Grandfather. People don't believe that stuff anymore. We live in a different world. We wear different clothes, live in different kinds of houses, and eat different kinds of food, so why shouldn't we think different kinds of thoughts? We're not Indians anymore, maybe. God knows what we are."

The old man watched Billy steadily for a moment and then added, "That's right, the Creator knows what we are. Them crows was talking yesterday when the big clouds come. You notice it was a funny kind of storm, with them clouds so way down and close to the ground?" He took a drink of the coffee and screwed his face up. "This is good coffee, Grandson."

"Not too strong?"

"Hell no. This here's Indian coffee." He grinned, and then just as quickly his face lost all trace of humor. "West," he said, watching the sun blossom in the east over the distant Manzano Range. "That darkening land is over there." He jerked his head backward toward the mountains to the west. "What our people call Nightland. You got to be careful about things that come from over there, Grandson. It's important that you stay awake."

"I believe I heard something about that before," Billy said vaguely.

"I guess there's lots of stuff you heard before, maybe. But like you just said, you think different now. You never did listen too much when you was a boy. Your daddy used to say you was a wild boy your mama found in the water. That's from a old story about First Man and First Woman and those Thunder Boys. I told you that story when you was little, you and Will both, but you probably forgot. You was always egging poor Willum into trouble, sneaking off to ride your daddy's steers and things like that." He nodded toward the risen sun. "You know what is over that way, now that you're growed up and think different?"

Billy shrugged. "I guess it must be Morningland."

"That's Sunland. Good things come from that way."

Billy nodded. "Makes sense, except that most of the white people came from the east. And they say Indians came from the northwest, down from Alaska."

The old man cocked his head and looked at Billy like one of the barn crows. "Nuts. We know when white people got here because we was already here waiting, but what do white people know about us?"

Billy shivered again and sipped the hot coffee, watching a pair of buzzards glide in a slow circle against the sunrise. Again he thought of the suitcase beneath his bed.

Siquani blew on the coffee and seemed to read the steam that rose from the cup. "Bodies was froze to the ground every morning. Little babies and the old ones. The people was crying for a long time."

Billy looked at his grandfather and then back toward the reddening mountains, hazy now with the smoke from chimneys far down in the Rio Grande valley. Where had the old man's thoughts drifted off to now, he wondered. A woodpecker began to hammer at a piñon tree near the barn, and he unsuccessfully scanned the tree to see if he could pick up the stark black and white of the bird.

"The government people said they had to count us and give us numbers. If we didn't let them give us numbers, then we didn't get none of our land. All them half-breeds was the first to get numbers, but a whole lot of the old-timers stayed back in the hills and never got numbers at all. That meant they couldn't be real Indians no more. Some of them decided to become invisible then. I did that for a while, but then I thought maybe I should be a crow. But I didn't have so much fun like those ones over there."

He nodded toward the barn, where the crows were engaged in what looked like a chaotic line dance along the tin ridge. "Sometime I should tell you about them crows."

"I've never heard you talk quite like this before, Grandfather. How come?"

The old man held the coffee securely in both hands and sipped, looking over the rim of the cup at the line of mountains miles away across the flat. "That was a very hard time, Grandson, when the old ones and young ones died. I guess now I'm getting to be a cranky old bastard. Maybe I think a young man should consider these things. Thinking is powerful. It's how we make everything."

Siquani squinted at the horizon and then closed his eyes fully. "Walk around this place, Grandson. Listen to what the animals are saying. Listen to what the wind is telling you, listen to the Thunders. They say it's a dangerous time. Soon it will be too late. You and Will are in a deep forest, Grandson, just like your pa and Will's pa. I couldn't do nothing then, neither."

"I'm a little confused, Grampa, but maybe you shouldn't get too down on white folks, since half of me is white."

"Which half you think it is?" The old man looked serious. "If you was lucky, the bottom half would be Indian, because us Indians is the best lovers. That's why all those white women was always sneaking into our towns, and then when they got caught they'd pretend that they was kidnapped. If you was unlucky, it'd be the top half, because then you'd always be thinking about how Indians got everything stolen. If you was white on top and Indian on the bottom, your top half could steal everybody's money and your bottom half could steal their women."

Billy rubbed the arch of a foot against his jeans and smiled at the old man. "Well, Grampa, I kind of think it's right down the middle, top to bottom."

"That's a shame, Grandson, because that way a man's just fighting with himself all the time."

Slinging the dregs from his cup into the weeds at the side of the deck, Billy let his eyes settle on the rock foundation a hundred

feet away. After a dozen years the stone chimney was still blackened, and the trunk of the juniper next to the foundation still
showed the effects of fire. The house had burned during a lightning
storm much like the one that had passed through yesterday. His
parents' room had been the one next to the butane tank, and they'd
never had a chance. The two Airstream trailers had come from
insurance money.

He looked away. "It's going to be a hot one today, Grampa."

"That's right. The crows said there ain't going to be no more
storms for a while. Something has to happen first."

"You need anything from town, Grampa?"

"I run out of peanut butter."

Billy stood up and patted his grandfather on the shoulder. "I'll
pick up one of those big jars."

"Get that clown kind. Don't get that crunchy kind."

"I'll be sure," Billy replied as he walked toward the barn.

Inside the barn, he glanced around in the dim light. Going to
a big, rusting toolbox, he lifted the lid and looked down at the
corroded pipe wrenches, ball-peen hammers, and other tools that
had been his father's. Somehow, water had gotten into the box,
and the tools at the bottom were welded into a layer of reddish
brown flaking metal. He dropped the lid and looked around him,
finally going to the open door of the long-abandoned tack room
and coming out with a moldy gunnysack.

In the trailer, he dragged the suitcase from beneath the bed and
threw the lid back, starting at once to transfer the money to the
sack. When the suitcase was empty, he looked out the window
and saw his grandfather's braids gleaming in the fresh sunlight. With
a shrug, he pushed the gunnysack to the wall beneath his bed and
then went to the trailer's closet. He bent and dragged a torn, wool
army blanket from the closet, tossing a pair of grease-stained coveralls out after the blanket. Finally, he shoved the suitcase into the
closet, arranging first the blanket and then the coveralls so that the
suitcase was hidden. Next, he gathered up his tackle box and fishing
vest and dropped them on top of the pile.

A few minutes later Billy emerged from the trailer in a white shirt, clean Levi's faded to a sky blue, the stained gray hat, and a shiny pair of brown Tony Lama boots. He waved at his grandfather and started walking down the half-mile ranch road toward the highway. The barn crows rose together and sailed out into the broad sky, circling over his head and cawing loudly. The flock tumbled and dodged above him until he reached the ranch gate. When he stepped onto the edge of the pavement and stuck his thumb out at an approaching cattle truck, the birds turned and flapped toward the barn, calling shrilly back and forth.

## 5

Will awoke with a hard jolt. He'd dreamed of the man in the tree. The dark body had begun to move, the hands grasping and pushing against the juniper trunk and the eyes seeking him out with a hard, shining stare. The man had smiled, and the teeth were as red as new blood. On the plain below, the white faces of the Array had turned in swift unison, each one a pale eye, and with their turning a vast sky of sharp-pointed stars had begun to tumble out of control. He'd realized then that it was all connected, the man in the tree and the machine that plunged at them from out of the rain, and the web of invisible wires that linked the Very Large Array to everything, including the stars in the summer sky. He'd opened his own mouth to say it wasn't his fault, but he felt a wire tighten and was hurled suddenly against the light breaking through his bedroom window. ·

He disentangled his legs from the single sheet and shoved his feet over the side of the bed, sitting up slowly. He'd come out of the nightmare with a certainty that they couldn't leave the body out there. Dreaming of ghosts could mean only one thing. More death. They'd have to tell somebody, or they'd have to bury it themselves. He'd also awakened with the certainty that the dead man was an Indian.

He went into the kitchen in his boxer shorts and put a pot of water on the gas stove, unable still to erase the image of the man in the tree. The day was dawning hot, and even within the thick adobe of the house he could feel the tight air of the summer monsoon season. Trouble was, the lightning storms came marching up out of the Sea of Cortez, kindling fires all across Arizona and New Mexico, but the rain they brought was no better than spit on a griddle. The land was as blistered and dry when the storms passed as it had been before they came. And the big fires often burned in the mountains for weeks at a time. He'd made good money with the D-6 a few times contracting for the Forest Service on project fires. On the big ones, especially when low humidity and high winds came together, they'd back the Hotshot crews off and tell him and the other dozer operators to put in a line sometimes a half-mile from the fire. He'd sat on the seat of the Cat more than once watching flames crown out a hundred feet above the ground, the distant fire jumping from ridge to ridge as it rode its own winds across the top of a forest. He liked a phrase the firefighters used: A fire makes its own weather, they said. That, he thought, just about summed it up. When a situation gets hot enough, it makes its own weather.

He walked toward the bathroom, hearing and feeling his bad knee click with each step and cursing the chronic constipation that troubled his mornings. He could date the beginnings of both. The knee on an October morning fifteen years before when Jezebel, with him in the saddle, had sidestepped into a fence post, tearing cartilage and tendons. The constipation not too long after Jace had packed up the Bronco and moved to Albuquerque almost four years ago, leaving him to his own fried potatoes and eggs. The wiry pain in his lower back he attributed to middle age and a lifetime of bucking grain sacks and hay bales. Every rancher or ranch hand he'd ever known, from middle to old age, had a little difficulty bending over and straightening up. You got what you paid for.

When he returned to the kitchen the water was boiling, and he lifted the lid of the enamel pot and dumped in two fistfuls of ground coffee. Jace had taken the plastic Mr. Coffee machine with her to Albuquerque, and he'd fallen back on boiled camp coffee with great satisfaction. Every morning without fail the smell reminded him of deer hunting with his father when he was fourteen and sixteen years old. They'd horse camp up high in the Magdalenas or farther south in the Gila wilderness, and he'd wake each daylight to the aroma of his father's coffee. Rediscovering boiled coffee was the first of two happy results of being abandoned by his true love. The other was the laxative properties of boiled coffee.

At the end of his second cup, he picked up the receiver on the old black telephone and dialed, hating the sound of the dial wheel as it rewound with each number. After a half dozen rings he hung up and headed back to the bedroom.

An hour later, he drove up to the two trailers on the Keene ranch. Seeing the old man on the little deck, he drove past Billy's trailer and parked in front of the other one.

"Good morning, Grampa Siquani," he said loudly as he climbed out of his pickup.

The old man nodded and smiled. "Good morning, Willum. I heard that thunder, so I knew you would come this morning. Are you here to learn the wisdom of the elders, some Cherokee love medicine maybe to get that wild wife of yours back?"

Will climbed up the steps and stood with his hands in his pockets, smiling back at Billy's grandfather. "I'm always ready to learn from your wisdom, Grampa, but I don't know if I want that particular woman back."

The old man cocked his head and looked up at Will. "Course you do. Why would that woman of yours want an old crow somewheres when she could have a sparrow hawk like Will Striker? I got just the thing for you, too. Listen: 'Ha! You White Woman, you hunt your lonely soul. The Sparrow Hawk has just flown in.' That's just a little tiny bit, not even the way it's supposed to be. It's what they call a teaser. I got some of that old tobacco, too. Nobody around here knows about that kind of stuff. Jace'll come running all the way back here."

"Well, like I said, Grampa . . ."

"Leave it to me, Grandson. A man by himself gets into trouble, like old Kanati. You growing any corn in that little garden of yours?"

Will shook his head and rubbed the bridge of his nose. "A few stalks. Not enough water for much else. Jace is just too smart to be stuck out in this godforsaken place all her life."

"Which god you talking about?"

"It's just an expression, Grampa. Godforsaken. It means 'dried up.' "

The old man looked out over the flat grazing land at the broad bottom of the canyon. "I know that expression. It was the animals that dried up this earth a long time ago when it was all mud. Billy said some buzzards come to your place."

"A dozen or so. Believe it or not, Grampa, these buzzards have been killing my chickens. You ever heard of buzzards killing anything?"

The old man looked at Will with a curious expression. "Old Buzzard was real important back in the beginning," he said. "There was nothing but water, you know, till Water Beetle dove down to the bottom and brought up mud to make this world. Then Buzzard flew all around over that mud to see where the animals could live, and he got so wore out he couldn't keep them big wings of his up. Everywhere his wings hit that mud, they made the mountains and valleys. Them other animals up in *Galunlati* got scared there wasn't going to be nothing but mountains, so they started yelling at Buzzard. He went back then, so some of this world is still flat."

Will smiled, remembering his father's version of the story. Before people came along, the animals had been in charge, getting things made by trial and error, screwing up and bickering and getting pissed off just like people. On the first try the animals put the sun too close to the earth so that Crawfish got his shell burned red. It took seven more tries to get the sun right. "Different people have different stories," Caleb Striker had said softly after telling the story of Water Beetle. "White people say that there wasn't anything at first and then God made the world just by talking. I always liked that story. You think maybe that's why white people talk so much?" Will remembered nights with his own son and daughter, one of them under each arm on the old couch, their little shoulders shoved up against his ribs. The earth, he'd explained, hearing his father's voice in his own, was an island floating in a great sea, suspended by a rope at each corner from the rock vault of the sky. Someday, if people didn't take care of the earth, the ropes might grow weak and break, dropping the earth back into that ocean. Someday a man might find himself looking at a world of water, seeing only his own reflection. Then he'd have to make a choice. "It's up to strong human beings like Holly and Si Striker to think good thoughts and keep those ropes in good shape," he'd explained to his children, looking in turn at each of their small, serious, beautiful faces.

"There's other kinds of buzzards, too," Siquani added. "Billy said they was black buzzards. You see which direction they come from?"

"Well, I guess they came in from the west. I saw a bunch of them out toward the foothills before they took up residence on my fence, so I guess they came from that direction."

"You got a problem," the old man said.

Will hesitated a moment and looked toward the barn and then back again. "What problem?"

"He's gone."

"Who's gone?" For an instant, Will thought the old man was talking about the body in the tree.

"He went walking off down the road this morning. I guess that four-wheel drive of his is broke again." The old man nodded toward the trailer. "Go get yourself a chair and sit down for a spell."

"He didn't tell you where he was going?"

"He's too wild, that one. Billy was always the wild boy and you was the one that always followed after him and got in trouble. I used to watch you two."

Will pushed his hat back on his head. "Well, Grampa, I wouldn't say I always followed Billy." But he remembered those days when Billy would seem ready to burst with ideas. At eight years old it had been hard to resist jumping out of the hayloft after Billy, but Billy had missed the tines of the hidden pitchfork that went all the way through Will's boot. It hadn't been any easier to say no to Billy's plan to ride the whiteface bull when they were twelve, the bull that had flung Billy against the barn wall like a sack of beans and would probably have caved Billy's chest in if Will hadn't distracted it with a two-by-four. It had always been hard to resist Billy, who seemed to appear out of the creek each day, running across the wooden bridge with a grin and a plan. Hot-wiring Caleb Striker's pickup to take out the Ruiz twins that first time had been the worst idea, since Will's dad had removed the brake master cylinder the day before. The old pickup had jerked spasmodically into life and, when Will slipped the clutch out, had flung itself nose down into the dry creek bed.

"I watched you two, Willum. You remember that time there was a great big thunderstorm and Billy talked you into letting both your daddies' steers out of that corral? I seen that. Them steers come out of that corral like a bunch of deer jumping out of a hole in the ground, with Billy trying to grab one and climb on its back and you trying to herd 'em all back in. I thought your daddies was going to feed you to the wolves for that one. You was the steady one, but Billy could talk you into most anything."

"Well . . ."

"It's just the way it's supposed to be, Willum. Billy said he'd buy me some peanut butter. I told him not to get that kind with all the little pieces of nuts in it. It hurts, that kind."

Will went into the little trailer and came out with a straight-backed chair like the one the old man sat in. He straddled it, with his arms over the back.

"Them crows told me something come on that storm last night. They say that storm went on but left something here." The old man looked sideways at Will. "You feel anything last night?"

Will chewed on the inside of his cheek and kept his eyes fixed on the eastern mountains. "I don't know," he said after a long silence. He stood up. "You know, Grampa, I'm about out of water at home. I think I better get that tank truck of mine running." He walked to the steps and stopped. "How're you and Billy fixed for drinking water?"

"We don't need none right now, I think."

"Maybe you could ask Billy to give me a call when he gets back."

The old man nodded, and Will added, "You need anything before I go, Grampa?"

"You got any beautiful young women you can spare?" His mouth curved in a slight grin, and then as Will was turning away he added, "I been hearing a screech owl, Willum. Three nights."

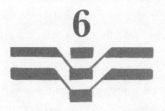

# 6

Driving the long dirt road from the highway back to the ranch house, Will listened to the clatter of the pickup's valves. Everything about the '51 Chevy was loose, and it rattled and ground against itself with every mile. He could feel and see in his mind the way the six pistons slopped around in their cylinders, the way oil seeped and probably splashed past worn rings and the rods wobbled on tired crankshaft bearings. He'd have to tear the whole thing down soon and start right back up from the bottom. The rear end sounded like a tin can full of rocks and the clutch was slipping. Sometimes he had to hit the solenoid with a wrench to make the starter turn over. The brakes, however, were hard and reassuring; he'd turned the drums, rebuilt the cylinders, and replaced the shoes only a month before. The mud tires he'd bought with a week's worth of cattle roundup, branding, castrating, and dehorning for Ruiz had deep new tread on them, and the old radio still pulled in country western stations all the way from Las Cruces and Albuquerque.

He eased the pickup to a stop in front of the barn and went inside, coming back out at once with a saddle, saddle blanket, and bridle. Going to the corral, he set the saddle, with the blanket on top, across the fence and let himself through the gate. He held the bridle up and whistled softly. With a clatter, three buzzards flapped up from the barn ridge and struggled into the sky above the barn. He watched the birds labor toward the scattering of cloud and longed to blast the creatures out of the air.

On the far end of the corral, the bay mare swung her nose up from where she'd been nuzzling the stale trough water and looked at him. With a sigh, she walked slowly to him and lowered her head to push it against his chest. He rubbed a hand along her neck and patted her shoulder before slipping the bit into her mouth and the halter over her head. He noted her ragged hooves with a twinge of guilt. He'd been letting things slip for a while. He'd ridden her so little in the last several years that he'd stopped shoeing her long ago. At least he'd trim the hooves, he told himself, when they got back from this ride.

"Just a little, slow walk, Jez. Nothing too hard on old bones."

As if in response, the mare farted and followed the expulsion of gas with a loud sigh.

"You trying to tell me something profound, old girl?" he said.

When he put the saddle on and began to tighten the cinch, the mare sucked in a great breath, barreling out her gut until he lifted a knee to gently touch her belly. It was a game they'd played since he'd bought her in his twenties, except that back then he'd had to actually use the knee. When she let the air whoosh out, he firmed the cinch, and went to the house, coming out with a small, lever-action rifle. Slipping the thirty-thirty into its scabbard in front of the right stirrup, he stepped around the horse and swung himself into the saddle.

As the mare stood waiting, her ears cocked forward, Maggie appeared from around the barn, straw sticking out of her thick coat. Seeing him on the horse, she came running up happily, shaking bits of straw into the air.

"You stay here, Maggie," he said. "Too many cactus spines out there for you."

The dog stopped and looked at him.

"You stay," he said. "And guard hard."

The dog turned reluctantly and walked back toward the house, where during the summer the door was invariably partway open, stopping once to look over her shoulder as Will reined the mare toward the canyon above the ranch.

He rode west from the house, up the wide vee of the canyon toward the foothills of the Magdalenas. The mare's hooves dragged in the loose dirt of the cow path as it wound through grama and rice grass, creosote brush and prickly pear, and up into the juniper and piñon. Off the trail, the pale gray earth, puckered into tufts around each bunch of grass, bore a fragile-looking crust pocked by the recent cloudburst. Despite the marks of rain, however, there was no sign of moisture anywhere.

Half an hour later, he came to the spring. From a distance he could see the shattered and partially blackened fork of the tall ponderosa pine and beneath the tree the silhouettes of the dozen white-face cattle near the pool, but as soon as they caught his scent the cattle scattered like deer. When he reached the water, the only signs of cattle were the stink in the air and the ploughed-up mud and shit along the edge of the shallow pool.

The water seeped out of a yellow, encrusted rock face so slowly that nothing about it could be called a stream, and it gathered in a stagnant pool that barely covered the bottom of the deep clay basin. Silty mud was still settling into hoofprints at the edges of the shallow pool, and he saw among the hardened tracks beyond the water signs of deer, elk, pronghorn, and, barely discernible among the crowd of signs, the soft pad marks of a mountain lion. Several feet above the level of the water, the end of a rusting pipe jutted from the cracked mud, the remains of his father's last, desperate attempt to bring water down to the barn.

The sulfur smell of the pool hung over the little basin, and he thought back to a time when he and Billy had climbed the rock face to dive into the cold water, a time when the stream tumbled in a little waterfall and the pool was deep and clear. Even when the wells below had dried up and the rains had begun to detour around to the east, for a while the pool had seemed unaffected. It had been common to find the tall blue herons and the squat night herons at the pool in the evenings and mornings, and in the thick grasses along the base of the cliff the frogs had seemed to never stop singing.

Now the grasses and ferns were gone, and there was no evidence of frogs. The ponderosa, one of the few tall trees that managed to grow this far below the real mountains, had obviously been struck by lightning only recently. Splintered wood lay at the base, and a blade of fire had slashed its way from tree tip to earth, leaving a raw strip snaking through the thin bark.

He looked around, wondering how his few scrawny cattle and the other creatures that had left tracks were able to survive on the tainted water, why the wild creatures didn't all move west, what held them to this dying place. He looked northward across Billy's ranch. The fence their fathers had put up between the two five hundreds stopped at the pool so that stock from either side could mingle there. The gap had made the fence relatively meaningless except as symbol, since the cattle tended to cross over one way or another and become a single herd. It had been several years since the last of the Keene cattle had died of old age or despair, and oddly it seemed that the dozen Striker cattle no longer ventured to the Keene side.

Satisfied that, bitter as it was, the water hadn't gone completely from the ranch, he turned and headed back toward the house, letting Jezebel set her own slow pace, dragging the rough ends of her hooves through the dust. His thoughts went to the duffel bag in the well. It was money he'd taken from a dead man, and if he was going to take it, he should do something with it. Eventually he could buy a new truck, but that wouldn't make much of a dent, and besides, the idea didn't appeal to him. He could rebuild the Chevy instead. He didn't need a new house. He didn't want a television or new clothes. He could build a new barn, but then he'd have to do something to justify a barn, and he felt an unexpected reluctance to get back into the cattle business. With surprise, he realized that he didn't want to work cattle any longer. What he wanted to do was ride the five hundred and up into the forest behind it, tie flies in his living room, and use them to catch and release fish on New Mexico and Arizona rivers. His thoughts shied away from deer hunting. Somehow, that desire had gone the same direction as cattle ranching.

A piñon jay screeched at him from a sprawling tree, and he looked up in time to see the luminous blue bird catapult itself away. He became aware suddenly of the shrill of cicadas that filled the midday, and isolated mutterings of dry thunder somewhere in the southwest. Only scraps of cirrus hung in the sky overhead. And then he remembered Billy's words. He could put in the well, the thousand-foot well the geologist had said he would need. He'd have cold, clear water in the house again, and he wouldn't have to make the weekly trips into Magdalena with the deuce-and-a-half. Maybe he'd put in a big garden, the kind his mother had had when he was little. Maybe even one of those raised swimming pools so that if he ever had grandkids, they would have a place to swim in the summer. If he went far enough down to free the waters trapped deep in the earth, he really could make the ranch bloom again. It was just a matter of money and technology.

He thought of the body and suddenly there was a crash of thunder as Jezebel began to crumple. When she collapsed sideways, he tried to push himself away, but one leg was under the horse, caught in the stirrup. His shoulder struck the rocky ground, and the air was driven from his chest.

For a few seconds he struggled to breathe, and then he felt the air rush back into his lungs. Even as he gasped for breath, he used his free foot to push against the saddle, realizing with relief that a large rock held the mare's shoulder a few inches from the ground. Only the rock had saved him from being trapped with a badly crushed leg. Quickly, he wiggled the foot out of the stirrup and began pulling it from under the quivering horse. There was a soft, thudding sound, and dust rose from the mare's shoulder. Something warm and damp splashed across his forehead. Then he heard the report of the rifle.

He jerked the thirty-thirty from its scabbard and at the same time worked his leg free of the now still horse. At once he was in a crouch and running awkwardly for a rock outcropping a few yards up the hill. The earth jumped in stitches at his feet, and he heard a chatter of rifle shots from somewhere below.

A bullet struck the rock in front of him and glanced away with a sharp crack, and he leapt and flattened himself behind the outcrop, scraping a forearm painfully against the rough granite and feeling his heart beat against his ribs. The metallic taste of panic rose in his mouth. He took several deep breaths and eased to one side so that he could look over the rock. Two black silhouettes were running up the slope below, sprinting fluidly away from the same place, bent low and carrying rifles. He scanned the juniper-dotted terrain between himself and the men and between them and the house. Seeing no other movement, he concentrated on the two, realizing at once that they were trying to flank his position.

He tried to assess his situation. His only advantage was that they couldn't be sure if he'd been hurt, and they might not have seen the thirty-thirty in the saddle scabbard. One of many disadvantages was that his hands were shaking like he had just let go of a jackhammer.

The outcropping climbed the hill to his right for ten yards and then collapsed in a jumble of boulders. He began to crawl along the rock line until he had reached the end. Once there, he squirmed to the edge and looked down the slope. At first he saw nothing, and then he spotted one of them crouched behind the trunk of a cedar, his outline showing darkly through the tangle of branches. The second man was nowhere to be seen.

Cursing himself for losing one of the two, he breathed deeply several times, noting with relief that his hands had steadied, then slid the thirty-thirty onto a flat rock and aimed at the man in the juniper thicket. The distance was scarcely a hundred yards, and he aimed for the dark bulk of the body, taking another deep breath and holding it. When he fired, the man simply slid from sight below the brushy tree. He worked the lever of the rifle, keeping his eyes on the tree. An explosion of rock next to his face stung and blinded him for an instant, and then he heard the rifle shot echo behind him. He jumped to his feet and half ran and half scrambled along the rock toward his original position, trying to put all the angles together as he did so. Another bullet and then another shattered the rock beside him, and he dove over the outcropping as still more shots struck the rock.

For a long moment he lay there, feeling abruptly calm and clear-minded, wishing that he hadn't lost his hat so he could stick it on the end of his rifle barrel and shove that up. That always seemed to work on television, and if you thought about it, there was no reason it shouldn't. Naturally the one shooting would take a chance on there being a head inside the hat. Anybody would. Finally, he looked over the top of the rock.

The man was walking calmly down the open hillside, the rifle against his shoulder and pointed toward Will.

Will eased the thirty-thirty over the edge of the rock, snugged it against his shoulder, and fired, seeing dirt kick up on the hill behind the man, who suddenly and inexplicably began running straight at the rocks.

Jerking the rifle back, Will grabbed frantically at the lever, feeling as though his hands were made of stone, willing his fingers to grip and pull. The thud of the running man's feet seemed to shake the earth, and as he felt he was about to be trampled Will stood and pointed the little thirty-thirty at the black blur coming toward him.

When he fired, the man folded in the middle as though reaching abruptly to tie his shoes. The man's rifle clattered to the ground as he dove gracefully in the direction of the earth, his body tucking into a full tumble that brought him flat on his back at Will's feet.

Holding his own empty rifle like a club, Will looked down at the man. The man's eyes blinked several times and shifted to focus, and thick tears formed and ran across the dark cheeks, while the mouth pursed as if in deep thought. The chest, where a bloody hole showed in the chambray shirt, rose and fell several times, and one hand lifted two inches from the ground, with the index finger pointed as if the dying man were about to make an observation.

Will picked up the assault rifle. The man had obviously brought only one clip and had squandered it. That last act had been something like a suicide run. As he turned toward the trail that led home, he felt a surge of pity followed by a rush of fear of whatever it was that could make a man that desperate.

Nearing the ranch house with Jezebel's saddle over his left shoulder and the bridle and rifle in his right hand, Will looked unsuccessfully for a vehicle before deciding that the two men must have approached the place on foot. Of course, he thought, they wouldn't have just driven up in plain sight. Nobody was that stupid. They would have left their car out on the highway and sneaked through the sparse junipers. He imagined their frustration when, after probably running and crawling nearly a mile from the main road, they had gone to the house before tracking him up the canyon. The heavy pine door stood open, and when he dropped the saddle and bridle and went through the door, the first thing he saw was the couch, upside down with the bottom slit open. The contents of kitchen cabinets and the chests in the bedrooms were scattered everywhere, and he was surprised to see Jace's clothing spread across the bed and floor, panties and bras and T-shirts and jeans. It hadn't occurred to him that she'd left anything in the cherry chest, and at the sight he stopped, shocked by the fact that she'd left so much behind. He picked up a lacy blue bra, the insubstantial kind that hooked in the front, and stared at it for a moment, a hot anger kindling just behind his eyes. They had thrown half the books from the shelves and torn the Navajo rugs off the walls, leaving rugs and books in a tangled pile. In his bedroom, the fly-tying table was on its side, hackle and dubbing and spools of thread strewn across the deep blue Pendleton blanket that lay beside the upside-down bed and gutted mattress.

As he bent to lift the wooden bed frame back to its feet, he heard a soft moan and only then did he notice the small, thin pool of blood that edged a corner of the blanket. When he raised the blanket, he saw Maggie's broad face, the eyes black and damp.

"Maggie, girl," he said, folding the blanket back to expose the length of her body.

The dog's nubby tail twitched, and when she raised her head he saw the matting of blood along her neck and shoulder.

7

The flattened half of a red sun lay snagged on black pines. Across the bloody face of the sun, framed in tatters of orange cloud, four buzzards circled evenly, the same four he'd scared up from the earth when he arrived with the pick and shovel. After studying the ground for a moment, Will dropped the shovel and backed out of the tangle of juniper branches. The body lay two yards away, and he grasped the feet to drag it inside the clutter of the tree's down-swept branches, backing carefully between the sharp limbs, reaching a hand behind him to push them away. The man had been large, tall, and big-gutted. Like the other, he was dressed in work clothes: chambray shirt, jeans, and lug-soled boots. His black hair was cut to within a half-inch of the blue scalp, and a few hairs of a sparse mustache lay over his upper lip. Will looked quickly away from the work of the buzzards and focused on the earth beneath the thick cedar.

Inside the perimeter of the tree, he cut and lifted away the top layer of sod in large squares. When he had a shallow hole dug, cutting through roots and shifting rocks, he used the shovel to pry the body over so that it rolled facedown into the grave. He scraped as much of the earth as possible back into the hole, tamping it with his feet and the handle of the shovel until it was hard packed, and then he carefully fitted the sod back into place. He distributed the remaining earth and rocks within the confines of the tree and lay several dead branches randomly across the grave. Finally, he scattered debris over the fresh earth and bent to back out of the juniper. From the outside the tree looked like all the other trees in the New Mexico landscape.

When he was satisfied, he gathered pick and shovel and walked up the slope toward the second body. The sun had vanished, leaving a red outline on the barbs of the distant ridge, and the buzzards had backed away until they were black motes on the horizon. He stopped at the rock outcropping for a moment, searching his mind once again for a different course and finding none. The two men sent to kill him would have to disappear. The only other option was to call the sheriff, but things had gone too far. The dead men had begun a journey some time before that led to this darkening canyon. He and Billy had ventured off their own familiar paths into something new, and now they'd have to follow that different trail to its end.

He stepped across the outcropping to where the other body

lay, the rigid form reminding him of Maggie lying on the rug at home. Because he'd known the old veterinarian all his life, and because the man had doctored cows and horses and dogs for Strikers more times than he could count, there hadn't been any questions. Guns did sometimes discharge accidentally, and dogs often were where they shouldn't be. The bullet had shattered the femur and continued through the flesh of the side and back. With a cast from foot to shoulder of one leg and gauze and bandages around the shaved chest and shoulder, Maggie would be a house dog for a long time.

He buried the body under the branches of a second juniper, scraping the rocky grave in the near-dark and spreading heavy stones and debris over the earth when he was done. He walked back down the canyon in utter blackness, following the lighter darkness of the path made by men and animals long dead. Around him the ranch and the growing night felt heavy with the presence of the dead. He'd have to find whatever the two men had driven and hide it in the barn for the time being.

8

Siquani Kaneequayokee closed his eyes. The evening was as tense as the skin of a water drum, and it tapped at his thoughts as it had for two days now. Something was happening. There was a disturbance in the earth and sky. He began to sing softly, a wavering monotone that remained caught within his own throat. In only a moment he had found the thing. It was approaching, and he felt it soaring on the still evening, gliding and swooping with outstretched wings, searching until it caught the trail of his song and came with a tumbled rush. And then it was there.

When he opened his eyes, he saw the image of a man standing on the top step before the porch. Dressed in a black suit and white shirt, the man was dark-skinned and wore an expression of despair. His hair hung down past his collar in hard-looking clumps and points. And just below where his heart would have been was a red-black stain that covered his shirt and disappeared beneath his suit coat on both sides. The hand that half rose in greeting bore a heavy turquoise and silver ring, the green stone veined with a thick darkness.

Siquani got up and went into the trailer, returning with the same straight-backed chair Will Striker had sat in. He placed the chair a couple of feet from his own, facing outward also, and with one hand on the back of the chair he motioned with the other hand.

The man smiled sadly and walked to the chair and sat down, his back and shoulders held rigid. Siquani stepped around to the front of the other chair and sat also. He looked at the blurry sky, where the stars seemed to be blowing slowly across one another, carried by distant winds. He pulled on the lobe of one ear and nodded to himself. Finally, still without looking at his guest, he said, "It's good you came."

"I sure was tired of that tree."

"I seen that tree," the old man replied.

"It was kind of you to call me."

Siquani shrugged, still looking straight ahead. "The sky was unhappy about you. The crows told me."

"I'm not too fond of birds these days." The young man shook his head and seemed to shiver.

"It's just what they're supposed to do. Like all of us." Siquani pulled on the ear again. "I ain't never called a ghost before."

"I hadn't thought of myself as a ghost," the other said. "I guess that's sure as heck what I am though, isn't it?"

The old man turned to look at the young man, his eyes focused on the air just over the ghost's shoulder. "Well, I can see plumb through you. And there ain't much else you can be but dead. So you must be a ghost."

"What do you think we're supposed to do now that you got me here?" He raised his shoulders and smiled faintly. "I have not done this thing before."

"Let's introduce ourselves. I am Siquani Kaneequayokee. This is my grandson's ranch."

"I'm very pleased to meet you, Grandfather," the ghost said. "My name is Arturo Cruz. I am from a pueblo up north. That's where I was from, anyway, till I got killed."

"Ain't you got someplace to go, Mister Cruz?"

Arturo Cruz shrugged deeply. "Who knows? In our pueblo, we always thought it was the job of the dead to bring rain. We would dress them up like rain clouds when we buried them and send them on their journey with prayers. But all I know is that I was out there and now I'm here. I thought maybe this was where I was supposed to go." He looked around the ranch, seeing the other trailer, the crippled barn with its shifting line of crows, broken fences, and weeds. "This doesn't look quite bad enough to be hell, and it sure isn't heaven. No offense, Mr. Siquani."

"It ain't so bad," the old man replied. "That allotment down there in Oklahoma was worse. We couldn't grow nothing but rattlesnake weed."

"Pigweed," the ghost said. "On my father's land we grow nothing but pigweed. He plants chiles, but pigweed comes up. That's why I went to the university."

"You can eat pigweed," Siquani said. "It tastes pretty good. Sort of like spinach I think. Poke salad kind of."

"Then I took up drug smuggling. It pays very well. See this suit?" He held an arm out toward the old man. "Twelve hundred bucks."

Siquani nodded. "Everything costs more today. Overalls cost thirty-two bucks now. Used to be four bucks. Maybe you can help me watch, Mister Cruz. Perhaps that is your job. I have laid down the pathway, but we will have to watch carefully."

Arturo Cruz shrugged. "I am at your service," he said. "Anything to get away from those birds." The shrug ended in a shiver.

"You play checkers, Arturo Cruz?"

"Damn right. But I think one of the rules of being a ghost is I cannot move things." He pushed at the chair, but his hand went right through the wood. "I could perhaps tell you where to move my pieces, and you could move them for me."

"Good. I'll get the board."

As Siquani started back into the trailer, Arturo Cruz shouted after him, "How do I know I can trust you to move my pieces?"

# 9

Will lay on his back, tightening the last bolt on the starter housing. Sweat ran from his forehead into his eyes, burning with salt. His hand slipped and he smashed a knuckle. Through his cursing, he heard the sound of a strange vehicle approaching. He reached for the shotgun that lay on the tarp beside him and pushed himself out from under the tank truck.

Inside a whirlwind of dust sat a shining new pickup, big and swollen with luxury. When the dust thinned, Billy stood in front of the truck.

"Isn't she a beauty?" Billy said. "Jesus Christ, Will, what's with the shotgun?"

Will stood the shotgun against the tank truck fender and blew on the bleeding knuckle as he looked from Billy to the pickup and back. "Goddammit, Billy," he said at last. "Goddammit to hell."

"What's wrong?" Billy's smile disappeared, and he turned to examine the pickup.

Will grabbed a rag from the fender of the Chevy and began gingerly wiping grease from his hands.

"Still got those buzzards over there, I see." Billy nodded toward the barn. "I guess they crossed with chicken hawks."

"Where the hell've you been for the last three days, Billy? I thought we agreed we wouldn't spend that money until we figured this thing out."

"Heck, Will, this truck didn't cost much at all. Besides, I was thinking about your plan." Billy lifted his hat from his head and pushed loose hair behind each ear before setting the hat back in place. "I hitched a ride up to Albuquerque and bought this from one of those car lots for cash. I paid the guy twenty thousand, but he wrote down nine thousand. It was his idea when he saw I had cash, because he said they have to report it if it's more than ten thousand. He talked like he did this stuff all the time. I told him I was an Osage Indian and it was my oil money."

Will shook his head.

"That's not all. See, I figured I could drive this for a little while and then sell it to somebody else. I'll get a check from them and take that to the bank. Nobody'll question that kind of deposit. It's like laundering money. And listen, the guy at Mad Anthony's car lot said I should make small deposits in different banks, never more than ten thousand, because banks don't have to report anything under ten thousand to the government."

"A guy at a car lot told you all that?" Will spat into the powdery dirt of the road, his spittle raising a little poof of dust and leaving a deep imprint. "I'm curious about what you told this guy."

Billy held out both hands. "Nothing. Just the Osage stuff. I don't think he believed me, but it didn't seem like he cared a whole heck of a lot. He mentioned all that other stuff on his own, like it was the kind of thing people talk about every day."

"Well, it's done now I guess." Will walked over to the pickup and ran a finger through the dust on the red fender. He leaned his arms on the bottom of the driver's window and studied the interior.

"Don't even have to get out to lock the hubs." He looked

over his shoulder at Billy. "Factory air," he said, his voice inflectionless.

"You can't get the good models without it, Will. Besides, it's essential for resale value."

Will stepped away from the cab of the truck and leaned against the front fender, his arms folded across his chest.

Billy reached through the truck window. "By the way," he said, "I picked up something in Albuquerque for you. They've got this paper called *New City*, spelled with a U." He opened a tabloid-size paper and folded it to the last pages. "This is the personals section. Listen." From his shirt pocket he took a pair of glasses with heavy black frames. "This one's called 'Nice Girls Do'—with three exclamation marks. Each one of these ads has a title. Listen to this. 'Queen-sized SBF'—that means Single Black Female—'in search of SWM, thirty-three to sixty, to explore sexual fantasies such as two men at once.'"

Billy lowered the paper and removed the glasses, gesturing with the glasses as he added, "See, I've been thinking about you out here all alone, Will. It's not natural. A man needs balance."

"And you think Queen Sized there might offer balance?" Will looked at Billy steadily.

"Well, hell, Will. Maybe she sounds a little extreme, but the ad also says, 'Relationship possible with right male.' You're the kind of man that could settle a woman like this down, the right male."

Will's mouth stretched faintly into the hint of a smile as Billy pushed the glasses back onto his nose and looked at the paper again. "You need something new and exciting in your life, Will. How about this one. 'Young and attractive lesbian couple in search of two B-i or S-t-r men to lose our virginity to—together!' What do you say? They want to buy two strong men."

Will pulled a bandanna out of his hip pocket and wrapped it around the still-bleeding knuckle. "Shut up, Billy. Just shut up and listen for a minute." Will looked off toward the western mountains and then back to the ground at his friend's feet. "I buried two men day before yesterday. Up there by the spring."

"What?" Billy dropped the newspaper, and the breeze caught it and tumbled it against the wheel of the pickup.

"They tried to kill me, and I got lucky. They shot Jezebel."

"Jesus, Will—"

"They were both Indians, Billy, just like that fellow with the suitcase."

"But how'd they find out?"

Will shook his head. "While you were gone, I went into town looking for you. I was afraid you'd run into some more like those two. I bought a newspaper."

"Geez, Will, if—"

"The police found pieces of that copter over by the Array. And they found a couple of bodies in the wreckage. The newspaper said one of the bodies had a bullet in it."

Billy took his hat off and wiped his forehead on the sleeve of his shirt, saying nothing.

Will's eyes locked on Billy's. "There's more. Joe told me a couple of guys'd been in the bar asking about an old Toyota Land Cruiser. They claimed they were collectors looking to buy one, but he said they didn't look like that. Joe didn't tell them anything, but he said they drove off in one of those Range Rovers."

Billy settled the hat back on his head. "How would they know I had an old Land Cruiser? And why'd they come after you?"

"They must've found that fender and somebody must've told them who had the only old Land Cruiser in the county. It probably wasn't too difficult to figure out."

"But why'd they come after you?"

Will removed the bandanna and examined the gashed knuckle, where the blood had stopped flowing. "I guess they couldn't find you, and somebody told them who your best friend was. My other guess is maybe those guys in the copter radioed somebody about us before they blew all to hell. It took me two days to put the house back together after they tore it up. You know what they were looking for."

"Jesus H. Christ." Billy removed his hat and ran a hand through his loose hair. "Those guys could've killed you."

"I don't think they wanted to kill me. That's why they shot Jez. They must've wanted information."

"I guess nobody could find those graves?" Billy said.

Will shook his head. "It won't be easy, but I guess anything can be found if somebody looks hard enough. I've got that black Range Rover in the barn right now."

Will looked at the edge of the dry creek bed a few feet away. An inch-long baby horned toad hugged the shadow of a rice-grass stalk, its knobby body strangely soothing to Will. He rubbed the greasy edge of his fist across his forehead and raised his eyes toward Billy. "You know," he said slowly, "it's either your bullet or mine in that body."

# 10

Billy left his friend's ranch and drove the ten miles into Magdalena, seeing the outline of Mary on the hillside above the little strip of town, the scarf pulled down around her beautiful hair. Outside the Tecolote Bar the dirt lot was crowded with pickup trucks and a scattering of big American autos. When he was sure he recognized every vehicle outside the bar, he parked the new pickup carefully along the street and went in.

The first thing he saw was Carla turning from the bar with a pint of beer in each hand. She saw him at the same time and gave him a kind of apologetic smile that dipped ruefully at one corner. With her blond hair pulled back, in a plaid blouse and denim skirt, she looked sixteen.

As they passed one another, he smiled and nodded, surprised

at how well he was taking his desertion. For a feeble moment he tried to dredge up old and familiar feelings of outrage, the kind of she-done-me-wrong sentiments cherished in the proximity of cowboy bars and rodeos, but what he thought of was the gunnysack beneath his bed. And what he felt was relief. He liked Carla. She was cute and smart and full of life and bored shitless by the end of two weeks on the ranch, and he couldn't blame her a bit. Even going into town every night and doing the Texas two-step at the Tecolote hadn't really been enough. She was twenty-one and looking for a good time before life closed in on her. He was forty-six and had already had his good time and plenty to boot on the rodeo circuit. And he was aware that the suitcase had altered his perspective. Proportion and dimension had changed; relations had changed. Even the familiar half-light and smoke of the bar, with its dingy linoleum, scarred counter, and dusty corners felt different. There was a sharp edge to the little bar that he'd sought but never found there before, as if it were the kind of place where things could happen. And he knew finally that he didn't want anything to happen, not a damned thing, ever again.

Carla had begun to make him a little bit tired anyway, even before the deer hunt. "I'm getting too damned old for this," he'd told himself late at night a week into their whirlwind passion. They'd lain in the little trailer bed, Carla stretched out beside him so that he breathed the fragrance of her young hair with every breath and his cupped palm felt the warmth of her breast. The evening hadn't been exactly a success as far as Carla was concerned. She'd been amorous, her mouth and tongue all over his body, until he felt like he was being assaulted by an infestation of soft-lipped locusts. Even when he became hard enough for her to sit atop his prone body and slip him inside her, he had felt an unusual kind of detachment. There she was moving up and down and grinding herself against him in little circular motions, her eyes closed and faint moans escaping from her young mouth while his mind wandered. His hands, like well-trained sheep dogs, went about their proper business, caressing her thighs and moving smoothly up the curve of her belly and rib cage, tracing the undershadow of each breast and sliding down her arms. When she said "oh god" for the fifth or sixth time, he looked up at her breasts with their erect, pink-brown nipples and thought about fly tying, remembering the problem he always had tying in the deer hair for the Adams Irresistible, the way the hair always spun too much and then the nerve-wracking job of trimming the hair body off with just the right taper, resting the little scissors precisely along a forefinger just beneath the fly clamped in its vise. And finally the problem of tying in hackle and wings without wrapping too far up the hook so the eye was obscured. There was nothing worse than getting out a new fly in the middle of a river and finding that you couldn't thread the tippet through the eye. Will's flies never had that problem. The wet sounds of Carla moving reminded him of a special place on the White River, where the water ran in fast and deep beneath the overhang of a rock face, slapping rhythmically and rippling against the dark granite. The trick was to float a dry fly downstream, something like a Blue Dun, avoiding all line drag. The big trout lay just beyond the in-sweeping curve of the current, hidden always in shadow.

"What's wrong, Billy?" she'd asked when she was finished with him. "You got about as much life tonight as an old cucumber."

He'd mumbled words about a long day, and she'd turned her back with the forgiveness of youth to snuggle in against him and drop off into a sudden and apparently bottomless sleep. He'd lain there, his body cupped to hers, knowing that something in his life was different. Feeling the tautness of her skin and the young heat of her, he sighed deeply with a new self-knowledge gained from realizing that he didn't want to screw Carla any longer. What he really wanted was to go fishing. He wanted an incoming low-pressure front that would make the fish restless. Or maybe a day of deer hunting would do, walking a forest with a rifle in the crook of his arm and all senses alert. At two in the morning he'd slipped out of bed and called Will Striker, waking his oldest and only friend to suggest a deer hunt the next day. And after Will had cursed bitterly and said yes, as he'd known Will would, he'd remained up, moving noiselessly to get ready for the hunt and realizing with certainty that Carla wouldn't be in the little trailer when he returned.

He sat on a stool at the bar, and the mournful little man behind the counter poured a draft beer and placed it in front of him. "How's tricks? You working anywhere these days, Billy?"

When Billy shook his head, the bartender said, "I hear Ruiz is hiring for hay."

"No hay bucking for me. I got enough hay under my skin already to last ten lifetimes."

"I thought you and Will might need the work. I heard he put in a fire line for the Forest Service a month or two ago with that D-6 of his, but that won't keep a man in filet mignon. By the way, did Will tell you some guys were in here buying beers for people and asking about a red Land Cruiser? Couple of hardcase Indians, said they were automobile collectors. Fat chance. Relatives of yours maybe?" The bartender tried a half-hearted smile.

"Yeah, Will told me," Billy replied. "That's really why I came in, Joe. What'd those guys find out?"

The bartender grimaced. "You know me, but there's plenty of loose mouths in this town. You can bet those guys know whose Cruiser it is. And I'd wager a week's pay they know he's driving a new red pickup."

"How'd you know—"

The bartender shrugged. "It's a little town, Billy. Somebody sees you drive through town in a fancy new rig and they tell somebody else. You know how it is. There ain't much happens here. You need help with anything?"

Billy reached out to tap the little man on the shoulder. "Thanks, Joe," he said. "Just let me or Will know if those guys come back."

"Well, you need some help, give me a call. How's your grampa?" As he spoke, the bartender's eyes focused on something behind Billy.

"He doing good, Joe. Grampa Siquani's going to outlive me and you and all the rest of this town."

"He sure as hell may outlive you, the way Mouse Meléndez there is looking at you."

Billy slowly revolved on the stool to face the direction in which the bartender was staring.

A very large man with light brown hair hanging loose past his shoulders was standing next to a booth along the far wall. Carla had both hands around the man's huge, tattooed forearm and was saying something to him in a hushed, urgent voice. The man, dressed in a leather vest open to show his hairy chest and large belly, and greasy Levi's and black boots, jerked his arm free and walked toward Billy.

There was a loud crash from the pool table at the opposite end of the small bar, and Billy turned toward the most beautiful woman he'd ever seen. She was bent over the pool table, where her break had just scattered the balls impressively. She held the cue stick ready as she calculated the angle of her next shot. Long, thick black hair fell over the shoulders of her white T-shirt and touched the green table, and as she lined up the shot her lips parted to expose teeth that looked amazingly white in her very brown face.

"Carla's done with you, Billy. You might as well accept it," a voice said.

Billy watched the woman make her shot, one arm pulling the stick back as she smiled and shifted her stance slightly. Her concentration on the shot was total, and the cue stick kissed the white ball and sent it into a solid so softly that the struck ball seemed to move of its own volition to disappear soundlessly into a side pocket. Her smile broadened at the shot, and Billy felt his own mouth smile in sympathy.

"Goddammit, Billy, are you listening to me?"

Billy turned back around to find Mouse Meléndez less than two feet away and leaning toward him.

"So you want to settle this outside?" Meléndez continued, his head wobbling a little as he spoke, as though unsure of exactly what posture it should assume.

"Settle what? I'm sorry, Mouse, I guess I was distracted." He felt the smile on his face but couldn't do anything about it.

Meléndez shook his head as if in disgust. "That always was your problem, Billy. You just don't pay attention. Never did when we was kids, and still don't I guess." He took a deep breath. "I'm talking about Carla. She's through with you. Carla's with me now."

"Oh, Carla." Billy looked toward the booth where Carla sat nervously over a beer. "That's okay. Carla and me had a good time, Mouse, but that's over."

"Bullshit." Meléndez paused as if confused, his eyes still seeming to have difficulty locating Billy. "You mean to say you don't want to fight me for Carla?"

Billy reached behind him for his beer, took a long drink, and shook his head before setting the glass back on the bar. "You mean do I want to see which one of us can use his doubled fists to inflict the most damage on the other one before one of us is too damaged to continue? No way. Now I've got to be going, Mouse."

"I never seen you turn down a fight before, Billy. Besides, we always use feet, too."

"These are the nineties, Mouse, damned near the twenty-first century. A woman has the right to choose who she wants to be with. I have no problem with that. So I wish you both the best of luck." He held out his hand. "No hard feelings."

Meléndez took a step closer. "I can't believe this shit," he said softly. "This is embarrassing. What's wrong with you?" His hand dipped and rose, and when it came back up the blade of a knife flashed. A glimmer of white teeth showed through the nearly blond beard, and his voice, when he spoke, was uncertain. "Maybe you'd like to get down on your hands and knees and crawl out of here, now that it's the fucking nineties?"

Billy fought against his desire to shrink back against the bar. "What kind of low-life shit is this, Mouse, some kind of crap you learned in California? Think about what you're doing; it's not like you. If you're trying to impress Carla, forget it. The only thing that impresses Carla is what you got between your legs and between your ears. Which in your case ain't much either place."

Mouse towered unsteadily over the stool where Billy sat. "You ain't going to embarrass me, Billy," he muttered.

"Goddammit, Mouse, you're drunk. You might hurt somebody by mistake, and you're going to feel pretty bad about it tomorrow. Now you'd better fold up that thing and put it away before you cut yourself." Billy measured the distance between the knife and himself, calculating the piss-poor leverage he would have in his sitting position. He imagined what it would feel like to get down on his hands and knees and crawl to the door, seeing himself as others would see him. It wouldn't look pretty, but it would feel a lot better than the knife would and probably look better, too. He tried to figure his odds. If he set one boot firmly against the rail below the bar and pushed off with that foot while aiming for Mouse's nuts with the other foot, maybe he could minimize the damage. He could go for the knife arm with his left hand and use the heel of his right hand on Mouse's nose, and if he also connected with his boot he'd be in luck. The odds, however, were very bad. His other option was to crawl out of the bar.

He had decided on the more sensible plan when he saw a blur and heard a dull thud. Meléndez's blue eyes rolled back in their sockets, spittle erupted from his big mouth and clung to his beard, and he fell, his forehead catching the edge of a padded stool on his way down.

Billy looked up to see the woman with the pool cue. She held the cue stick like a baseball player who'd just hit a home run, her hands gripping the thin end of the stick and her eyes on the man she had clubbed. Her wild black hair had fallen forward over her shoulders, framing the thin, even wilder-looking face. Eyes the color of black coffee gleamed above arching cheekbones, and Billy had the impression of looking into the face of a hunting bird. But in the darkness of her face, her smile was brilliant. The muscles of her arms looked hard and corded in the sleeveless T-shirt, and the tight Levi's showed off impressively long legs.

Carla walked slowly from the booth and gazed down at her new boyfriend. She turned to look up at the woman with the cue stick. "You killed Mouse," she said, more in wonder than accusation.

The bartender squatted next to the body and felt for a pulse on the neck. "Naw," he said. "Better luck next time."

He picked up the butterfly knife and closed it, slipping it into the pocket of his western shirt and then stood up. "This turd'll be okay. But I think you two better clear out. When Mouse wakes up, I'm going to throw his ass out of here. Unless this knocked some sense into him, if I know him, and I've known him since he was a baby, he'll go get some of those friends of his and come back looking for both of you."

Billy looked at the woman. Apache or Ute, he guessed, definitely not Navajo or Pueblo. And no spring chicken either. Judging by the fine laugh lines around her beautiful eyes, she was probably in her mid-thirties or older.

She smiled at him and walked back to the table and set the cue stick in its rack. He scanned the dozen other customers, all of whom were watching her with apparently the same fascination he felt, and when she went through the door, he was a step behind her.

Outside the bar, she stopped and stood with her hands on her hips, her back to him. "Would you look at that sky," she said.

He stopped beside her and looked at the sky. The stars were bright, forming vaguely familiar patterns across the moonless arc. The afternoon heat had faded, and a cool edge encroached on the little town from the nearby mountains.

"Thanks," he said.

She turned and the smile had disappeared. "Don't mention it. I might have done the same for a white man."

He made a wry expression at the old joke. "I haven't seen you around here before," he said.

"That's because I've never been here before. Although I lived pretty close to here when I was a baby." She nodded toward the southeast. "Over at Mescalero. I'm Apache."

"And you've never been in Magdalena?"

"You know someplace else we can get a beer? I sure as fuck didn't see any other bars in this metropolis."

He raised his eyebrows and pretended to think.

"You find me another beer and I'll tell you why I have never seen this one-street town before."

"Well, I don't know. There's a place about half an hour from here. It's very exclusive, but I have connections."

"What are we waiting for?" She hooked her arm through his. "What kind of mixed-blood are you, anyway? It's easy to see you're some kind."

He led her toward the new pickup, admiring the way even through the dust the bar lights played dully on the red paint. He thought again of the gunnysack. He'd be a fool to bring this woman he didn't know into his trailer with all that money under his bed. He turned toward her, seeing the flash of smile and light glint in her nearly black eyes. "I guess I'm Cherokee, Irish, and God knows what all," he said. "My dad was full-blood Cherokee, and my mom's folks came from Ireland."

"Was?"

"They both died a few years ago."

"I'm sorry. You were going to crawl out of that bar, weren't you?"

He hesitated. "I've known Mouse a good part of his life. He's not a bad guy really, but when he gets drunk like that he doesn't think at all. That knife must be a bad habit he picked up in California."

They both looked at the stars for a moment longer before he added, "I've probably fought Mouse Meléndez a couple dozen times since we were kids, and I haven't beat him yet. He's too goddamned big. Mouse's descended from those Spaniards who came up from Mexico about a thousand years ago. That's one reason he looks so white. The other reason is he's half white."

She laughed out loud. "I'm glad you didn't hurt him. I almost waited to see if you had enough sense to crawl out. But I was afraid you wouldn't be that smart, and you were too sexy to lose before we even met."

In the pickup, she sat against the door, her eyes studying the scenery as if memorizing the route. "That girl was cute," she said after a long silence. "I'll bet she's a great fuck."

He cocked his head and looked at her.

"Only you macho men are supposed to talk like that, right?" She cocked her own head back at him with the thousand-watt smile. "Sorry."

He drove through the town slowly, wondering if he should turn around and take this woman back to the bar. He felt an uneasiness about the whole evening, the way Mouse had acted so out of character, the funny feeling of the bar, and now this woman he didn't know sitting beside him in a pickup that smelled of new leather, new plastic, and new money. He covered the five blocks of the main street at twenty miles an hour, and then, fighting an instinct to turn back, accelerated west into the dark. His passenger leaned against the door, watching the shadowed scenery flow by. When they turned into the ranch gate, she looked behind them at the paved road for a moment.

"Planning your escape route?" he asked.

She brushed the long hair back from her face and the white teeth flashed. "Why do you say escape? Maybe I'm planning an attack. I like cowboys."

"Really?" He looked sideways at her. "Did you know that most of the real old-time cowboys were queer?"

She laughed, and he went on. "It's true. I read it in a new history of the West. I read a lot. This professor from Kansas who wrote the book found hundreds of secret letters and diaries. He found out that most of the cowboys were queer. They had a kind of underground recruiting network all over the east coast, and they'd get all these young guys to come out and sign on. You had to be recommended by a queer cowboy to get hired on almost all the big spreads. The whole West was controlled by a kind of queer cowboys' union. It was a brilliantly kept secret."

"I'm sure it was," she said.

"It's true. How else do you think they'd get those guys to go on trail drives or work in bunkhouses and line shacks with nothing but men around? The working conditions were terrible and the pay was worse, but they loved it. They were having orgies in the bunkhouses, big queer parties with grizzled old cowpunchers and young guys prancing around butt naked in nothing but chaps. This historian quoted from diaries and journals and letters they wrote to their boyfriends back East and in cities like San Francisco trying to convince them to come out. It's all documented. Statistics show that over ninety percent of real working cowboys in the nineteenth century were homosexual. The book is called *When Men Were Men: The Real History of the West*. Of course cowboys are different now, since most cowboys these days are Indians."

"Today you're all real men," she replied.

He looked sternly at her. "Well, at least we half-breed cowboys are. It's genetically impossible for Indians to handle their liquor, step on twigs, or be homosexual. You might say evolution is responsible."

"I'll have to take that up with some of my friends over at Zuni," she said.

He stopped in front of the darkened Airstream, the pickup's headlights glinting for a moment on the lightless bulk of his grandfather's trailer before he killed the engine. "This is Billy Keene's club," he said, gesturing with a sweep of his hand. "Don't be deceived by the modest appearance."

"You're Billy Keene?"

He lifted the rifle from the rack over the seat. "Billy Kaneequayokee actually, though in the everyday world like my father before me I use the shortened version. And you?"

"You're a strange man, Billy Keene. It took you a long time to ask. My name is Odessa Whitehawk, and since your next words will be a question, I'll tell you how I got the name. I was conceived when my parents' car broke down in Texas. In the backseat, I'm sure."

"Do I call you Odie?"

"You call me Ms. Whitehawk, or Doctor Whitehawk, if you like."

"Doctor?" he said as he held the trailer door open for her.

"Doctor of Philosophy from U.C. Berkeley," she said as she stepped past him into the little trailer. "American Indian religion and law. I sort of specialized in Indian sovereignty."

"Sovereignty?" He leaned the rifle next to the door and took two beers from the refrigerator.

"That means independence, self-government. Indian tribes are independent nations, you know, or should be by treaty rights."

He held a can toward her. "Glass?"

She shook her head as she took a seat on the edge of the bed, and he handed her the red and black can as he pulled a chair around so that he could see both her face and the trailer door.

"How'd you come by that attractive scar?" she asked, holding the can on her knee and watching him.

"Steer's horn when I was a kid."

"I suppose people've told you it looks like a lightning bolt?"

"A few. So, professor, tell me why were you born so close but . . . ?"

She took a long pull on the beer and looked around. Clothes hung on every angled projection, and boxes of shotgun and deer rifle cartridges and open tackle boxes full of lures and small, exotic trout flies sat on the floor and counter by the sink. A two-piece fly rod and a spinning rod and reel leaned against the wall on the opposite side of the door from the rifle.

"You run a neat establishment here, Mr. Keene," she said before taking another drink. "To begin with, I'm not a professor. Let's say I didn't take well to academic life once I had the degree. To answer your next question, my parents are both from Mescalero but I grew up in Los Angeles. My mom and dad were sent there for relocation just after I was born. My dad became a pipe fitter and they bought a little house in the San Fernando Valley. Dad mowed the lawn on Saturday and Mom joined the PTA. In their hearts, I think, they wanted me to be a val gal, just like the little blond Barbie dolls they bought me. They obviously thought my life would be easier that way, but they overlooked one thing."

"Your beautiful brown skin." He watched her without smiling. "What about brothers or sisters?"

"Only child. The Indian Health Service doctors tied Mom's tubes after I was born. Without telling her, of course. Standard operating procedure back then to help along the Vanishing American syndrome."

"Yeah, I've heard they did that. So why the college Indian thing?"

"It's a question of freedom, isn't it, Billy? Of knowing who you are?"

He took a long drink and then looked at the top of the can. When he raised his eyes, he looked thoughtful for a moment. "It is beautiful, you know—your skin."

He stood and picked up a box of shotgun shells from the floor next to the bed before reaching for a pump shotgun that stood in a corner. As he pushed shells into the gun, he said, "So you don't know too much about your Indian roots?"

She watched him load the twelve-gauge. "My mother told stories sometimes, and my dad talked once in a while. And I've read a hell of a lot. Funny how Indians read books by white people to find out who they are, isn't it?"

"I don't know. Do they?" He leaned the shotgun back in the corner and went to the narrow closet next to the bed. Out of the closet he took a big, heavy-looking revolver, returning to the chair. He laid the gun across his lap and opened the loaded cylinder. "So how—" He snapped the cylinder closed as she cut him off.

"You expecting the bluecoats to attack your trailer, Billy Keene? Maybe somebody else trying to steal your girlfriend?"

He shook his head. "Just a habit, I guess. Let's just say there's a few guys who might have a grudge against me."

"You want to explain the situation?"

He shook his head again. "Not now."

"Why not now?"

"I don't know. Maybe because I can't. Or maybe it's because like my grampa says, words have power."

"Fair enough, I'll wait. But what about you, Billy? Do you know about your Indian roots? Are you enrolled?" She smiled over the can. "Can you prove you're a real Indian?"

He picked up the can of beer, leaving the pistol in his lap. "You mean with papers, like one of those polled Hereford bulls? I never thought about it. If I ever was, the papers would've probably burned up with our house." He shrugged. "I suppose that means I can't make any money putting myself out to stud, since I don't have any papers. I guess I'll just have to be American."

"Don't count on that, Billy. But I thought you wanted to know how I ended up in Magdalena." She brushed her hair back and smiled at him, and he stood up to slip the pistol under the pillow of his narrow bed before resuming his seat in the chair.

"I got dumped," she continued. "My boyfriend and I were driving across from Phoenix to Austin, and he wanted to take the scenic route. We got in an argument, and he dumped me. I went in that bar to get a beer and figure out my next move."

"A man dumped you?" He shook his head. "That's a hard one for me to swallow."

"Why?" She smiled the mocking smile again.

"Well, you sort of look like the type that dumps, not the kind that gets dumped."

"I told him to go fuck himself, and he stopped the car and said, 'Get out.' So I got out."

He looked at her skeptically. "And he fucked himself?"

"Better him than me." She stood up, setting the beer on the counter, and stepped close to his chair. She cupped his face in both hands and kissed him.

When they came up for breath, she said, "You want to really tell me about the guns?"

He rose from the chair, took a half-step backward, and squinted at her with his head cocked. "Just a habit of mine, like I said."

She tossed her head and her hair whipped over her shoulders. "I'm sure you can take care of Mouse, but right now I want to take care of you." She released the top buttons of his shirt and pushed her hands inside, running them over his chest.

"All you women ever want is sex," he said, and she ran her tongue up his neck and began to nibble on his ear. Her thick hair shrouded his face, and he breathed in a heavy, exciting aroma. "You never stop to think that sometimes men just want to talk."

She pulled his shirt free of his pants and finished unbuttoning it, and she sank slowly to her knees, sliding her lips and tongue down his chest and across his stomach. When she reached the big rodeo belt buckle, she looked up at him and smiled. "All women ever really want is one thing," she said. She unbuckled the belt and popped the buttons of his Levi's open with a single motion. "And we always get it."

## 11

When he became aware that he was outside the plane, tumbling through that damp infinity of gray cloud, he felt himself enveloped in an overwhelming sadness. It stemmed not from the fact that he had been pushed, nor even from the boundless panorama of death that swelled up at him from the beautiful earth hidden somewhere below, but from his realization that the caress of air was more like love than anything he had ever known. A great pity formed a lump in his chest that rose into his throat and emerged as a wail soundless in the rush of sky. With the release of pity came clarity, and he told himself that his free fall was a metaphor for life itself. Pushed gently from the plane, suitcase in hand, he had the experience of these few seconds before his body struck the earth and sent his soul off to wherever souls went. Wasn't that like life, wherein time was meaningless and we might as well live seconds instead of years? Like those insects that are born merely to breed and die within hours or days. Seconds, days, or years—who could tell the difference? Our moment of life was a ripple in a great spiraling current, where beginning and end were but illusions.

Clarity gave way to anger, and he was mad, furious, vengeful, and bitter. They had killed him because he was a nuisance, the way someone might swat a fly with little thought. An incidental gesture. Death should be meaningful, tragic, full of implications. But he had died so that someone could have more money, and why did anyone want money except to purchase material pleasures? He had died so that someone might for a brief time be more comfortable before that person died in turn.

A picture came to him of the yellow cottonwoods near his family's home, and the irrigation ditches that led from the little river to the cornfields. His grandfather's small patch of alfalfa on the northern edge of the pueblo was a fine blue against the yellow summer day, and a single jackrabbit crept along the edge of the field. A golden eagle spun in widening circles out of the sun, and the breath of the earth was sweet and unending.

The suitcase jerked suddenly away, buoyed by the drag chute attached to it, and then he struck and felt his soul catapult from his body like a clown shot out of a cannon.

# 12

The fragrance of coffee floated above the surface of an irritating, high-pitched roar. He pulled the sheet away from his face and saw Odessa, dressed and holding a mug six inches from his eyes.

"I let you sleep in," she said. "After last night I figured you needed your rest."

He sat up, pushing his hair from his face, and accepted the coffee. "Thanks," he replied. "I feel like a used-up bronc buster. What the hell's that?"

"That?" She went to the trailer door and lifted the pillowcase that served as a curtain. She came back to the bed and sat down with a cup of coffee, sipping slowly before she said, "That looks like your friend from the bar, the one I cold-cocked, with about a dozen of his friends. They're all on Harleys, except for one ass-whipped pickup."

"Oh, shit." He struggled to free his legs from the sheets and swung them to the floor. Coffee splashed on his bare leg and he shouted "Ouch!" before throwing the cup in the sink and reaching for the rifle. "Mouse brought a bunch of his biker friends out here from Oakland," he said.

With the gun in one hand, he pulled the pillowcase back and looked out into the scowling face of Mouse Meléndez.

Mouse's fist slammed into the door three times, the noise like an explosion in the little trailer. "Open up, Keene," he shouted. "I seen you in there."

Billy threw the door open and jumped back at the same time,

so that suddenly he stood facing Mouse, the rifle held half raised across his naked chest. Behind Mouse, at least fifteen bikers, men and women, stood beside their machines, their faces ripe with amusement.

A huge man who towered behind Mouse, with a black beard and long straight hair that hung over his shoulders, yelled, "Look at that crazy sumbitch. Is he trying to scare us with his gun or his dick?"

Mouse Meléndez grinned and then held a hand to his temple. "Jesus H. Christ my head hurts. I hope I didn't wake you up."

Billy saw Carla a couple of yards behind Mouse, looking shy and a little worried.

Mouse craned his head to peer around Billy. "Good morning, ma'am," he said, nodding toward Odessa. "You do swing a mean pool cue."

"What do you want, Mouse?" Billy said.

Mouse turned around and shouted, "Bring her up, Gordo."

The bearded biker lifted a silver keg from the bed of the pickup and carried it to the steps. "Morning, Billy," he said as he set it on the ground.

"It's my apology," Mouse said, nodding toward the keg. "I believe I didn't act right last night. It was the demon rum again. Carla give me all kinds of hell after my head stopped whirling around. I realized I was just a asshole. I mean first I take a man's woman and then I try to kick his ass." He shook his head and looked sorrowful. "You know I ain't like that. So I come to make it up to you."

"You don't have to make anything up to me, Mouse." Billy looked past Meléndez to the grinning bunch behind him. "I understand. You were drunk."

"We brung you a party, Billy," Mouse said. "Hell, we got three more of them kegs. When Joe found out what we was going to do, he give us a extra one free of charge. Said he wants his best customers to get along. Maybe you want to put on a loincloth or something before we get this party going."

Billy looked down at himself and turned to search for his pants. Odessa sat on the edge of the bed holding his Levi's up and grinning. "I don't want a goddamned party, Mouse," he said over his shoulder. "What I want is for you all to get out of here."

Billy slipped the pants and a T-shirt on, hearing the sounds of breaking wood and shouts from outside. He pulled his boots on over bare feet and went to look out the trailer door. The bikers had torn down half a dozen fence posts and were smashing them over rocks. He glanced toward his grandfather's trailer and for a moment seemed to see a pair of silver braids floating all alone above the deck.

"Ain't you got something we can kill and cook?"

Billy jerked his vision back toward the huge man in front of him.

Mouse was looking around the ranch with one hand on his hip, the other hand holding a bottle of beer in front of his expansive belly. "I don't see nothing, not even a goat." He turned back to Billy. "Ain't you got even a wiener pig somewheres?"

"I don't have anything you can barbecue, Mouse. There ain't a living thing on this ranch but me and my grampa and Odessa here, unless you want to cook those damned crows on the barn." Billy looked toward the other trailer, where the torso of his grandfather appeared to be floating above a wooden chair.

"Man, the old Meléndez Grant has gone to hell in a handbasket, ain't it? I hope Will's doing better with his half."

When Billy shifted his gaze back to the speaker, Mouse was studying the ground and shaking his head sadly. "My great-grampa must be spinning in his grave."

"Go away, Mouse," Billy said, shaking his own head. "There's nothing to cook, and your friends are tearing down the last fence on the ranch."

"Hell, it don't matter." Mouse tossed the bottle over his shoulder. "We probably got half a cow anyway. Everybody brought hotdogs and hamburger and shit like that in their saddlebags, too. It's beer and barbecue time on the old Meléndez Grant for sure."

Mouse went to his pickup and rummaged in the bed of the truck. He made a wide circle through the busy bikers, and then came over to the trailer steps where Billy now sat running his hands through his hair. As if by magic, a paper cup of beer appeared in the hand Mouse held toward Billy. "Why'nt you introduce me to the beautiful woman who brained me last night?" Mouse said.

Billy accepted the beer and felt Odessa's knees in his back as he heard her say, "I'm pleased to meet you, Mr. Meléndez. My name's Odessa Whitehawk."

Mouse held his hand out and they shook solemnly. "Judging by the goose egg on the back of my head, Miss Whitehawk, you are my kind of woman." He patted Billy on the head. "But don't worry, Billy. I don't take more'n one woman a week from a man."

Billy looked toward his grandfather's porch, where now there was only a pair of empty chairs in front of a small table. A checkers board sat on the table, and behind the chairs the silver trailer caught the morning sun in a slow burn.

"Real funny, Mouse. She's Doctor Whitehawk to you." Billy waved toward the men and women who had siphoned gas out of the pickup and used it to start a bonfire with the splintered fence posts. "Please tell them not to tear down my whole ranch."

"You just wait till we get a good bed of coals out there, Billy. I can almost smell them ribs already."

"I thought you said you had hamburger and hotdogs."

Mouse held up a finger. "Don't go away, Miss Odessa. We got steaks, too." He held out his big fist and opened it slowly, one finger at a time. In his palm lay a pair of turquoise earrings. "Just to show there's no hard feelings," he said.

"I don't wear earrings," Billy said.

Odessa held her hand out and Mouse dropped the earrings into her palm. "Shouldn't you give these to your lady friend?" Odessa said, nodding toward Carla who stood by the fire.

"Naw. I have showered Carla with gifts already."

He turned to Billy. "I hope you're studying this, Billy. You need to learn how to make a woman happy, especially now that you ain't a young buck no more." He shifted his attention back to Odessa. "Women just don't stay with Billy very long. Look at this place; it get's 'em down. And Billy here ain't exactly a ball of fire. Course he was when he was young. Ain't that right, Billy. Did he tell you yet that he was all-around champeen cowboy at the New Mexico State Fair one year and then number one at the Indian Rodeo in Albuquerque the next year? He's got them big damned belt buckles to prove it, somewheres. Even though he sure don't look very much Indian does he? What kind of doctor are you, anyway? Maybe you ought to look at the back of my head."

Billy drank from the cup and squinted up at Mouse. "Listen to this blond-haired Mexican tell me I don't look Indian. What kind of man named Meléndez has blue eyes and blond hair?"

Mouse grinned. Another cup of beer had magically appeared in his fist. When he lowered the cup a ring of foam lined his bushy mouth. "Not Mexican, *pendejo*, Spanish. My family come up here," he looked at Odessa, "in the eighteenth century with Oñate. There's lots of blond Spaniards."

"Come off it, Mouse. There was a Swede in your mama's woodpile."

"So Billy's a cowboy," Odessa said, looking down at Billy inquisitively. "That's funny. He told me that all the real old-time cowboys were queer."

Mouse laughed, spraying beer. "Only the best ones," he said. "Truth of the matter is my mom is a Georgia cracker who come through here with her family and just swept my dad right off his feet. Her dad worked in the mines, and she must've been the prettiest thing to ever hit Magdalena."

"Judging by the looks of her son, there's certainly no doubt about that," Billy said. Turning to Odessa, he added, "Mouse hates to talk about himself."

"It made my grampa mad enough to eat nails when she married my dad," Mouse went on. "She raised me after my dad got killed by a Texas bull before I was old enough to walk. That's how I come to live out there in California. She got tired of listening to all those Meléndezes talk about how rich they used to be and what kind of white trash she was. Did Billy tell you how my family used to own this ranch and the one next to it, too?"

"Since Billy and I just met last night, there is much he hasn't had time to tell me," she replied.

"Well, Billy's dad and old Will Striker's dad bought both their places from my grampa. This used to all be ours." He waved his hand generally in the air. "About a million acres I think. One of my ancestors was give all this by the King of Spain. The Meléndez Grant it was called. By the time Billy and Will's dads come through here with their pockets full of cash back in the thirties, it was mostly all gone. Some stole by those Texans that came during Billy the Kid's time, some lost to gambling, some sold off, and a whole chunk stolen by the government because my great-grampa couldn't pay the taxes." He waved toward the mountains. "That national forest back there was all Meléndez land. The feds got that for taxes in the twenties. And then Billy and Will's dads come driving through with some spending money and my grampa couldn't resist. Could he, Billy?"

Billy sipped the beer. "I guess not," he said. "Or at least he didn't want to resist."

"Billy knows why Grampa was happy to unload it, too. You remember that part, Billy?"

Billy finished the beer and looked morosely into the empty cup. "The land is cursed," he said.

"That's right. You should've heard the stories my grampa used to tell," Mouse went on. "This was all Indian land." He paused for a drink. "Of course the whole fuckin' country was Indian land once, wasn't it? But this was Apache country. They didn't want to leave. They liked to hunt up there in the Magdalenas, and I guess now and then after the Spanish come the Indians'd kill a cow and eat it. Grampa told me his grampa found a whole bunch of them roasting a steer up by the big water hole—back then it was a regular stream—and him and his vaqueros killed every one. They shot the grown ones and cut the throats of the little ones. Him and his vaqueros." He looked at the ground and shook his head. "They buried them up there. Twenty or thirty of them, he said. Can you imagine how bad a man must've wanted land to do something like that?"

He finished the beer and crumpled the plastic cup. "Hell, you couldn't give me this land. Grampa said that was when the curse started." He looked out over the ranch and shook his head. "This used to be all green, he said, with grass up to a man's waist and a nice stream that run year round over on what's Will Striker's place now. You could dig a hole anywhere and find good water. All this was covered with cattle back then, and the mountains was full of elk. But the water started to dry up right after the massacre. Grampa told me when he was a boy he used to lay there in his room in that old adobe Will Striker's dad fixed up and he'd hear the screams of those women and kids. Every night they got killed over and over. Everybody knew the stories, and everybody'd seen the land dry up, so Grampa couldn't of got ten cents an acre for the place from anybody around here. But when two ignorant Injuns from Oklahoma showed up wanting to buy the last thousand, Grampa was happy as a clam."

"And you believe this about the curse?" Odessa asked, looking into the big man's eyes.

He looked away. "Ask Billy does he believe," he said. "Ask Will Striker. Gimme that cup, Billy. We need some more beers." He walked toward one of the kegs that had been set up on a mound of rocks.

Odessa looked at Billy. "My parents never mentioned that story. Why did Mouse say to ask you and Will Striker?"

Billy stood up. "I guess we've got us a beer barbecue here, Odessa," he replied. "Like you said, there's a whole hell of a lot I haven't told you. Just look around." He started toward the beer keg, shouting, "Let's barbecue those goddamned crows." As if on cue, the birds came wheeling from the barn, cawing raggedly and loosing streams of white shit toward the revelers. Billy stopped and dodged back to the trailer, where Odessa stood on the first step watching.

"I think I'll call Will," he said. "Will hasn't been to a party in ten years, and I want him to meet you."

When Will drove up in the old Chevy, the burning man was surrounded by a dozen people hurling beer at him from plastic cups. Will jumped from the truck, dragging the seat blanket behind him and throwing it over the man. Together they tumbled to the ground.

When the flames were out, Will became aware of loud clapping, whistles and cheers.

"It's the Cisco Kid," Mouse Meléndez shouted.

The one who'd been on fire sat on the ground looking bewilderedly at his burned fatigue jacket.

"The Crisco Kid, you mean. Hell, he was mostly out already," the long-haired biker called Gordo said, looking at his empty cup. "The flames didn't get to his flesh, I bet."

On the porch of his trailer, Siquani sat in the straight-backed chair. He watched the revelers curiously, occasionally addressing comments to the empty chair beside him.

"This is part of it," the old man said. "It started a long time ago."

Arturo Cruz nodded solemnly. "Those crows make me nervous." His eyes were on Odessa, watching her movements with care. "You keep making me nervous, too, Grandfather, the way some of you disappears and then comes back again. Your grandson may notice pretty soon."

"Us Cherokees don't normally like crows a whole lot neither, but these crows are different. Besides, you have to learn to accept some things, Grandson, especially now you're dead. I'm afraid there's more bad things coming to this place, and I ain't used to this disappearing yet, neither. Seems like a hundred years since I done it."

"The bad things are already here," Arturo sighed. "The earth is broken, and like me you see the one who comes in darkness."

"Yesterday there was blue lightning, Arturo. And last night I heard that big diamondback rattler coming down from the hills. He's coming slow, but he'll be here soon. Together we will all do what we can. And maybe that's why you are here, Grandson. Maybe these are important things for you to see. Who knows? I been old a long time," Siquani held his wrinkled hands up and examined them. "I was already growed up when the white people come and paid us to kill all the deer where we had lived forever. Back when they sold our people for slaves."

"They did that here in this land, too. They sold the Navajo and Pueblo people for slaves down in Mexico and up there in Santa Fe."

Siquani nodded. "It was a pretty country where my people came from. Big trees and streams and black earth, Arturo, to make the corn heavy. It was a land that made an old man's bones sing. This is nice country, but that Cherokee land was the best. When my people was put in cages and then made to walk with death, I went with the old ones. And when this one's father asked me to come with him to this country, I thought maybe I should continue that journey a little bit longer, though I wondered if my bones would carry me. So much has been forgot. Cherokee people like that boy don't remember where they came from or how to talk right. The stories tell them of those sacred places, but they only see those places in the stories. And they stop listening."

Siquani rubbed the heels of both hands on his knees and watched the carousing mob. "You see, Grandson, I know the story of how my own line will end in that boy over there, and because of that I had to come out here. The story was give to me whole by the little ones way back before the whites came, and I knew I had to come here for the story to be complete. Old people are sometimes given the gift of knowing things like that, but only few receive the gift of changing those things. I never got that second gift."

He gestured toward the beer drinkers with his chin. "My own blood is there, and I know the terrible things that will happen to my blood. Things that have already happened." He turned to look almost directly at Arturo. "Night walkers are coming here. You feel them, too?"

Arturo Cruz shook his head sadly. "Anyone can feel it, like when a big lightning storm is coming in from that Navajo country. You feel it walking across all that land with heavy steps, and everyone just waits. I'm sorry now I got mixed up in the drug business. It was my uncle who started everything. When I was just a baby, some white men came and said they would pay him if he would show them where to land their planes with drugs way out on one of the mesas. He told me that part. I guess he showed them where to land, but when he understood everything they were doing I think he just made those white men disappear so that he could take over. He's like that. Some people have said he has help from the witches or maybe he is one of them."

Siquani watched the porch near Arturo's feet, nodding with his eyes closed. "I've seen that man, your uncle," he said softly. "He is part of it."

Arturo went on as if he had not heard the old man. "At first my uncle had me do little, easy things, and he gave me money each time. That's how I paid for college, and I thought maybe he was doing it that way because he didn't want to embarrass my family by just giving me money. Now I know he was testing me. He would always say, 'Remember that money is not important. It is only the white man's weapon which we must learn to use against him in the long war.' But I liked the money, and I said to myself, 'The white people have cheated and killed us Indians forever, so who cares if their children have drugs? Who cares if white people suffer for this? Maybe that's good.' I listened to my uncle, and I didn't understand it was part of their plan to make us kill each other. Like that one." He gestured with his chin toward the celebrants. "When I graduated from college, my uncle had bigger things for me to do, and more money. Now I think he's part of their plan, too, and he doesn't understand either. I think those first white men with the plane were witches."

The old man nodded at the eastern mountains. "I've felt your uncle in the north. His presence is growing stronger, and closer. Red mountain lion passed by this morning, rubbing his shoulder right there against the corner of my little trailer. You can see his tracks. Here's a story, Grandson. There was a big flood and on all the earth only one man survived with his family. The man heard the sounds of dancing, but when he climbed to the top of a ridge and looked he saw only bones, so many bones that the earth was covered. Then he knew it had been the bones that danced. You see, white people are not real. White people invented themselves. Then they came here and invented us Indians. For a long time they've forgot that truth, and they think they're not alone. But it's just the bones always dancing, Arturo."

"You talk like my grandfather back home. He never makes sense neither."

"Both them boys was born in a thunderstorm." Siquani shook his head. "Witches don't like thunder."

"Watch that one, Grandfather." Arturo nodded. "That one has a story forming now."

Will sat on the steps of the trailer, drinking a beer and watching Mouse's dozen friends suck on barbecued ribs and hotdogs. He'd planned to tell Billy that they had to cut the body down and bury it, but he hadn't had a chance to speak to his best friend. Now, Billy sat on the remains of a fence post near one of the fires, seemingly lost in conversation with a tall, skinny, heavily tattooed biker. In front of Will, sprawled on a woven plastic chair he'd found somewhere, Mouse held a cup in one fist and looked at the wood between Will's feet.

"You and Billy better have *mucho cuidado*," Mouse was saying. "Those guys asking about Billy's Cruiser are very bad shit."

When Will didn't respond, Mouse went on. "I don't know what Billy did to get his feathers wet, but I do know those guys are connected way up. Me and the boys do a little business, you know, just mom-and-pop stuff."

When Will still remained silent, looking into his beer, Mouse said, "See it works like this, Will. When some shit goes down wrong, the guys at the top get real pissed. So they lean on the guys in the middle, and those guys lean on the ones at the bottom. The ones at the bottom are supposed to go out and fix things. It's their ass, so they do whatever it *pinche* takes, *comprende?* Them guys got nothing to lose but their ass."

Will looked up from the beer and said, "Thanks, Mouse. I appreciate it."

Mouse nodded. "It's best to stay clear of guys like that. They ain't no fun at all. But this here's our home. If you and Billy need some help, you let me or Gordo know. This is our home." He got slowly to his feet and placed a hand on Will's shoulder before lumbering away.

"Maybe not," Will said aloud to himself.

Behind Will, Odessa materialized in the trailer doorway. "Mouse is a fascinating character, isn't he? A mass of mestizo contradictions," she said above Will's head. "Far more complex than a person would think at first glance."

Will watched the bikers throw empty beer kegs into the pickup and mount their Harleys. As abruptly as they'd appeared several hours before, the group vanished in a torrent of noise, leaving the big fire smoldering and the area between the trailers littered with plastic cups, bottles, and animal bones.

While Billy walked around putting the litter in a plastic bag, the crows swooped down on the debris with shouts, flapping and hopping from bone to bone.

Still seated in the chair, Siquani looked from the other trailer back to Arturo Cruz. "You mean I must watch the Apache woman," the old man said. "Yes. The dead are calling her, too. She has come on their business."

# 13

Odessa held the little black-and-white photograph closer beneath the overhead lamp and bent to scrutinize the blurred faces. "You're the perfect combination of your parents," she said. "It's funny how they look so different from one another but you look just like both of them."

Billy leaned across her shoulder and arm to look at the ancient picture with its odd, serrated edge. The couple in the photo were younger than he was as he sat there dizzy with the clean smell of Odessa's thick hair and feeling the curve of her breast against his arm. The couple, with their clothing in shades of gray and white against a gray car fronting angular and rounding forms of gray trees, rocks, and distant mountains, might have lived a thousand years and miles away. He leaned closer to look at the man, whose thin, sharp-planed face held darker shadows of the camera and whose angular eyes seemed to recede into personal distance. The black hair was all but hidden beneath a snap-brim hat, and the suit coat and slacks were at the same time too small and yet loose on the man's tall, lanky body. The woman beside him, in her flower-print dress and cocked hat, stared confidently at the camera, as if daring a future, any future, to find fault. It was clear that the woman had come to an understanding with her own existence. Everything about her face was there to be seen: the little curved nose and full, smiling lips, the pale-looking eyes and strong chin.

"I've never seen that before," he said.

Odessa turned toward him, the photograph held gingerly by

one edge between thumb and forefinger. He was conscious of the firmness of her breast as she moved, and his face pulled back from hers to seek a focus.

"They're a beautiful couple," she said. "Your mother looks very strong."

He looked again at the picture she held at an angle to his vision. "I guess she had to be back then."

"Back then?"

"To marry an Indian man in Oklahoma. White men married Indian women all the time, mostly to get their hands on allotment land, but white women didn't marry Indian men. Her parents wouldn't let her in their house again."

"Really? I guess I shouldn't be surprised."

"Really. I suppose that's part of the reason they decided to come out here with Will's folks."

"How come you've never seen this picture before?"

He shrugged and nodded at the cardboard box full of little gray-and-white squares. "Will found that box in his house after the fire. His mom had a whole bunch of pictures she'd taken of my folks. He figured I should have them, but I never felt like looking until you showed up."

"So why now?"

He brushed her hair back from her shoulder and traced a finger down the sharp edge of her cheek. "I suppose I thought you should see where I came from." He reached into the box and picked up another photo. "Maybe I thought I should see where I came from. Look at this one."

He held up a photograph of two boys in tight, stained T-shirts and rolled-up blue jeans. Both boys had shaggy dark hair as they stood shoulder-to-shoulder facing the camera. The stockier boy held a jackrabbit by the feet, the rabbit's long, bloodied ears touching the earth beside him, and the other boy cradled a small rifle with the barrel pointing away.

"You and Will," Odessa said, a slight tone of wonder in her voice. "How old were you?"

He held the picture closer, remembering how the jackrabbit had run, wheeling away from the spring in bounding leaps to abruptly stop the way rabbits always did and sit rocklike near a cluster of sage. The air of early fall had felt swollen with coming rain and the fragrance of sage and cedar, and he'd been the one to pull the trigger because it had been his turn with the rifle. He had made Will hold the rabbit for the photograph because, as he'd explained, it hadn't really mattered who fired the shot.

Now, sunlight slanting through pictured junipers in the west cut across the thirty-plus years of the photo, stilled in gray and white, to cast doubt across Will's face. It was an expression of caution and almost perplexity, which, Billy realized, had always been there in his friend's eyes but had gone unseen for most of a lifetime.

"He hasn't changed, has he?" Odessa said.

Billy laid the picture back on the pile in the box. "I don't know. Maybe nobody changes."

She set the other photo in the box. "I think some people change incredibly, that they metamorphose like those cicadas that crawl out of the ground and split their skins to fly away."

He reached for her thin, powerful-feeling hand and held it in both of his own, stroking the palm with his index finger. "Or maybe the way a caterpillar turns into a butterfly?"

"Pretty to think so," she replied, smiling thinly. "Your parents were beautiful. Your father had a warrior's face."

"I'm older than they ever got," he said. "That feels strange."

"You still have Grampa Siquani."

"He's not really my grampa, exactly." He paused, feeling the little muscles of her palm. "He's my dad's grandfather or something like that. I never have known exactly."

She gently extracted her hand from his and pushed the hair back from her face again. "How old is he?"

Billy shook his head. "I don't know. Three or four hundred years, I think."

Odessa laughed. "He's a sorcerer then."

She picked another photo from the box. "Who's this?" she said.

Billy took the picture and held it close. "That's Will and Jace, the year they got married." In the photo, Will stood in front of his family's house, his arms folded across his chest and a wide smile on his sunburned face. Jace, her long hair falling in a thick braid over one shoulder, leaned against his side, one arm around his waist and the other in her jeans pocket, her own smile matching Will's.

"She's beautiful, isn't she?" Odessa said, moving closer to Billy to see the picture again. "She reminds me of a friend I had once."

Billy dropped the photo back in the box. "That was taken right after Will dropped out of college. Jace, too, but she went back."

"Do you think Will ever regretted quitting like that?"

Billy shrugged. "It's hard to say about Will. He always was good in school. Had his nose stuck in books all the time. In more than twenty years I've never heard him say a word about not finishing college. But Will isn't a person to talk about his problems."

"Even with his best friend?"

"Even with God, I suspect."

Billy rose and picked up the box, lifting it to the top shelf of the closet and shutting the door. "You know what Grampa's name, Siquani, means?"

She shook her head. "I've forgotten my Cherokee."

"Suckling Pig," he said, smiling. "How could an old man named Suckling Pig be a witch?"

"Maybe he's a trickster witch, Billy. Maybe you don't know your grandfather as well as you think you do."

He went to the refrigerator and brought out two cans of beer. "Maybe I don't know anybody, Doctor Whitehawk." He handed her one of the beers and then pushed the trailer door open and stood facing the eastern horizon. Overhead, the stars of Orion showed in the dark, gray-streaked sky as the hunter wheeled slowly westward.

# 14

Will squatted to pour the bucket of water into the well of the cornstalk, watching the parched earth turn first brown and then black as the water sank out of sight. When only a white stain was left on the mud circling the stalk, he stood and looked around. The dog and pig lay side by side outside the wire gate, watching him, Maggie's filthy cast stretched out in front of her.

"You'd like to get those little choppers on this corn, wouldn't you, Molly?" Will said. "Well it ain't going to happen, Piglet." Behind the dog and pig, he could see both threadbare-looking bulls nosed up against the wooden barn fence, their gazes fixed on him. On the barn ridge above the bulls, four buzzards perched facing him, like stoop-shouldered old men. Maybe, he thought, they're all afraid I'm wasting the last of the water.

He set the bucket down, slapping dust off the seat of his pants, and surveyed his corn crop. Seven stalks had survived to maturity and now carried big, well-tasseled ears. It was the smallest garden on the ranch in his memory. He'd started with the usual squash, pole beans, tomatoes, turnips, and carrots, but the plants had either chosen to stay as dry seed in the ground or had pushed their way up only to wither and vanish. The tomatoes had bravely forced vine and leaf into the sun, but the blossoms had appeared brittle and weak, dropping fruitless to the earth. A fraction of the corn had survived because he'd begun early to carry buckets of water from the barn trough. Without enough water, you had to cut your losses and make decisions. He'd decided to save some of the corn.

He couldn't remember a summer without cornstalks whispering in the August winds.

He ran a forefinger up the sloping side of a heavy ear, careful not to touch the yellow-green tassels. "Selu," he said. He'd loved his father's often-told story about first man and Selu. Kanati, the hunter, was all alone upon the earth and bored to death, so he started killing too many of the little deer and other animals, just because he was bored. The animals went to the Creator and complained, and the Creator said, "Oh yes, I forgot something." Then a cornstalk grew up beside Kanati, and when the hunter awakened there was a tall green stalk with a beautiful woman rising out of the top of the stalk. That was how Selu, Corn Woman, had become Kanati's wife. Will loved the image of the dark, black-haired Selu rising above the golden tassels of the cornstalk. He could still see her swaying there in the breeze above the sleeping hunter. "That's why Cherokee people always plant corn," his father had explained. "Corn is our mother."

When Maggie started barking, he turned toward the road. A county patrol car had already pulled to a stop in front of the house, and he watched as the sheriff maneuvered his big gut from behind the steering wheel and climbed out of the vehicle. The sheriff looked around, obviously trying to locate the barking dog, and then started toward the closed barn door.

"Over here, Nate," Will shouted. He opened the gate, closing it behind him, and walked toward the sheriff. Maggie hobbled in front of him, swinging the cast in half-circles as she moved and braying powerfully. Out of the corner of his eye he saw Molly trotting toward the back of the barn, frightened as always by any sign of strangers.

The sheriff turned and raised a hand in a half-wave and began walking to meet him. When he was a few feet away, the sheriff stopped and said, "That there peg-leg dog bite?"

Will reached for Maggie's collar and pulled her into a sitting position. Maggie growled, her black muzzle flecked with foam. "Well, Nate, I'm afraid she's in a bad mood these days," Will replied. "Come on in the house."

"Can't say I blame her for being a little pissed off. Rumor around town says you accidentally shot your own dog. That's a fine crop you got." The sheriff nodded toward the garden. "You plan to hire any hands for the harvest?"

Will half grinned. "It's a dry year, Nate. I just grew enough so the earth wouldn't forget."

"You wouldn't have any coffee in that house?"

"If you can drink it, you can have it," Will answered as they both started toward the house. Maggie scraped along beside Will, her shoulder touching his thigh.

When they were sitting in the kitchen with cups of flat black coffee, the sheriff said, "You hear about that helicopter blew up over near the Array?"

Will nodded. "I read about it in the paper."

The sheriff sipped the coffee and frowned. "You better get that wife of yours back, Will, before you kill yourself with your own cooking."

"How about a little cream?"

The sheriff's frown deepened. "Cream's for faggots. I like strong coffee." He took another sip as though to verify his statement. "You and Billy used to hunt over in that country south of the Array, if I remember correctly. In fact, I believe you and Billy and me hunted together over there about ten years ago."

"Sure, I remember that. You got that little forked horn."

"Scrawny sonofabitch as I recall. I believe I was using that old thirty-forty of mine and you and Billy was both shooting ought-sixes." The sheriff lifted his tan Stetson off his head and set it on the table, running a plump hand through his sweaty hair. "Me and Brice found thirty-ought-six cartridges out there not too far from where the helicopter crashed. You still got that ought-six?"

"Sure. That was my dad's gun. Right over there in the cabinet."

The sheriff nodded. "You always took good care of your guns, I recall. I bet that ought-six has been cleaned and oiled and everything just recently. Probably can't tell when it was fired last or who even touched it."

Will nodded. "I like to take care of things."

"A man that lets a gun rust ought to be shot with the same gun," the sheriff responded. He pushed the coffee a few inches toward the center of the table. "We found four-wheel-drive tracks out there too, Will. Kind it'd be pretty easy to match if we locate the vehicle that made them."

"Why are you telling me all of this, Nate? What do I have to do with a helicopter crashing? My truck's right out there. You can match all you want."

"Now don't get your nuts in a sling, Will. I got to ask questions if I want to keep this pissant job." He reached for the hat and placed it carefully on his head. "There was two bodies in that crashed copter, Will, and one of 'em had an ought-six slug in his guts. Both were burned pretty good, but the lab boys figured out who they were. Dope pushers. Personally, I figure that whoever helped blow 'em to hell deserves a reward. But if I don't do my job I lose it. There's people in Santa Fe interested in this, not to mention the feds because it crashed close to that radar shit of theirs."

The sheriff stood up. "Thanks for the coffee, Will. It'll sure clean out a man's parasites."

"You're welcome, Nate. Anytime."

"I stopped by Billy's place before I came here. Nobody was there, not even his grampa. I got no choice except to get a court order to search both your ranches and take your rifles over to Socorro for matching. But it'll probably take a few days to get the paperwork ready. Just thought I'd let you know. You seen Billy's Land Cruiser around?"

Will shook his head. "I'd guess it was where it always is, unless he left it somewhere to be worked on."

"Well, keep your eyes peeled, Will. By the way, I see you still got that D-6 of yours out there. You think about selling that thing, you let me know. My wife's dad's looking for a Cat for his gravel pit. Hell, you got no use for a machine like that. I bet you don't even start that old thing more'n once a year. He'd make a good offer on it."

"I'll think about it, Nate," Will replied.

"You do that. A decent D-6 like that's worth some *dinero*. Meanwhile, you keep your eyes peeled."

# 15

As soon as the dust from the sheriff's car had disappeared, Will went to the telephone and dialed Billy's number. When there was no answer, he left the house and walked rapidly to the side of the barn, where a big D-6 Caterpillar crouched under the tin-roofed lean-to.

At the front of the tractor, he grasped a steel crank with both hands and jerked. The starter motor gasped twice and fell silent. Again he cranked the small motor, and again it sputtered and died. Going to the cab, he pulled a can from beneath the seat, shook it, and listened, and then went back to the front. He shot fluid from the can into the carburetor of the starter motor, dropped the can on the ground behind him, and cranked again. This time the motor caught, choked, and came to life with a small shriek.

Walking back toward the cab, he worked the compression release and climbed onto the badly sprung seat. After a moment, he slipped the clutch and the big diesel roared to life. A streak of black shot out from the corner of the barn, bursting past Maggie and through the open back door of the house. "Go ahead and shit on the bed for all I care," he shouted after the disappearing pig.

After listening for a couple of minutes longer, he kicked the throttle and the great machine began to crawl out from under the shed, swiveling prehistorically around the side of the barn to a huge manure pile in back.

He lowered the massive blade and began to cut into the tons of bull shit and horse shit scraped out of the corral over many years, cleaving the mass of composting manure in two and backing up for a second run.

In a few minutes he had moved the entire pile. Then he pivoted the D-6 to the side of the dark place once covered by manure, lowered the blade further, and began to rip a gradually deepening trough in the earth, pushing the dirt out the other side.

After thirty minutes he wheeled the tractor past the earth buttress and climbed off the seat, letting the machine idle while he went to the front of the barn and slid the big door open, disappearing inside. Seconds later, the black Range Rover backed out of the barn and then flowed smoothly around the corner and down into the newly gouged trough.

Quickly, he was back in the seat of the Caterpillar and maneuvering the tractor toward the hole he had made. For an instant the Cat's tracks balanced on the edge of the crumbling hole, and then the tractor tilted forward and seemed to half stumble into the hole. The roof of the Range Rover gave with a metallic cough, the windows exploded, and the vehicle sank abruptly beneath the full weight of the bulldozer.

Reversing the tractor, he backed out of the sloping end of the hole, the track ripping across the compressed metal, and then he swiveled the D-6 around to plunge once more onto the Range Rover. When he backed out the second time, the Range Rover was a third of its original height. Satisfied, he began to blade earth back into the hole, using the weight of the Caterpillar to compress the fill again and again until it was level with the surroundings. Next, he spread the excess dirt across the hole and used the bulldozer to reform the manure pile over the bladed earth.

For long minutes, he stood on the tractor and stared at his work. Someone looking would see a freshly stirred mound of very old shit surrounded by signs of tractor work, a common sight on any ranch. Satisfied, he parked the Cat beneath the shed once more and went to his pickup, fishtailing away from the house toward the highway.

# 16

Odessa stood for a moment in the empty frame of the small door, staring into the huge shadow of the barn. Along the near wall to her right, light came through wide cracks in the planking, and dust motes floated between bars of black and white. When she stepped into the barn, there was a feathery shuffling high up in the rafters, and her eyes searched the dark peak for a moment before shifting back to the objects closer at hand.

She walked slowly past the tack room, her eyes taking in the ancient machinery of farming and ranching, her nostrils flaring at the sweet scent of rotting hay and rodents. She walked close to the Land Cruiser and ran her hand carefully along the hood where a line of dimpled holes ran up to the missing windshield; then she moved around the vehicle and studied the space where the fender had been. Cupping both hands around her eyes, she peered through the back windows of the Land Cruiser and then moved around so that she could look into the space in front of the seats.

She had turned toward the fallen bales of composting hay when suddenly she froze. A soft whisper as of shuffling feet had come from the edge of the tumbled bales close by. She stared at the place where the sound had originated, seeing only the shadowed hay and beyond that the far wall of the barn with its slats of faint light. A warm surge of air surrounded her with the fragrance of cedar, and she stepped backward, continuing to place one foot behind the other with precise care as she backed toward the light of the doorway. At the door, she stepped into the sun and then turned and walked rapidly toward Billy's trailer.

From inside the barn, Siquani watched her go, his bony arms folded across his chest and his eyes black in the gray light. Overhead, he heard the owl ruffling her feathers and the scrabble of crows' feet on the tin roof. Behind him, from the mountains in the west, came rumblings of thunder, a deep, steady sound answered by a sudden snap of impatience.

# 17

Billy's ranch was deserted, the new pickup gone and both trailers empty. After knocking loudly at first Billy's and then his grandfather's door, Will stepped off the old man's deck and started back to his truck.

Halfway to the truck he heard his name called. When he turned, Siquani was sitting in one of the straight-backed chairs, a hand raised in greeting.

"Come and visit an old man, Grandson," Siquani said.

Will stood in silence for a moment studying the scene, and then he slowly climbed back onto the deck.

"I don't think I'm even going to ask," Will said.

The old man chuckled. "You can sit in that chair, because Arturo ain't here right now."

"Arturo?"

"Me and him play checkers."

"How—"

"I been practicing my disappearing magic, Will. It's old Cherokee medicine. The kind Billy Pigeon used to get away from the sheriffs with."

Will stood looking down at the shriveled old man. "You weren't here two minutes ago," he said.

Siquani nodded. "It was hard, but I got it figured out. It took me a while. Thought it might come in handy."

"Okay, Grampa. My dad used to tell me about Billy Pigeon. He called him the Cherokee Jesse James. I always meant to look him up in the library at the university."

"Billy was better than Jesse James. He never killed people like them James boys. Well, hardly any. He knew a lot of powerful medicine."

"Like disappearing."

"Love medicine, too, they say."

"You seen your own grandson Billy recently?"

Siquani nodded, lifting a hand to point.

Will turned to see the shiny pickup coming toward the trailers, trailing a high plume of dust. "I need to talk to Billy," he said.

"Listen to the thunder, Grandson."

Will cocked his head toward the mostly clear sky, hearing nothing. "You got to walk careful," the old man said. "Billy is on the path to the darkening land now. Black ones are coming here. I seen them and I been hearing the thunder."

Will looked toward the crowless barn and then back again as Billy parked the truck and jumped out. On the other side of the pickup, Odessa climbed out and, with a wave at Will, went into the trailer while Billy walked toward them.

"I think I'll go home, Will, soon's this thing is over."

Will looked up sharply at the old man. "What thing, Grampa?" he said.

Siquani seemed to be watching the sky for something that might appear. "Maybe it was my fault. This one's mother washed deer meat in that creek. I never told her the story of blood."

"What kind of story is my grandfather telling you now?" Billy said loudly when he was a few yards away. "Some kind of Cherokee hocus-pocus like always?"

"Don't worry, I'll watch out for Billy. I'll be careful," Will said quietly to the old man before he walked out to meet his friend.

"Come on, Billy," he said. "We need to talk."

With a surprised look, Billy followed Will toward the remains of the burned house. When Will sat on the stone foundation, Billy settled beside him, waiting in silence.

"Nate was at my place," Will said at last. When Billy didn't reply, he went on. "He's going to get a court order to search both our ranches."

Billy studied the toes of his boots for a moment before replying. "I guess we better get rid of our rifles."

"I don't think they can prove anything by the tires tracks, not with all that rain. But those bullet holes in the Land Cruiser are a different story, and I think it was your gun, Billy. I'm pretty sure I hit that fellow with your rifle."

"I guess I'll lose it somewhere."

"Nate said it would probably take him a few days to get the court order."

Billy pulled a small pocket knife from his pants pocket, opened it, and began to clean his fingernails. "I'll talk to Mouse. Mouse can get rid of anything." He curled the fingers of his left hand and studied the nails.

"Good idea," Will said. "The sooner the better." He paused to watch a column of large red ants moving back and forth at a hole in the base of the wall. Each ant seemed to be carrying a seed of some kind, and he wondered idly if any of those seeds ever sprouted in the earth. Was that the real purpose of ants, to farm the deep earth?

"You ever think much about our parents, Billy?" he added.

"All the time. Sometimes I dream there's fire everywhere and Grampa Siquani's dragging me out through the smoke again. Once I dreamed that I saw my mother's hair on fire. She was standing in the doorway of their room, her hands reaching out, and instead of hair her head was surrounded by flames."

He folded the pocket knife and put it back in his pocket. "You know, I can't stop thinking about the way her hair used to look at night, after she'd worked her tail off all day and her hair would be hanging down beside her face. She'd be so tired she could hardly stand up, and she'd come into my room and read me a story. And all those times I'd come in busted up by some goddamned Brahma bull in Albuquerque or Gallup or somewhere, and she'd be waiting with Band-Aids and some kind of Indian salve she'd learned about from my dad's mom back in Oklahoma. I don't remember them ever having any fun. My dad never took her down to Socorro for a movie or dinner. He was so damned desperate to make this ranch work. I think she liked to dance. I don't know why, but for some reason I think so. But he never took her dancing.

"And him. You remember how he used to just stand there with his arms crossed and look at you and me like he knew exactly what we were thinking and there wasn't a damned thing he could do about it? I used to wonder about the expression his face always had at those times. I couldn't figure it out. But after all these years, Will, I finally understand that it was just love, a word I never heard him say, not once."

"It was love, all right. I think that's why he worked so hard at this ranch, why he and your mom took out that mortgage. It was for you."

Billy shook his head. "It's funny, isn't it? Sometimes I think about what it must have been like back there in Oklahoma. What it would have been like for you and me if our folks had stayed. Most of the time I think to hell with all that Indian stuff. I mean we're just human beings and here we are like everybody else, so why keep trying to remember something everybody else is forgetting. But then sometimes I think Jesus Christ, there's a whole Cherokee nation back there that we don't know shit about."

"I guess it was a stupid question," Will said. "They weren't as old as we are right now."

Billy stared off toward the east for a moment. "You remember that time we followed my mom out to the corn shed that morning? She was praying in there in some kind of Indian way even though she was a white woman. She must have learned that from my grandma in Oklahoma, too."

Will nodded. "I remember looking through the cracks in the wall. You thought maybe it was witchcraft or something. Your own mother."

"Well hell, I was only ten or eleven, but it was odd for a white woman to pray like that." He bent down to pick up a dried twig, breaking it into small pieces and dropping them between his feet. "I never paid much attention, Will. I never wanted to be like them. I figured if I was half white I could just choose what I wanted to be. Even in the Indian rodeos I never really felt like I was one of them—you know, an Indian like those Navajos and Apaches. Now sometimes when I'm laying in there at night I get a kind of funny feeling that the fire was my fault, even though I know it wasn't."

"It was just lightning, Billy, nobody's fault. But I know what you mean. My parents were coming up to Albuquerque to see me when they got in that accident. So it was sort of my fault.

"Maybe Mouse is right, Billy. Maybe there's a curse. Sometimes I pick up a handful of dirt at my place and I feel something in there like fire."

"There's no such thing as curses, Will. There's just things that happen. We remember the bad stuff. But a lot of it's good, and we forget that part. There's accidents like a butane tank that gets hit by lightning or a drunk that crosses the line and kills a man's family."

Billy dropped the remains of the stick and seemed to reflect for a moment. "I'll tell you what, though. This feels like the end of something. Do you feel it all around you? You know what I'm going to do?"

Pushing the hat back on his forehead, he turned to look closely at Will. "I've given this a lot of thought. I'm going to take that money and build a house just like the one my dad built, exactly the same, right on top of this same foundation. I'm going to do every damned thing myself, from the plumbing to the shake roof. And I'm going to ask Odessa to marry me. You had your family, and back then I thought you were tied down while I was free and lucky. Now I think of you alone over there with that dog and pig, but I know you at least have Si and Holly out there somewhere. And Jace, too. No matter how you feel, you aren't really alone. Hell, I'm not too old to have a few good seeds left. Me and Odessa could have a brood of Cherokee-Apache-Irish mixed-breeds right here. We could even turn this into a real cattle ranch again. The Keene and Striker spreads can be something again, Will, even if we have to drill all the way to China for water. We can do it together. Like we've always done everything. I'll just be a little later than you on the family part."

Will turned away toward the eastern mountains. In the background, he heard the barn crows taunting and teasing one another with treble cries. "That sounds awfully good, Billy," he said softly. "Maybe we can. But be careful. You don't know Odessa. You don't really know anything about her, where she came from or anything."

"I know enough. I know plenty. Hell, Odessa's the first Indian woman I've ever really known, and she's smarter than you and me put together. She likes it here, and she likes me. She's in love with me. Everything's about to change, Will. Can't you feel it? That suitcase was just the beginning." He gripped Will's shoulder hard and looked directly into his face. "We can do what our parents tried to do, what nobody's been able to do. We can turn this whole damned thousand acres into a garden. All it takes is money. And I'm not going to make the same mistake my father made. Odessa and me are going to have some fun."

# 18

"There used to be railroad tracks down through here," Billy said, motioning below the road toward steep, rock-broken switchbacks that angled down to the Rio Grande Valley. "They'd drive cattle over from Arizona and ship them out from Magdalena."

"I wonder what they did with them?" Odessa said, peering through the broad, curved windshield at the dry landscape. The late afternoon sun spread thin cloud patterns across the few trees and rock outcroppings and sent the pickup's shadow racing ahead of it on the black road.

"Hamburger, steaks, glue, and shoes I guess."

"No. The railroad tracks. I wonder what they do with all of that steel when they tear up old tracks like that. I always used to think they were beautiful, all those long straight lines of steel. When I was about twelve, I had a friend whose family lived on the railroad tracks. Her father worked for the railroad, and they lived in a railroad car on a siding in the middle of nowhere."

"They lived in a railroad car, like a house?"

Odessa nodded as she watched the burned landscape slip past. A ground squirrel dashed across the road and Billy braked sharply. The pickup flinched and then the rocks and shrubs began to flow at the same smooth pace again.

"It had a door and windows like a house, and a wood stove with a chimney sticking out the top of the car. To me it felt like a playhouse for grown-ups, not even as much of a house as the

Indians had. When a train went by, everything shook like some-body with chills."

She reached for a strand of her own hair and held it between her fingers, examining it as though comparing it with the childhood memory. "She was beautiful, with long, straight blond hair, green eyes, and a huge smile. There was a band of freckles across her nose, and she was almost as brown as me from being in the sun all the time. She used to hunt rabbits with her father, and a couple of times I saw them both come walking back to the railroad car, each one carrying a rabbit by the feet in one hand and a rifle in the other hand. For a whole year I'd run over there and get her so we could walk around in the hills and talk, and then one day they were gone. She didn't even tell me, or maybe nobody told her. They must have just come and hooked an engine up to the car. I remember standing and looking at those railroad tracks that just went straight forever. White Sands was right across the road, with the white gypsum blowing around, and the sun was running along the edge of the track like fire."

"You didn't have any idea she was leaving?"

"I guess she knew that would happen one day. Maybe that was why she always seemed to be hovering off in the distance a little, like a hummingbird. If I reached my hand out to touch her, she'd be just a couple of inches too far away, so all I'd touch would be air."

"I thought you grew up in California."

"I stayed with my grandmother that year down near Three Rivers. You know, one time I couldn't find my friend. Her mother didn't know where she was. So I started walking around the arroyos behind the siding and yelling her name. She never answered, but finally I stumbled across her. She'd dug a hole and had a piece of tin over it for a roof, and she was sitting there in the dark watching me through a little space between the tin and the side of the hole. Not saying anything. She looked like a beautiful and very fright-ened badger staring up into the light like that, and I had a terrible thought for a moment she'd been changed. Then she laughed and pushed the tin back so I could climb in, too."

"She sounds lonely," Billy said. "What was her name?"

Odessa kept her eyes on the dry country outside the pickup, and when she spoke her voice was soft and as dry as the clumps of sage along the fenceline at the edge of the road. Billy thought of the white sound a snake made as it slid across summer grass.

"She was the best friend I ever had." Odessa pushed her hair back from her face with both hands and turned to smile at him. "I would have left her pretty soon anyway, since I had to go back to California, but I still think about her. I wonder where she went, whether she stayed on the railroad tracks, wherever they led, and kept making homes in the earth, or if she broke away. I like to imagine that she's somewhere beautiful now, maybe in a perfect little house close to the ocean miles from any railroad tracks, where nobody can ever come in the middle of the night and take everything away, where someone can touch her. Her name was Jemmie, and she was the only purely good person I ever knew."

Billy shifted into fifth and let the pickup gather momentum down a long, steep straightaway. "I guess I'm real lucky," he said. "I've always had Will. I can't remember a time when he wasn't there. I guess there wasn't anything we didn't do together."

"Anything?"

He smiled. "Pretty much, I guess. We even lost our virginity together in my dad's old car. One Ruiz sister in the front with Will and one in the back with me." He laughed out loud. "And for the life of me I can't remember which one was in the back."

"I'll bet they tell the same story." She rolled the window down a crack and took a deep breath of the summer air. To the south and west lightning menaced faintly from a bank of thin gray cloud. She shivered and rolled the window back up. "Are you really sure we should be doing this?" she said. "Maybe we should just turn around and go back."

"You've earned one evening of fun. Everything'll be fine. Everything will be great, in fact."

"I'm fine at the ranch. I don't need an evening of fun. Besides, are you sure your grandfather will be okay?"

"Grampa Siquani will be okay. He can call Will. Will's always there." He turned to look directly at her. "When we get back home, I'm going to show you something you won't believe."

"What?" She lowered her sunglasses and looked steadily at him over the top of them, her eyes serious.

"I can't tell you, but it's going to change both our lives. You won't believe it, Odessa."

"There isn't much I don't believe," she replied.

He took a hand from the wheel to stroke her leg. "I think you're always afraid that somebody's going to come along and hook on to your life and drag you up some shiny railroad tracks."

She looked out the window and exhaled slowly, as though resigned to something. "Imagine what it would have been like," she said.

"Staying home?"

"No. Five hundred years ago. Imagine us meeting, a Cherokee and an Apache. It would have been like people from different planets." She gave him an enigmatic look. "I don't think my family would have approved."

"Of course they would've. The Cherokee were royalty."

"Right, that fact slipped my mind. But it took white people to herd you Cherokees halfway across the continent with bayonets just so we could meet."

"It took white people to make me, too, don't forget that. Look." He held his much paler hand upon her arm and then slid the hand down her thigh and along the taut line to her knee, his hand rising at the end to rest on the pickup's gearshift.

"Have you ever wondered what it would have been like, Billy, if Europeans had never come? If Native Americans had been allowed to evolve our own cultures in our own ways? Think about it. Indian people are among the most adaptive on the face of the earth. If we hadn't been, we'd all have been dead a long time ago. So what would we be today if we'd been left alone?"

"The great communal capitalists of the world maybe, sitting behind desks in beaded ties and business buckskins. Tribes might be multinational corporations by now." He watched a coyote walking slowly up the dry arroyo below the road, mouth open in what looked like a grin and apparently oblivious to the pickup on the road three hundred yards away. The animal's shabby summer coat ruffled in a wind snaking up the arroyo from the distant valley, a thermal rising that shimmered gray fur and shivered the grass tufts of the wash. The coyote moved like sand lifted and carried on the invisible currents of the earth.

He started to call her attention to the animal, but then the coyote paused and looked up, the grin widening so that he could see its pink tongue and yellow teeth. He had a feeling of shared intelligence, some kind of sarcastic communication for an instant as if the coyote knew something he didn't, and then the animal turned, lowered its head, and resumed its shambling trot. He watched it slip out of sight around an angle of rock, the gray-brown sides blending perfectly with sandstone and sage.

"Maybe we'd have evolved into the ecological saviors of the world," she said, her words trailing off with a cynical edge.

"Maybe we'd be a theme park, a kind of ocean-to-ocean Disneyland where we could charge Frenchmen and Germans five thousand bucks for a weekend vision quest, thirty thousand for a shaman school diploma."

She shook her head and adjusted her sunglasses. "You don't take anything seriously, do you, Billy?"

"I take you seriously." He ran his fingers along her bare upper arm to the edge of her sleeveless white blouse.

She sniffled. "I think I'm allergic to cedar pollen. Do you have any tissues?"

Before he could respond, she opened the glove compartment. After glancing at him and back to where her hand still rested, she pulled out the forty-four. Laying it across her lap, she ran a finger along the barrel and then traced each concavity of the cylinder before following the line down along the curved handle.

"Is it loaded?"

He nodded. "It's legal, you know, to carry a loaded gun in your glove compartment in New Mexico."

"You think I was going to ask if it was legal?" She flipped the cylinder open and ejected one of the heavy cartridges into her palm. She held the large, hollow-point forty-four slug up to the light of the window and then slipped it back into the gun. Spinning the cylinder, she said, "Uranium turns into lead if given enough time to decay. So these bullets are really like tiny atomic bombs. Inside a person, the lead flowers like a mushroom cloud, and that person has his own personal Trinity Site."

"How do you know so much about guns?" Billy took his eyes from the road for a moment to look at Odessa.

She pulled back the hammer on the pistol. "There are more than a thousand uranium mines left in Indian country, each one a death hole. Sometimes they fill up with water and the animals drink slow death. Sometimes they leach into the drinking water of Indian families. Sometimes they just sit there making radon gas. A lot of Indian families are living in houses made out of uranium ore. It's like Indians had our own Hiroshima right at home, except that it's taking more time."

"Maybe you should put that thing away." He glanced at the pistol and back at the road, where a raven flapped up from the flattened remains of a small brown creature.

"All those Navajo and Pueblo people live with death pointed at them every second. And most of them don't even know it." She studied the side of his face for a moment. "Do you know what they call the elements released by the breakdown of radon? They're called radon daughters. Maybe the breakdown of cultures releases the same kind of poison. Maybe I'm a radon daughter, Billy. Perhaps it took five hundred years to create me."

With his right hand he reached for the gun, gently pushing the barrel away and then taking the pistol from her and uncocking it, steadying the steering wheel with his forearms as he did so. With one hand he flipped the cylinder out and turned it carefully. "I like to keep the hammer on an empty chamber," he said as he pushed the cylinder back into place. "Now put it away."

Odessa took the gun by the barrel and replaced it in the glove compartment. "I like it when you're firm." She rested her hand on his thigh for a moment and then let it slide between his legs.

In front of them the land swept down toward the Rio Grande Valley, the distant view a pastel layering of brown, pink, and green, with a shadowy, uneven line of black mountains far to the east across the river valley. He watched a jackrabbit climb the side of the old railroad bed beside the road and pause at the low summit, its ears sharp against the sky where the earth dropped away.

"You're no radon daughter," he said. "You're a goddamned atomic explosion all by yourself."

The pickup floated quietly down the last long stretch of asphalt toward the town of Socorro. Pale buildings gathered and glimmered tin roofs at them, with the Rio Grande forming a line of dull green in the background. Brownish hills descended toward the town with the road from Magdalena, and car windshields and semis flashed amidst trees lining the interstate along the town's eastern edge. As they followed the curving road into town, Billy pointed to a square sand-colored building.

On the faded paint of the two-story brick structure an owl stood against a pale yellow moon, the bird's round, almost invisible eyes fixed on the street and its curving wings seeming ready to enfold everything into itself. The colors had nearly vanished over many years, leaving a ghost owl of gray against the wind-blasted moon.

Odessa stared at the painting as they drove past, waiting until they were a block beyond the structure to say, "That's creepy as hell." She shivered and rubbed her shoulders with crossed hands.

"I know what you mean. Grampa Siquani won't go past it. He always makes me drive around the back way." He swung the truck through a curve back onto the town's main street. Halfway down the ten blocks of the street, he pulled in beneath a lighted sign hung at a broken angle, a cocktail glass tilted as though it would spill at every flash of light. Above the painted glass RUDY'S looked like it had been scrawled across the sign in red lipstick.

"You sure about this place?" She kept her hand on his leg.

"Have I been wrong yet?" he replied.

# 19

Siquani arose before dawn, glanced around the trailer without seeing the shadow of Arturo Cruz, and went out the aluminum door toward the barn, looking like a figure of sticks in his loose jean jacket, overalls, and hat. In the dark he found a shovel and walked a hundred yards up the road from the two trailers. Chipping and levering painfully at the gravelly earth, he managed in a few minutes to scrape a hole nearly a foot deep and a foot across in the middle of the road. He dropped the shovel on the road and turned to confront with surprise the dark form of Arturo Cruz.

"You didn't wake me," Arturo said.

"I didn't know you was asleep. I didn't know spirits slept."

"I was dreaming," Arturo replied. "That I was flying like the eagle again, but I couldn't see anything because the world was all dark. I could only hear sounds coming from below like little animals calling for help. Then I woke up and felt you gone."

The old man shook his head and walked past Arturo, saying over his shoulder, "I thought you was out practicing to be a ghost."

In a few minutes Siquani returned with an armful of splintery sticks, which he carried back to the hole. As Arturo watched, the old man built a small pyramid of splinters that he lighted with a match. In a moment he had a fire going, leaning the larger slivers against the smaller ones until, almost as quickly, the splinters and sticks of pine had become thin embers at the bottom of the hole.

With the embers still smoldering, he shoveled dirt back over the hole and returned to his trailer, walking determinedly with Arturo following.

From behind, Arturo said, "That was lightning wood from that pine by the spring, wasn't it, protection from the dark ones, those you called night walkers?"

Siquani leaned the shovel against the little deck and went into the trailer, coming back out with a small clay pipe that he lit before he walked several paces to the east, blowing a puff of smoke toward the still unrisen sun.

He cast an irritated look at Arturo and then turned to his right, walking to the south of the trailer before again blowing a faint puff from the pipe. Arturo stood at his shoulder, watching intently.

"You know, you're making me more interested in the medicine of my own people," Arturo said at Siquani's elbow. "I always thought anthropologists were sort of like corpse diddlers, but I'm beginning to see how it could be interesting. This is a trap for those dark ones, isn't it, Grandfather, like the web of a spider?"

The old man turned to face Arturo. "I ain't never heard of anybody doing work with a dead person pestering him every minute," he said.

Arturo cupped his chin in his hand. "I was thinking about that, Grandfather. At first it worried me, too, but I've decided that I can help you."

"How?"

"Moral support."

Still trailed doggedly by the translucent shadow of Arturo, Siquani moved to the west behind both of the little silver trailers, blew a puff of smoke in that direction, and then continued to the north side of Billy's trailer, repeating the action. When he stood once again in front of his trailer, the sun had begun to rise, causing objects to step out of the dark around him. Ignoring Arturo, he went inside and reappeared quickly without the pipe, going to the barn and pushing the big door open just enough to squeeze through.

In the shadowy interior of the barn, the Land Cruiser loomed like a rock outcropping. Siquani approached the machine carefully, touching the rear corner the way he would have patted the flank of a dangerous horse.

"This is a classic automobile, a collector's item," Arturo said from behind him.

Siquani turned to see the silhouette of a man, the faintly slatted light of the barn planks showing through the form. From the corrugated roof above, he heard the sound of crows' feet on tin and the quarrelsome arguing of the birds.

"See if the key is in it," Arturo said.

The old man pried on the door handle awkwardly until finally the door swung open. He stuck his head in and withdrew it quickly, shutting the door. "The key is there," he said.

"Good. You get in and I'll show you what to do."

Siquani looked at his friend for a long minute before opening the door once more and climbing with difficulty up onto the driver's seat. He pulled the door closed and peered around the big steering wheel at the key in the ignition.

"Okay," Arturo said from the passenger seat. "See that pedal by your left foot? That's called the clutch. Push that down with your foot."

Siquani touched the toe of his tennis shoe to the pedal and gave a delicate, experimental push.

"Push it all the way and hold it down," Arturo said.

The old man scooted forward and shoved his leg farther under the wheel to depress the clutch.

"Now this lever here is for shifting." Arturo held his hand over the gearshift sticking out of the middle of the floor. "Keep that pedal in and pull that lever back to the middle place there. Feel how it's loose now? That's called neutral. The car won't go when the gearshift is there. Now look over here on the glove compartment."

"Billy don't wear gloves when he drives."

"That's just what people call it; I don't know why. But see this diagram here on the outside? That shows you where the gears are. You have to put the gearshift in this place, where it says One, to start moving, and then when the car is going you change it to these other places. I can tell you when to change it. And each time you change it you must push the clutch pedal to the floor and hold it there until the lever is in the new position. Then you let the pedal out slowly."

Siquani turned in the seat and stared at Arturo Cruz for a long time, his face without expression.

"It's okay, Grandfather," Arturo said. "You will be a very fine driver. I've always been a good judge of such things. I'll show you how to lock the hubs and shift this little lever here when we need four-wheel drive. Now maybe you should practice moving the gearshift lever to the different positions."

Siquani held the clutch down with his left leg extended awkwardly while he tilted to the right and manipulated the gearshift. When he had gone through the pattern of four gears several times, Arturo said, "*Muy bien, Abuelo*, now you see that little knob right there?"

The old man squinted at the metal dash and nodded. "That's called the choke. You have to pull that out the first time you start the engine and then push it back in once the motor is running good."

Siquani pulled the choke out and waited.

"Okay, now keep the shift lever in that middle position and turn the key."

The old man turned the key and the motor shrieked.

"Push the choke halfway in," Arturo yelled.

Siquani reached for the knob, and the vehicle leapt forward with a grinding thud into the piled hay bales. The motor belched and died.

"That was excellent," Arturo said. "But you must be careful not to bump that gearshift lever. Now you must push the clutch pedal to the floor and move that gearshift lever to the middle place before you start the motor again."

Siquani peered through the windshield at the gray-black bales of rotting hay that had tumbled down onto the front of the Land Cruiser, and he looked over at Arturo. Motes of dust hovered in the bars of light still visible through Arturo's outline, with a keener light shining between barn planks beyond the vehicle.

"You ain't as substantial as you used to be, Mr. Cruz."

Arturo shrugged. "Maybe it is time for the next part of my journey. Perhaps we'd better hurry. Okay, you got it in neutral so turn that key again."

This time when the motor caught and screamed the Land Cruiser remained nosed up against the fallen bales and shivered violently. "Excellent," Arturo shouted. "Now you push that knob in about halfway."

Siquani pushed the choke in and the motor quieted to a muted roar.

"You are a natural with machines," Arturo said, smiling. "I can tell that you have a feel for them. Now push it in a little bit more."

Siquani pushed the choke in almost all the way, and the motor slowed to an even rush.

"Fantastic. Now we are ready. Push the clutch pedal, that one on the left, all the way to the floor and hold it there. Good. Now pull the gearshift lever over to that 'R' position. Okay. Now you must lift your foot very slowly off the pedal to make the car go."

Siquani looked at Arturo and then peered down through the steering wheel at his foot. Slowly he lifted his foot off the pedal. The gears caught and the Land Cruiser shot backward with a terrible grinding. Siquani grabbed the steering wheel and leaned forward to stare out the windshield.

"No," Arturo shouted. "You have to look behind us."

As Siquani turned to look, the vast, closed door of the barn loomed in a gray, light-fractured wall, and then the Land Cruiser smashed into the door and through it with an explosion of brittle gray planking.

Once outside, the vehicle spun in a backward half-circle to

crash against the massive silver trunk of a cedar, lurch twice, and die.

When they were still, Siquani stared at the front of the barn for a long time, where a gaping hole showed the shadowy interior. A broken bale of hay clung to the brush guard on the front of the Land Cruiser, and small clumps of decomposing straw were lodged in the windshield wipers.

"Fine," Arturo said. "Now start the motor again like before, with that lever right in the middle."

**20**

From Tramway to the Big-I, traffic crawled, and Jace cursed herself for not cutting across to Gibson at the edge of the air force base to escape the freeway jam. Beside her, a lowrider's Chevy purred on its out-thrust, too-small tires, the driver staring straight ahead behind his shades. Ahead of him, a jacked-up pickup showed a gunrack in the back window, a lever-action rifle in the rack, and a working rope dangling from one hook of the rack. Everybody's in a costume of some kind, she thought, glancing down at her own western boots, jeans, and catalog-ordered chambray shirt.

Once through the sweeping exit to southbound 25, she cut in front of a stainless steel tanker in the fast lane and punched the accelerator. The Jeep gulped and leapt ahead with a satisfying growl, and she settled in at seventy in the fifty-five zone bisecting the heart of Albuquerque. In a few minutes the interstate swung west across the Rio Grande and then south again past the Isleta

Pueblo and into the desolation of the Rio Grande Valley where rock and earth lay exposed for all to see.

Watching the road ahead and the rearview mirror for troopers, she accelerated to seventy-five, pushed the cruise control, and turned on the radio. The classical station from Santa Fe was booming an Italian tenor, so she punched the scanner, stopping when she caught the strains of Dwight Yokum and Buck Owens twanging about the streets of Bakersfield.

Something was going on with Will. It vibrated in his voice over the telephone and seemed to emanate from the air she breathed. Something about the dry electrical storms of the past two weeks had worked its way into the marrow of her bones and played through the nerves of her spine like plucked chords. She'd found herself watching the southern sky at night, fixed on the play of splintery storm-light down that way. Their phone calls always flared with anger, no matter how she tried to avoid it. But the last few calls had been unique. His voice was different, and behind his anger she could hear a kind of resonance, a hollow space beyond which she seemed to hear the snap of sheet lightning.

She'd awakened in the dark that morning with a feeling of unease, exhausted from a sleepless night, to be startled by the man beside her. For what felt like minutes, she couldn't remember who the blond touseled hair and muscular shoulders belonged to, and then the memory of the evening before returned. It had started with a couple hours of late work together at the office, a logical dinner, and a few drinks. He was the youngest partner at the firm, a man some years younger than she, and it had ended in her bed with what, in the dark predawn, she remembered as hours of his mouth and tongue touching and kissing every inch of her from the instep of her foot to the soft indentation beneath her rib cage to breast and nipple and lips. She had felt as though she were being devoured, and she'd given herself up to it with a delicious totality that, in reflection, shocked her. And then him inside her, at first incredibly gentle and slow but ending with the two of them clutching one another in a kind of desperation she had never experienced.

She remembered forcing him to turn over, so that she could be on top, so that she could be the one fucking him.

As she had lain there before daylight, remembering with a vague astonishment, he'd stirred and reached for her, a hand sliding up her arm and onto a breast, and when he moved closer she had been amazed to find him hard. The strange, timeless warp of morning and memory had created an unfamiliar arousal in her, and she felt herself growing wet with desire. As if from a distant height she had been aware of her own body turning to his and her hips widening to encourage his first gentle and then stronger thrusts. Then he had been fully inside her, and as though from a balcony she had watched them making love again, herself straining to take him as deeply as possible and her hands cupping his buttocks to pull him tighter as he came, as though this near stranger could fill some void deep in her center.

He had kissed her cheek and shifted to one side, his breathing becoming deep and regular again, and when she knew he was once more asleep, she slipped from the bed and showered quickly. Carrying her clothes into the living room, she dressed and wrote a note, which she left next to the coffee machine in the kitchen.

"So now that you've fucked your boss, you go running to your husband," she said aloud as Dwight sang about people who had never walked the streets of Bakersfield. But she knew that wasn't it, at least not all of it. She wasn't seeking out Will because of the man she'd left in her bed. For whatever reason, she simply could no longer resist the urge that had tugged at her for the last two weeks to drive down to the ranch and find the man she was married to. The night and morning had broken down some kind of resistance. The image of Will Striker rose in her thoughts. She tried to imagine him in bed with another woman, even desired such imagining, and the picture refused to form. It didn't seem possible for Will. His life was monastic. He rose with the sun, having formed already a pattern for each day. From the beginning she'd felt that the man she married was but the frontispiece to something else, that behind the gentle, serious man were landscapes she couldn't conceive of, canyons and ranges to which there were no maps. She had always thought of that region as Indian in some vague and perhaps romantic way, a place requiring a map she would never have. And she'd watched their children curl into their father's lap, snuggle against his broad chest and try to burrow into his soul only to seemingly find themselves, too, lost in that other landscape. How could someone remain a stranger after half a lifetime? She thought of the photograph of his parents over the fireplace, the dark-faced man in neck-buttoned shirt and western hat beside the white woman whose face betrayed nothing but love. Somehow that infinite measure of resistance had merged with simple love to produce Will Striker.

Sex had ceased to be part of their life together several years before she left. He'd simply lost interest. Kisses and caresses had engendered nothing. "I don't know, Jace," he'd said, as together they looked down at his limp cock. "Something's busted, I guess." She'd suggested counseling, without success, and had not argued with force because she'd known already what was busted. Will had seemed to note the failure of his sexual apparatus with only mild interest and less curiosity, as though somehow it were to be expected. As the ranch grew more dry with each searing wind, the straggling cattle baring ribs to the same wind, Will had grown more disengaged. When son and daughter, one after another, spun off into lives of their own, she had watched and felt her husband drift away from their life together, coming home from working other men's cattle or building other men's fences to stalk the gray regions of his own, separate existence. Their bed had become a place for sleep, two bodies that recoiled with each touch. Finally, she had found herself in the place where she had begun: alone with a stranger. When she had told him of her plans to move closer to the university in Albuquerque, Will had nodded, saying nothing, and that night he began to sleep in the small back room that had been their son's. The day she moved, he had saddled the mare for a ride up the canyon, and she'd been gone before he returned.

Part of her own family had been to Bakersfield and back again, a rare portion of the Dust Bowl exodus that still had enough gas and patched tires to turn around and go home from the promised land. "They ain't nothin' out there but two kinds of people," her grandmother had told her when she was little. "Poor folks and rich folks that hate each other like tarnation. Trouble is, poor folks want to get rich and rich folks don't want to get poor." In Jace's memory, California was a faded gray, white-bordered photograph of an old car with canvas water bags hanging from every sharp projection of mirror, fender, and hood ornament. Her grampa sat behind the wheel and stared bleakly ahead under a narrow-brimmed hat, with the head of her father just visible in the backseat. Behind the car the gray desert floor looked like a shallow ocean banked up to the two-lane highway. A flash flood somewhere in Arizona or the California desert had stopped them for a day, and her grandma had snapped the picture with a Brownie camera. Now the photograph had become part of Jace's memory, putting her there in the old car crossing a desert. She remembered the confusion of loss and the torched desert in the depths of her soul and the pores of her dry flesh, though she had not yet been born and would not be for years when her father and grandparents traveled that circle.

Passing one of the two or three microscopic towns along the river between Albuquerque and Socorro, she began to probe her own feelings for motive and intention. She lowered the sun visor and looked into the mirror on the visor's back. Her sandy brown hair was short and neat, lying straight and healthy-looking to the bottom of her chambray collar. Her eyes looked surprisingly clear, their gray deepening with the growing daylight. She knew she looked younger than her forty-four years. Her jeans were comfortably snug, fitting a moderately lean and adequate body. Aerobics and swimming and strategic use of minimal makeup had turned back the clock since she'd left the ranch and moved to Albuquerque. Men came on to her often, but usually in subtle ways. She knew she intimidated men, and that was their problem. She was comfortable with the woman who had walked away from a dying ranch.

Frank and last night weren't sending her on this drive south-ward. For a reason she didn't try to fathom she felt no guilt at all about that, nothing but a kind of pleasant sensation that filled her body, a kind of sensation she hadn't known in too many years. She knew she wouldn't let it happen again with Frank. Maybe she'd leave the law firm; she'd felt the urge to quit for some time. But none of it seemed to have anything to do with Will Striker. Can I love one man and sleep with another, she wondered, answering yes before tumbling into the deeper question of loving her husband. Maybe it wasn't love at all, but simply a long habit of caring.

She conjured up his face, trying to see him as he would be at six in the morning. She saw him at the wooden table, already dressed in a flannel shirt, jeans, and boots, unshaven, his graying hair tangled into odd points and curls. Getting up early for a day of what? A sliver of sun would be angling through the too-small kitchen window, showing the enamel-painted gouges and pits of the countertop. How many mornings in twenty-five years of mar-riage had they faced each other like that? A pleasant, burning sen-sation grew in her abdomen and rose, spreading through her chest and ending with a sweet, salty taste in her mouth. For an instant she wondered if the feeling came from memories of her life with Will Striker or if it was just a remnant from the night and morn-ing. And then she saw him as he had been at the funeral. She had stood beside him, holding his callused hand and wishing she had known the couple who were being buried. Inside her, even then, she had felt the weight of their first child who was but an infini-tesimal speck of life. But she knew that life would carry whatever it was they were burying, Indian and white, foreign and irresis-tible.

Winding up the switchbacks above Socorro, she began to feel nervous. At Magdalena she watched for familiar figures going into the one café but found none, and when she turned off the blacktop onto the ranch road she felt something like panic surge through her. Something was wrong. There was imbalance in the air, in the way the morning light slanted across the barbed wire fence, the tilted quality of the few clouds piling up in the west. The sky seemed closer to the earth than she could recall, the shreds of cloud somehow damp with either promise or threat, she couldn't tell which. Is it just me? she wondered. Have I gone so far away that my own life threatens me? Or was it the loss of the children, the fact that her daughter and son had gone off to lives of their own, leaving an uninhabitable barrenness behind?

Will saw the Jeep as he walked back from the chicken run. In both hands were rocks he had intended to chuck at the buzzards, but the birds hadn't shown up that morning from wherever it was they roosted.

He stood with his hands hanging down, watching the shiny, dark green vehicle approach. It wasn't until she was stepping from the Jeep that he recognized his wife.

She walked toward him, stopping a few feet away with arms folded across her chest and looking at him with her head slightly cocked.

"You bought a Cherokee," he said, letting the rocks fall from his hands.

She smiled faintly. "I thought you might have a little trouble with that."

He shrugged. "Why don't they make Jeep Japanese or Jeep Germans? But what the hell. You look good, Jace."

"You look awful. I'll bet under that hat you haven't even combed your hair."

"I have coffee on. It's not the kind you prefer, but it's hot."

"I'd like that," she said, and she walked ahead of him toward the house.

In the kitchen he poured two cups of black coffee and set one in front of her. "I'm afraid I don't have any milk. I don't use it anymore."

"It smells good. You still put eggshells in the pot?"

He nodded, lifting his hat off and hanging it on the back of an empty chair.

"I was right about your hair. It looks like a pack rat's nest. And you need a haircut." She looked from him toward the recesses of the kitchen, scanning the counter and shelves as though searching for evidence.

"I think I'll grow it long," he replied, brushing it back with both hands. "Like Billy's."

"You're serious?"

"I think so. It feels good."

"There are brushes in the bathroom then."

He ran both hands through his hair with some difficulty, brushing it back from his forehead. "Yeah."

They sat in silence for a long moment as Jace continued to look around the familiar kitchen. The patterns of all the years seemed worn into the air itself, invisible paths from bedroom to stove, to sink, to cupboard.

"I still do that, too," he said.

"Do what?"

"Look for Si and Holly. I miss the cereal boxes spilled on the counter and the milk glasses they never rinsed. You'd think a person would adjust after a while, wouldn't you?"

"It's not like they're very far away," she replied. "We could give them a call. Maybe they could come up for a visit."

He nodded. "Maybe later."

"How have you been, Will?"

He shrugged and raised his eyes slowly from the cup to her face. "Fair to middlin', I guess."

As he spoke, there was a sudden crash from the back of the house followed by an anguished howl. Jace started, splashing coffee on the table, and he stood up quickly. "Maggie must've smelled you," he said, "and I guess the door wasn't all the way open. She's still a dog of very little brain."

Jace grabbed the towel from the refrigerator handle and wiped up the spilled coffee. "All the way open?" she said as she tossed the towel on the counter and sat back down in the chair.

"I keep it open a little for Maggie and Molly."

"Molly comes into the house? When I wanted her, you said only on the condition that she lived in the barn."

He made a wry face and spoke as he headed into the hallway leading toward the back. "They wore me down. Besides, she's a hell of a clean pig. Hates mud, not that she could find any around here."

With a great banging and scraping, Maggie came sprawling into the kitchen, whining loudly, the cast on her front leg making her attempt to wriggle look like an elaborate dance. Before Jace could get up, the dog plunged into her lap. Too late, Jace reached for the table's edge at the same instant that Molly streaked into the room like an elliptical torpedo.

The chair tilted and fell backward, Maggie arcing across Jace with the stained cast jutting out beside the chair. With a piercing squeal, the pig exploded from beneath the collapsing chair, in the process tumbling woman and dog sideways onto the wooden floor and then racing for the hallway. Instantly, Maggie began to emit a moaning bark and flail with the cast for footing.

Will moved quickly around the table, picking the dog up with both arms around her midsection and hoisting her to a standing position beside the sink, where they both turned toward Jace.

On the floor beside the overturned chair, Jace lay on her side, looking up with an expression of shock. And then she began to laugh.

Will stepped around the dog and reached a hand down to his wife. As she gathered her legs beneath her and rose, he placed his other hand on her shoulder.

"You all right, Jace?"

She spoke in the middle of a laugh. "This is how you've been living, Will Striker? What happened to Maggie?" She crouched and put both arms around the dog's large shoulders, nuzzling her face into the thick fur above the bandage. "Poor girl."

"A little accident. But remember, they're your dog and your pig."

Jace continued to nuzzle the dog, who squirmed with pleasure.

With her voice muffled, Jace said, "I give them both to you. It's clear you've all bonded."

"Funny. Ha ha. I don't want them. Billy suggested a barbecue."

"Too late, and it's Billy who'll get his ass barbecued if he messes with Molly."

When Jace was sitting at the table again, with Maggie at her feet, Will turned to the stove, lifting the lid to the coffeepot and peering into it. "Maybe I'd better heat up this coffee again."

Jace grimaced. "That's okay. I think I've had enough coffee this morning."

He struck a match and lit the burner under the pot and returned to the table. "What's going on, Jace?"

"I don't know. I had an urge to see the ranch. To see how you were doing."

He watched her, his eyes probing hers.

"You don't answer the phone. You don't call. Not even once in three months," she said.

He got up and poured the coffee from his cup into the sink before refilling the cup from the pot. He gestured with the pot. "You sure?" When she shook her head, he turned the burner off and sat back down, taking a gingerly sip of the heavy black liquid.

"Something's wrong. I heard it in your voice when I called."

"Nothing's wrong."

She studied his face for a moment. "Have you had any work?"

He shrugged. "I've been doing contract work for the Forest Service once in a while, put in a fire break over near Quemado. Worked some cattle for Ruiz last month." He lifted his eyebrows. "Old man Kenden asked me to help him inoculate his turkeys a couple weeks ago. One of those damned toms just about busted my arm."

"You ought to sell that Caterpillar. You could get a lot for it."

"That's funny, Nate just said the same thing. But that Cat meant a lot to my dad."

She shook her head. "I remember. You said he was planning

to put in stock tanks from here to hell and back, but he never did and you never will either, will you?"

He formed a tight-lipped smile. "A stock tank isn't worth much without water, I guess. Or stock. Besides, who wants to keep gouging big damned holes in the earth?"

"Well, I'm glad, but you know I could help out." She looked at the bare kitchen. A twenty-five pound burlap sack of dried pinto beans leaned against the cupboard by the sink, and a ten-pound plastic bag of potatoes lay next to the beans. A giant bottle of cooking oil stood beside the potatoes. "You aren't watching your cholesterol, are you?"

He grimaced. "Everything is just fine, Jace. How are things with you?"

"Maybe I will have some more of that coffee if it's still hot?"

He reached for the coffee-sogged towel and tossed it onto the counter beside the sink and then stood up and brought the pot to the table. "Everything okay with your job and all?" he said as he poured.

She paused before saying, "I'm thinking about quitting the firm. Maybe it's time to try something new."

"You've only been there two years, right? I thought being in a big firm like that was what you always wanted."

She shrugged. "People change."

"So what're you going to do?"

"I don't know. Maybe comb your hair for you."

He looked at his cup and the rough knuckles of the hand holding it. A small, pale lightning bolt lay across the back of the hand, and he thought of the dying foal whose hoof had flicked out suddenly to slice the hand open as he reached to cradle the animal in his lap. The deaths of young things had always been hardest. He remembered his desire to pour his own vitality into the newborn foal, to share his life to save the strange new spirit he could feel slipping away.

"I've been combing my own hair for a long time, Jace," he said.

After a moment, she replied, "And doing a lousy job."

He thought of the money. Maybe if he told her about it the money wouldn't seem such a weight. He hadn't been near the well since he'd hidden the duffel there. He'd tried to make himself think of what he could, or should, do with it, but his mind shied away from the subject. He felt a great curiosity about how she would react. What would she say?

He looked into her gray eyes and realized he couldn't say anything about it. The telling would require an intimacy that felt dangerous.

The ringing phone jarred the kitchen, and they both looked toward the sound. He picked up the receiver with a sense of relief.

"Will?"

"Yeah," he answered.

"This is Billy. The Land Cruiser's gone."

"What do you mean gone?"

"It's fucking gone. It's not in the barn."

"How long's it been gone? Did Grampa Siquani see anything?"

"It was gone when I went out there this morning, and the whole damn barn door's been smashed. Grampa's gone too."

Will held the receiver and glanced at his wife.

"I'll come over," he said.

He hung up the phone and turned toward her. "That was Billy. I have to go over there."

"I'd like to go. I haven't seen Billy in a long time." She pushed the chair back and stood up, the dog scrambling to its feet and watching her alertly.

Will shook his head. "It's not a good idea."

"Why not?"

"I can't tell you right now, Jace. It's just not a good idea. You can stay here if you want."

She folded her arms and stared at him skeptically, and he thought of what she must look like in a courtroom, if she did things in courtrooms. "I appreciate your permission to stay in my house," she said.

"You know what I mean, Jace. Spend some time with your dog and pig. Maggie's already afraid you're leaving again. And that pig is developing some kind of pig complex." He went to the gun cabinet and took out the thirty-thirty, slipping a box of shells into his pocket.

Jace glanced down at the dog and spoke without looking at her husband. "What's going on, Will?"

"Nothing."

"Since when do you take a rifle for nothing?"

He picked up his hat and headed for the door. "Is the key in your Jeep?" he asked abruptly.

When she nodded, he said, "I'll park it in the barn before I leave. The ought-six in the cabinet's loaded, and Maggie will let you know if anybody comes."

"Goddammit to hell, Will, if you don't tell me what's wrong, I'll leave right now and never set foot on this place again."

He stopped at the door and looked over his shoulder. "That's for you to decide, Jace."

## 21

The first thing Will noticed when he arrived at Billy's ranch was the hole in the front of the barn. The large sliding door had exploded outward, leaving splintered planks hanging from the metal track like jagged teeth.

Billy came walking out of the darkened interior of the barn, the shadows seeming to cling to him as he emerged into the wan sunlight of morning. Will got out of the pickup and walked to the barn, pushing his hat back to better see the destruction.

"The Cruiser did it," Billy said. He pointed at the ground. "It came out through that hole and went in a crazy circle right into that tree over there."

Will glanced at the skidding crescent left by the tires and then went to examine the gouged bark of the tree. He walked to the barn and looked through the door.

"Odessa and me spent the night down in Socorro," Billy explained from behind Will. "We found this when we got home about six-thirty this morning."

Will stepped into the barn and emerged again a moment later. "Grampa Siquani's gone?" he said.

Billy nodded.

"Grampa Siquani can't drive, can he?"

Billy shook his head. "Never drove in his life that I know of."

"Well this beats all," Will replied.

"I shouldn't have been gone. Somebody must've come while we were gone."

"Why would they take Grampa Siquani? That doesn't make any sense."

Billy shook his head, his face grim. "I followed the tracks out to the highway. They headed west."

The trailer door closed and both turned toward the sound to see Odessa walking toward them. Her long hair was loose over her white T-shirt, and the black Levi's looked molded to her long legs. Will felt an unfamiliar stirring in his belly as he watched her.

"Good morning, Will." She flashed the dazzling smile at him. "Billy says Grampa Siquani and the Land Cruiser are both gone."

"I guess me and Will better go look for him," Billy said. "I'll get my rifle."

"My thirty-thirty is in the pickup," Will replied.

Billy continued toward the trailer, saying over his shoulder, "I think I'll take the two-seventy."

When Billy was inside the trailer, Odessa stepped close to Will and placed a hand on his arm. "What's this all about, Will?" she said.

He breathed in the strange sharp scent of her, trying to decide what it reminded him of. After a moment, he said, "I can't explain it right now. I'm not sure I could explain it if I wanted to. You can ask Billy later."

She looked directly into his eyes, and her hand tightened faintly on his arm. He felt engulfed in her, like a man who had stepped into a shadow and lost his bearings. He was deeply aware of every aspect of her suddenly, from the dark eyes and long black hair to the curves of her small breasts and nipples through the white T-shirt and the long legs in their tight jeans. And surrounding it all an aroma that seemed tangible, playing like lightning around her and probing through the pores of his skin.

"Billy won't tell me anything, either. Don't you think I have a right to know, if people are being kidnapped off the ranch where I'm staying?"

He struggled for words, finally saying, "I'll talk to Billy. Maybe he'll explain it when we get back."

Billy emerged from the trailer, the rifle in one hand, and waved as he headed for Will's pickup, his gaze taking in the scene of Will and Odessa fully as he walked. "Let's go," he yelled.

Odessa removed her hand slowly from Will's arm, the tips of her fingers tracing a line from shoulder to elbow. "Please?" she said.

He nodded, feeling his body shiver as he turned to walk away from her.

In the pickup, Billy looked at him strangely. "What was that about?" he asked.

Will squinted at the gas gauge and said, "She asked me what's going on. She says you won't tell her."

"You think I should?"

"Not yet."

# 22

The boy led a black horse toward the stream. Yellow leaves spun down from white cottonwoods in a steady, sparse pattern, moving with the green-black water, catching on the willows and rounding back in slow eddies. Like a blue spark struck from the clear sky, a kestrel flashed amidst the leaf-rain and dodged higher to settle on a bare gray branch, watching the boy and black horse move through pale stubble.

Paco Ortega watched the hawk, horse, and boy flow together into the beginning of fall, though the true season had come only to the high country. Up there in the pine and aspen life would be in its final, frantic rush before winter settled fully. Down here, cedar smoke rose from the earth-brown pueblo and vanished in the light wind, leaving a sweet, clean scent that he breathed deeply into his broad chest. A pleasant exhaustion hung over him, and the sacrifice of rising early for the red sun hummed in his slow blood. The deer had danced in the pueblo the night before, and the sleeping village still pulsed with the impact of drum and foot. Out of the corner of one eye he caught the jarring fold of a television antenna protruding from an adobe roof, and he shifted his head away from the image.

With his jean jacket buttoned to the neck and a black hat pushed back from his forehead, he leaned against the fence of twisted piñon, his forearms resting on a rail, his hands held together as though in prayer. The boy was himself, was his own father, his grandfather, and his grandson yet unborn. The river was like that, running down through the miles of deep canyon until it opened here by the pueblo and broadened toward the lands below, the water always changing but holding in its mirroring face the same sky, trees, hawk, boy, and horse. Looking into the water, one seemed at first to see a reflection of a person, but then the outlines always blurred and the reflection gave way to depths unending. The river had always flowed through the canyon, cutting the sandstone and granite, carving motion into the rock the same way it had carved the people into its own shape. Over generations they had learned the seasons and motions of the water, the blood that coursed through them beginning with the river and returning like the water to earth and sky.

He looked down at the brown, sloping backs of his hands, the rise of branching veins beneath smooth skin, and he felt the current of the river in his body. The whites built dams everywhere, and that was like stopping the blood of one's heart; everything flowed in a circle, and when the flow was stopped the body died. It wasn't complicated at all; the simplest child should understand it.

The boy with the horse reminded him of his nephew, Arturo Cruz, showing the same easy movement upon the earth, the straight back and curve of shoulders leaning subtly toward the horse's flank. There had been a time just a few years before when they'd ridden together up the long arroyo to the west, out onto the big mesa on a morning when the air felt so fragile and brittle that one might shatter it with a single word. The dust of yellow and red rock had stirred around the horses' feet, and the animals' breaths made blue clouds of steam as they labored up the final switchback of trail, and as they broke the surface of the mesa the scream of a red-tailed hawk had cut across the sky. He'd felt it was a good omen. Even then, he knew now, he had been planning the boy's future. Just back from the Indian school in Santa Fe, the nephew was already preparing to go down to the university in Albuquerque. Four years at the university would be very little time, and then the boy would be ready to take his place in the story that was forming. Arturo was steady and large-hearted, but there was also a streak of ambition in the boy, something absorbed from the white world. Arturo Cruz, his sister's son, would one day take Paco Ortega's place in the bigger plan, and the white world would help educate him to destroy it. But something had gone wrong. The boy who came home from the university was different. He saw things only at close hand, material things. Paco had brought the boy into the operation but had held much back, waiting for signs that the boy's heart would allow him to see through the hard, resistant surfaces of things. And for this process the old ceremonies would not work.

But there had been a different feeling on the morning of that ride. His own heart had seemed to expand to take in the whole world. As far as he could see in every direction there was an Indian world, the same as it had always been, only the creak of their saddles reminding him of what was behind them. He had on that perfect morning longed to tell the boy of his plan, to share the vision that had grown so slowly over a lifetime, but he knew that he'd have to keep it to himself for a while longer.

The older village was upstream, built high on top of a rock face. As a young man he'd walked there for the sunrise one time and had not gone again, for the place was crowded, the breaths and cries of his ancestors heavy in the closed air. There had always been enemies. "Be good or those Navajos will get you," a mother might have warned a wayward child long before the whites came. And always there had been the Apaches who swept down the canyons like eagles with outstretched talons. But the Europeans were a new kind of enemy. In the beginning they enslaved and killed the people until those first ones were driven back to the southland, their churches burned. But the Spanish had returned more powerful than before, and with the other Europeans they had remained.

Upon their return, the Spanish had destroyed the town upstream, killing many, and the people had moved away to this place farther downriver at a wide spot in the canyon, taking the names of their conquerors, their earthen homes seemingly gathered around the mission church but in fact turned to embrace the rising sun. That had always been the people's way: not confrontation but avoidance. And finally, after five hundred years and near the beginning of a new millennium, an ancient seed from the New World had blossomed in the invaders' flesh, sending its powdery white roots deep into tissue and bone, a beautiful plant that luxuriated in the conqueror's fears.

Paco tried to imagine the Incan priests forced to watch the Spaniards smash the sacred stone that tethered the sun each winter, knowing in his blood that the priests must have clutched even then in their tight fists the plant that would one day poison the foreigner's own seed. He liked to look at the white powder that made its way northward to him, imagining the labyrinth of time and historical irony represented there. Surely the priests had foreseen it all.

However, complications had arisen near a town called Magdalena. His nephew had disappeared along with a great deal of money. Arturo wouldn't steal, but there were others who had also disappeared, and the signs were ominous. Paco straightened and turned away as the boy and horse dropped from sight over the riverbank. Looking toward the north, he studied the hard outline of the escarpment that rose ledge by ledge toward the narrower canyon. The day was spilling richly down from the mountaintops, riding the wings of great birds. Shadows hung thickly up there. Walking with quick, determined strides, he went to a battered pickup truck at the edge of the field. He opened the door and pulled out a cellular telephone, quickly punching buttons and then lifting the phone to his ear.

"It's time to go," he said into the phone. "Prepare well, Duane."

He put the phone down and turned toward the south. Something was going on down there, and the heat in his blood reminded him of distant times and stories heard with snow on the ground. The boy with the black horse, the blue hawk and yellow leaves, and the whiteness of the bare branch seemed to weave a web for the deepening red of the sun.

# 23

As soon as Will's truck was out of sight, Odessa went into the trailer and came out carrying Billy's keys. She jumped into the big Dodge and started it up, sending gravel flying as she skidded it around and accelerated toward the gate, causing the flock of crows to scramble toward the cloudy sky, their cries lost in the truck's roar as the horde of black birds followed the bucking pickup over the cattle guard to the asphalt.

At the blacktop the birds wheeled and tumbled over one another back toward the barn while a spindle of lightning split over the Magdalenas. Odessa glanced at the lost flash in the pickup mirror and listened as the thunder seemed to almost speak. A language of consonants was what the thunder spoke, she thought, pushing the accelerator pedal deeper. A strange, foreign language that someone, sometime, must have understood. But lost tongues and lost times were things she'd given up on long before. All the real stories happened right now, were happening right now. The past was a white man's illusion, the future a white man's dream. Stories were what Indians had, and the story was born anew with every telling. What mattered was the telling, and every story could be changed, had to be. It depended upon who did the telling.

She rolled the window down and drew a deep breath of damp, electric air laced with sage and *chamiza*. They'd been telling the stories for too long. Now it would be her turn. Fuck their words and their worlds. She turned on the radio and laughed at the country-western song proclaiming that lonely women made good lovers.

When she knew she was alone, Jace walked to the gun cabinet and looked through the glass. Opening the door, she lifted the thirty-ought-six and then set it back down and closed the cabinet. She looked about the room, noticing the blasted television for the first time. Clearly, Will had swept up and removed all shards of glass but had left the shattered set there for some bizarre reason.

She went down the hallway to what for almost half of her life had been her bedroom. Maggie limped after her, and when Jace opened the door and turned on the light, the dog went directly to the bed and, with a clumsy swing of the cast, clambered up onto the down comforter, settling on her side with a contented sigh.

"Maggie!" Jace yelled. "Bad dog."

Maggie's head shot up, and she struggled wildly for purchase before managing to propel herself to the edge of the bed, where she tumbled to the floor with a painful yelp and sat looking confusedly at Jace.

"You know you're not allowed on the bed," Jace said, and then she walked close to the bed and saw the mud stains and the layer of dog hair.

"That sonofabitch," she said to herself. She turned to Maggie and ruffled the dog's head. "It's okay, girl. I should have known. He's probably had Molly sleeping here, too, hasn't he?" She glanced around at the dust and cobwebs that looked as if they'd been stirred once or twice with a rag and then allowed to reform to some kind of bizarre pattern. Some of the books appeared to be spotless while others bore a heavy layer of dust. Cobwebs hung tattered from the corners, light fixture, and bookshelves, while new webs stretched in beautiful symmetry here and there. After staring at the mess for a moment, she went out of the room and farther toward the back of the house, the dog at her heels.

The room Will had made his own was spotless. The fly-tying table was neatly arranged, the fly-tying books stacked on an apple crate next to the table. The walls were still covered with bridles, ancient reatas, bits and other assorted debris her husband cherished, and the narrow cot was covered with a red and orange Pendleton blanket stretched so taut that not a wrinkle showed. On a second crate at the head of the bed, a hardbound book lay open. She bent to read the title at the top of a page. "Killing Custer. Good God," she said aloud.

Picking up the book, she sat down on the bed, propping the pillow against the wall and leaning back to read. As Maggie settled on the little Navajo rug beside the bed, there was a snuffling at the door and the pig came waddling in, her round body shivering with obvious happiness at finding a room more stable than the kitchen. After shoving her nose into Jace's thigh and grunting, the pig lay down on the rug beside Maggie and shut her eyes.

Maggie's roar ripped Jace out of a deep sleep. For a moment she frantically tried to remember where she was, recalling the man who had been beside her and an image of Will Striker in a doorway, and then she saw the face of a woman whose eyes seemed hooded and almost as dark as the hair that framed them.

"I'm so sorry," the woman said, and Jace awakened fully to see Maggie on her toes, the hackles of her shoulders upright and a profound growl emanating from her chest. The object of the dog's fury stood in the doorway to the small room, a tall, dark woman with amazingly long black hair and a very white smile.

"I was looking for Billy and Will," the woman said. "I thought they might be talking back here and didn't hear me knocking."

Jace swung her legs to the edge of the bed and stood up, causing the book to fall to the floor and feeling the wriggling form of Molly shoved as far beneath the bed as her bulk would allow. "Who are you?" Jace said, feeling still fuzzy with midday sleep.

The woman smiled again. "I'm Odessa Whitehawk. I'm a friend of Billy's."

Jace felt the muscles of her back grow more tense as the woman spoke.

"I'm really awfully sorry I surprised you like that," Odessa said. "I didn't expect anybody to be here except Will or Billy."

"Do you always walk into my husband's house like this?"

"Oh." Odessa took a half step forward. "You're Jace. Billy's told me a lot about you." She shrugged apologetically. "Actually, I've never been here before. I'm so embarrassed at barging in like this. I was sure Billy and Will were here. I'll go."

As Odessa moved toward the door, Jace spoke quickly, surprising herself. "No. Please wait. I think there's still some coffee in the kitchen, if you don't mind it reheated."

Odessa turned back with what looked like a grateful smile, and Jace felt a sudden warmth flush through her still-sleepy body. "That would be wonderful."

Jace reached down to pat Maggie, and her fingers vibrated with the silent growl still reverberating through the dog's massive shoulders. "Come on into the kitchen," she said to Odessa.

As Odessa stepped aside and then followed Jace, with Maggie scraping along behind the two of them, Jace said over her shoulder, "You just came from Billy's place, I guess?"

After an almost imperceptible pause, Odessa said, "Yes. Billy and Will took off in Will's truck without telling me anything and I thought they must have come over here." She laughed in a slight, self-deprecating tone. "I guess I was a little mad. I don't like being left out. Billy's kind of an old-fashioned sexist, I'm afraid."

"But a very attractive one, no?" Jace glanced back. "I don't like being left out either." She went to the stove and, with precisely the same motion her husband had used earlier that morning, raised the lid of the enamel pot to peer at the contents. Shaking her head, she lit the burner and motioned toward a chair.

"This coffee will probably scar us both for life, but I'm afraid the options are limited. Have a seat."

"I like strong coffee," Odessa said when they were both seated. "I think it's a genetic characteristic of Indians."

Jace peered around the kitchen, feeling that it was somehow different from the way it had been earlier that morning. She scanned the cabinets and drawers, seeing nothing that seemed out of place, but still unable to shake the feeling.

"You're Indian," Jace said.

Odessa nodded. "Mescalero."

"From across the valley."

"From San Francisco, actually. Though my parents are originally from the reservation."

Jace looked quickly at the other woman and then stood up, feeling that she wanted to keep staring at the dark, slanting eyes, angled cheekbones, and deep, rich-looking lips. If I were a man, she thought, I'd want to kiss Odessa Whitehawk. No, if I were a man I'd want a lot more than that.

"Have you known Billy long?"

"I'm afraid not. Just a week or so."

"You're living together?"

When Odessa looked at her in silence, Jace added quickly, "I'm sorry. I guess my law practice has screwed up my social skills. I'm too used to asking questions."

"Apology accepted."

"So what's going on, Odessa?"

"That coffee's boiling," Odessa replied, and as Jace turned to the stove, she added, "You think something's going on? With Billy?"

Jace found two stained cups in the cabinet and poured the very black coffee. "Something with Will at least. Sugar? I'm afraid Will doesn't have milk." She held a cup toward Odessa.

Odessa took the cup with both hands and held it close to her mouth. "I like black coffee."

Jace sat down. "Did Billy take a gun with him when they left?"

"Yes."

"So did Will. I don't mean to pry, but you *are* staying at Billy's trailer, right?"

"You really are a lawyer, aren't you?"

"Have you noticed anything strange about Billy? Or Will?"

Odessa shook her head. "I'm afraid I've barely seen your husband. Billy and I have been getting to know one another."

Jace raised her eyebrows. "I've known Billy Keene for twenty years," she said. "He and Will are like brothers. Maybe closer than brothers."

"I can tell that from the way Billy talks about Will. Not too many people have anybody they're that close to. What about you, do you have any friends like that?"

Jace thought for a moment, and her life, which twenty-four hours before she would have described as full, even exciting, felt abruptly barren. She shook her head. "I have my children."

"They're grown?"

Jace studied the younger woman's face. "They're both a little younger than you, I'd guess."

"Do you and Will see them often?"

"You know how it is. They have their own lives."

"I didn't mean to pry."

"Will and I have been sort of separated for a while, to answer your next question," Jace said. "Since I moved to Albuquerque to finish law school. It was supposed to just be for a little while at first, but . . . I don't know. We used to see each other every week or two, and then every month, and then it just became easier not to."

"He's a powerful man. In an Indian kind of way, I mean."

"I know what you mean." Jace reached a hand up to rub the back of her neck and shoulder. "I guess I fell asleep in the wrong position in there."

Odessa pushed the chair back and walked around the table. "Let me see what I can do."

"Oh, I . . ."

Before Jace could say more, Odessa was standing behind her chair with her hands already kneading the muscles of Jace's shoulders.

Jace closed her eyes. "That feels great," she said.

"I took a couple of courses in massage therapy while I was writing my dissertation," Odessa replied. "I thought I could teach my boyfriend and then he could help take the stress out of my life."

"Did it work?" Jace asked, her eyes still closed.

"Get serious. That asshole never did anything for anyone but himself. He even had to be on the bottom in bed." Her hands moved up the back of Jace's neck and then down, kneading across the tops of the shoulders to the upper arms.

Jace laughed out loud. "God, that feels fantastic. What was your dissertation on?"

"Tribal law and sovereignty. Back then I thought I wanted to be a famous professor at Stanford or Harvard."

"Now you don't? And you have a Ph.D.?"

"I finished the doctorate, but I got sick of anal retentive academics. Like the boyfriend. I forgot to mention that he was a law professor."

"You could get rich doing massage therapy, I think," Jace murmured.

"You're very tense. This would work a lot better if you were lying down. How about lying down on that cot where you were sleeping?"

After a moment's silence, Jace said, "Okay. You're really good at this."

Odessa followed her back to the room, and as soon as they were inside said, "It would work best if you took off your shirt and bra."

When Jace didn't reply immediately, Odessa added, "Don't worry, I'm a confirmed heterosexual, some might even say a flaming heterosexual."

Jace laughed and began unbuttoning her chambray shirt.

"Women, I've always thought, lack a certain something I find essential as far as sex is concerned," Odessa said as Jace unhooked her bra and laid shirt and bra together on the apple crate beside the bed.

When Jace was lying on her stomach, Odessa sat on the side of the bed and began massaging the shoulder muscles once more and then moved her hands slowly down the back.

"God, this feels absolutely wonderful," Jace murmured.

"Spread your legs a little," Odessa said, pushing Jace's legs apart so that she could kneel on the bed with one knee between Jace's thighs. "I can't really get the proper angle sitting like that." Her hands moved back up Jace's spine and across to the triceps of each arm and then down the sides, the fingers probing around into the soft perimeter of the breasts.

Jace felt her nipples harden against the Pendleton blanket, and she shifted her legs slightly. Odessa's hands moved down across the ribs to the base of the spine and lower still, the heels of both hands pressing deeply into the blue jean–covered buttocks and each thigh.

Jace shifted slightly. An extraordinary warmth was spreading from her belly in all directions like a delicious electricity. When Odessa's hands closed gently on her left shoulder and lifted, Jace let her body follow the hands' urging and roll from stomach to back, keeping her eyes tightly closed all the while.

Odessa's hands began to massage the deltoid muscles, the fingers spreading fire up Jace's neck and down each arm, and then Jace felt a blend of irresistible pleasure and pure panic when the hands descended, the heels pressing into the pectoral muscles and the fingers shifting to the circumference of her breasts.

"You are very beautiful," Odessa said in a near whisper as her hands descended across Jace's ribs to touch and probe the depression between thigh and groin and then move lightly upward again. "You remind me of someone I knew a long time ago."

Jace felt her nipples taken softly between thumb and forefinger, and she tried to summon the essential force to say "stop." But her body seemed to have slipped into a dream state that kept her tongue still and silent. And then she felt lips touch her own, strange, ghostlike lips that belonged to no one, and soft hair falling around her face and keeping her from the light. With blank astonishment, she felt herself responding, seeking the lips touching hers, her tongue reaching out to taste that which was tasting her. And then the lips were on her breasts, the tongue gently caressing her nipples and moving down across her belly like a torch. She felt a flood building within her, a dam filled to bursting.

"I think I'd better go," a far-off voice whispered.

When Jace opened her eyes, Odessa was kneeling above her, her closed lips smiling softly.

Jace tried to open her own mouth to speak, but her tongue seemed welded in place, her lips incapable of motion. In silence she watched Odessa rise from the bed and, still smiling, disappear through the doorway.

For a long time Jace lay on her back, seeing the cracked plaster of the adobe ceiling and listening to Maggie's sleeping breath. Idly, she wondered what had become of Molly.

Finally the other impulse that had been working its way into consciousness came to her. She imagined her husband and Odessa Whitehawk, his heavy-muscled body and Odessa's long legs and broad shoulders together. It was impossible. The Will Striker she had found in the kitchen that morning carried an air of solitude with him that seemed impenetrable. Had he made love with Odessa Whitehawk, he would have carried the impression of her like a bruise.

Jace lay a forearm across her eyes to block out the light, and she felt the heat burning steadily inside her. Her mind sought to move toward rationality, an interrogation of recent events, of Odessa Whitehawk, but those doors swung abruptly shut, shunting her thoughts in darker directions. Again she felt the sense of imminent change. From outside came the sound of muted thunder, the kind that accompanied rainless heat lightning. She took a deep breath and uncovered her eyes, simultaneously swinging her legs to the floor and rising to her feet.

Back in the kitchen, she took a sip of the foul coffee to wake herself up and then looked around the room carefully. Finally she realized what had been bothering her. The door of the broom closet was ajar, and she felt certain it had been closed that morning. She went into the living room. Everything looked normal. She walked back to the hallway, opening the hall closet where they had always kept heavy winter things. The closet was a mess, with a couple of sullen-looking wool coats bunched on top of boots and abandoned gloves. A broom with a jagged broken handle leaned against the wall. She closed the closet door and went into the bedroom.

Everything in the room looked just as it had earlier. She grabbed the comforter and dragged it from the bed, throwing it in a pile on the floor. She shook her head and used both hands to wipe dust and dog hair from her face and then ripped the blankets and moldy sheets off and dropped them on top of the comforter. Bunching her arms around the pile, she half carried and half dragged it out of the room.

A few minutes later she returned with the broken broom and several kitchen towels. Wrapping the largest of the towels around the straw of the broom, she tore a strip off a second one and tied the towel in place. Straining to reach with the broom, she began brushing cobwebs harshly from the ceiling corners, swiping violently along the ceiling and the tops of the bookshelves. When the ceiling was free of webs, she unlatched the window, shoving both sides outward so that weak light and damp, late-summer air flooded into the room. She turned back to the bed, hooking both arms beneath the mattress and bending her legs to lift and shove the big, queen-size mattress until it slid off the far side of the bed. Climbing onto the box spring, she pushed until the mattress toppled over, and then she walked across the bed and stepped down before beginning to lever the mattress back onto the bed, the top side now on the bottom. As she worked, she kept seeing Odessa Whitehawk as she had first seen her when she awakened. There was an unnatural clarity to Odessa's outline, a sharp boundary that set her apart from her surroundings in a way Jace had never seen or felt before. The feel of Odessa's hands lingered in the muscles of her shoulders, back, and thighs.

She left the room and returned with a vacuum, beginning at once to suck webs, dust, and moth wings from the long shelves of books. When the books looked clean, she pushed the vacuum out the door and tore the cloth off the broom, wiping her forehead with the sleeve of her shirt before starting to sweep at one corner and driving dust, dirt, and animal hair before her out the door of the bedroom. In minutes she was back with a bucket and rag mop.

When the bedroom smelled of Pine Sol and seemed steeped in

the grayish light from the open window, she left mop and bucket outside the door and walked to the bathroom at the end of the hall. Standing before the mirror she had made Will hang on the back of the door years before, she began to undress, dropping her clothes to the floor and shoving them into a tight pile with one foot. The body in front of her seemed to stand back in the depths of the mirror, infinitely removed from her and unfamiliar.

She shifted to one side and looked out the small bathroom window at the rising juniper slope outside. A shiver passed through her chest as a beautiful, gray-winged hawk darted across the slope, its pointed wings tilting as it dove and pulled up to bank away toward the light. She felt her breath catch, and she began to cry without sound.

When she turned the handle of the shower, a weak spray of rusty water sputtered and then merged to form a small, dark waterfall. She looked at the splattering of liquid for a long time before stepping into the shower stall and turning her body slowly under the trickle so that it dampened first one side and then the other, and she heard herself begin to sob.

24

The shadow of a man crossed the sun's arch. Fire burned at the shadow's edges, and a red-gold light flamed through the chest. The sun, just beginning to touch the far ridge, cast a warm light over the second figure of a man squatting close to the earth.

Siquani stood up, the clay pipe held with both hands in front of him. He walked to one of the cedars growing nearby and pinched part of a frond, crumbling the green cedar into the

tobacco-filled bowl of the pipe; then he fumbled in his shirt pocket
and brought out a single wooden match, which he struck on the
seat of his pants. Holding the match to the bowl of the pipe, he
puffed and turned in a slow circle, blowing a small whiff of pungent
smoke in four directions. When he had completed his circle, he
turned back toward the ghost of Arturo Cruz, which at that moment stepped down from the sun.

"This here's what we call remade tobacco," Siquani said. "And
that's strong cedar, so maybe this'll work." He frowned at Arturo.
"But I don't know. It's generally considered a pretty bad idea to
have dead folks around when a person is working like this."

"You mean making medicine to protect everything. You want
me to go back down to the four-wheel drive so this doesn't seem
kind of futile?"

Siquani shook his head, causing the gray braids to sway on his
thin chest, and squinted past Arturo toward the west. The sun now
seemed to be poised on the crest of the far western ridge, a pre-
cariously balanced ball of red. "Now that I made medicine for this
grandfather tree and for what we got to do, I think you better stay.
A person's got to try new things. The important thing isn't this
tobacco, but what is in the heart."

"You're a strong man to drive that machine so far. I don't
think you hurt it too much. You could be one of those race-car
drivers like the Unsers up in Albuquerque."

Siquani turned a mistrustful eye upon a chain saw that lay on
the ground where he had been squatting. "I should have learned
to drive one of those things a long time ago; it ain't so hard. I
hope that old saw will start."

He bent and lifted the saw, turning with it and walked toward
the twisted cedar a few yards farther up the hill. He put it down
and went back for a burlap sack, which he dropped near the saw.
The eastern sky seemed to suddenly catch a spark from the sun,
and a golden fire spread from one end of the sky to the other,
deepening in the borders of piled clouds. Atop the tree, the body
looked dark and angular, a scrawny bird.

"I hope this old saw will start." Siquani placed one small tennis-shoe-covered foot inside the handle of the saw to hold it down and grasped the pull-rope with both hands. He pulled and jerked upright, and the saw sputtered and choked. Bending again, he clasped both hands over the rope and jerked a second time. This time the saw sputtered and caught, bursting into ear-splitting life.

"I wish," Arturo began loudly, but the old man waved him silent and picked up the saw.

Propping the saw against his thin, blue-jeaned leg, Siquani leaned the blade into the tree. Instantly, the chain bit into the wood and the saw jumped out of his hands, landing on its side and rolling a few feet down the hill.

"I think you got to go a little slow," Arturo said. "I think maybe you got to hold the saw tighter."

Saying nothing, the old man picked up the still-running saw and walked back to the tree. Again he rested the saw on his thigh and leaned the bar into the tree. This time as the teeth cut into the wood he held firm, easing the saw backward halfway around the trunk. When the cut was made, he turned off the saw and sat it on the ground, collapsing beside it and staring up in disgust at the ghost of Arturo Cruz.

Arturo came and sat beside him. "You know, I used to be a real good woodcutter," he said. "We'd cut wood in the *bosque* when I was a kid and make great big piles by the houses. I was real good at it. Sometimes we'd go out in the snow and cut wood, too, and then when you burn that wood it smells sweet." Arturo looked at his hands clasped between his knees. "I think I'll miss that. The way everything gets so quiet in the winter snow, and you smell the piñon and cedar burning in all the houses, and all those little birds with the dark heads are out there in the snow. My grandmother used to gather that new snow in a big pot and mix syrup and a little bit of cream with it. Us kids would eat it like ice cream."

Siquani nodded, his head now tilted to look up at the sky. "Yes," he said. "Sometimes when Billy is gone and I don't see no one for a long time, I feel like Kanati, the hunter, back in time immemorial when he was all alone on the earth, before First

Woman come. I think maybe it's time for me to go back home, too." He took one of his braids in his hand and examined it. "I was like many others when those white men first come. I thought it would be okay, that we could live together with them like we did with others. Even when we started fighting a little, I thought that would be okay because we always had fights sometimes with other peoples. That was the way. When Indian people started killing all the deer to trade those skins to the white men, Awi Usdi, the Little Deer, come and asked me to help. My people will go away, he said, unless something is done. But nobody would listen, and the deer had to go hide in the deep places where even Indians couldn't find them. Then I saw the white people take all our land and put little children and old people in pens to die. And then they made us walk toward the Darkening Land. All the way there, we saw the black ravens and buzzards watching us, and we heard the Thunder Boys warning us. And one night when it was very cold and I could hear the babies crying everywhere, Awi Usdi come and told me I was supposed to watch and remember everything. That was my job, they said. Someday, they said, Indians and the deer, too, would be strong again. You got to remember everything, they said."

The old man rose and bent over the chain saw. Again steadying the handle with his foot through the guard, he started the saw with a single pull.

When he had cut a wide notch out of one side of the tree, he walked slowly around to the uphill side, again leaning the saw into the trunk.

In a few minutes, the cedar began to quiver all over and then to crack. Very slowly it began to lean, bending like an old man, its branches reaching like hands toward the earth. Slowly the tree twisted, carried sideways by the weight of its branches, causing Siquani to jump backward as the branches curved down through the ghost of Arturo Cruz.

"Hey, old man," Arturo shouted as he stepped free of the shattered tree. "Look what you did."

Siquani turned off the saw and dropped it to the ground. Walking around the crushed branches of the big tree, he looked carefully at Arturo.

"It went right through you. You ain't hurt none."

"Not me," Arturo said, pointing. "That."

The body's head was cradled all alone between two branches, its empty sockets staring at them. A few feet from the tree, the torso lay among lichen-covered rocks, and other parts of Arturo Cruz were scattered amidst the silver debris of the dead cedar.

"I guess it was them birds, plus all that weather," Siquani said.

"You Cherokees must not have reverence for your dead."

"Of course we do. You ain't hurt none." The old man went to the burlap bag and brought out a white sheet, which he spread on the ground. He stood looking at the empty bag for a moment. "Funny thing about this bag, you know. We used to call them kind toad sacks, but then somebody said it was supposed to be tote sack. Then somebody else said we ought to call them gunnysacks. Then they said they was burlap sacks."

He looked away from the bag and sheet toward the body parts tangled in the splintered tree and spread across the low-growing grama and bunched sage. "Cherokees don't like ghosts no more than other folks do. This here's a dangerous thing, Arturo. That other time, when so many died on the trail, the other old ones were more powerful than me."

"The tobacco will protect you, maybe," Arturo responded. "Besides, I suppose the fact that I'm the ghost in this particular case must make it somewhat different."

Siquani looked at Arturo for a long moment and pursed his lips. "It sort of beats all get-out, don't it," he said, and then he began to gather the pieces of body, placing them on the sheet. Suddenly a raven that had been watching from a nearby juniper swooped down and grabbed something, flapping powerfully away toward the foothills.

"My hand," Arturo shouted. "He took my hand."

Siquani watched the bird disappear into the higher forest. "It was probably that ring he wanted," he said. "Maybe we'd better take you back to your people so they can do this right."

Arturo studied the direction the bird had taken, shaking his head sadly. "No, Grandfather. I don't think we can do that."

"But that is the proper thing. We can drive that machine there."

Arturo shook his head, turning to survey the body parts on the sheet. "What's left of me don't smell too good," he said. "We can't take me back because my family will ask questions about me. They will call the tribal police and those police will call the FBI. The FBI will find out everything."

"Maybe that's the way this has to be," Siquani replied. "Maybe it's the only way."

Arturo shook his head. "The police will arrest your grandson and his friend. No, I think we got to bury me on your grandson's ranch like we planned, perhaps over where you got that lightning wood for your fire." He pointed a few feet from where they stood. "There's some of me over there. That way Billy and Will can keep that money."

Siquani picked up the fragment and dropped it on the sheet. "I think perhaps they should not keep that money."

"Maybe they can use the money to help this land," Arturo said. "Maybe if they put it into the earth here somehow it will break the evil power of that money."

Siquani looked at the western horizon, where the sun had disappeared. "But my grandson's pathway lies toward the Nightland. Some things can't be changed." He folded the corners of the sheet and tied them together with great effort. "We can come back for that saw, but now we got to get you down to that machine. We will bury you up by the spring. Running water has great power."

"For my people the dead have an important job," Arturo said as they walked together down the hill, Siquani bent over by the weight of the sheet. "The dead bring the rain to the people."

# 25

"Look at those fucking things. Like a bunch of goddamned eyes watching everything. That's what this fucking country's done to all of us, especially you Indians. I bet they got those things aimed straight at Indian country. See if you redskins are about to go on the fucking warpath again."

On one side of the two-lane road, the white dishes of the Very Large Array sprawled across the high, barren plain, each tripod-mounted dish mobile on its own steel tracks, the twenty-seven faces of the radio telescopes pointed northward. Behind the Array, the earth rose up to a sprinkling of low, twisted trees that thickened gradually toward a range of dark mountains. Wiry, ghostlike currents of blue-white lightning wavered over the mountains. A black steel-mesh fence cut the government project off from the road and surrounded the dishes on all sides.

"I read that they have those things hooked up to other ones all over the fucking planet. They link them through computers and look billions of light years out in space. What they don't tell you is that they can look anywhere they want right down here. They can take a photograph of a wart on your ass from a thousand miles away. And they're fucking doing it, too."

Rolling the window down, the speaker leaned out to look at himself in the pickup's cracked side mirror. He smiled, using a fingernail to pry at something between his front teeth, and then, satisfied, ran the same hand across his black, buzz-cut hair, causing the dark scalp to writhe.

"You hear about that new shit they developed up at Sandia Labs? It's a kind of gun that shoots plastic ooze that can stick you right to a wall or something. They can shoot that shit all over a crowd, and it'd be like flies in molasses. Look at those pronghorns." He watched the white rumps of half a dozen animals bound away from the opposite side of the road ahead of them. "People think they're antelope, but they're not even related. Those big god-damned oryx they got over at White Sands, those seven-hundred-pound motherfuckers from Africa, those are real antelope. Those bastards have six-foot-long horns. They can fight off African lions. Think how a scrawny fucking little coyote feels looking at one of those suckers. Those yoties must be thinking holy shit where the hell did that thing come from."

"Coyote would use his brain," Paco Ortega said. "You can bet he's out there right now smooth-talking those African antelope right into the frying pan. Probably learning a few new African dance steps and a couple of songs at the same time." He smiled with closed lips, and a web of fine lines radiated in the dark skin at the corners of his sunglasses. "Coyote never met a surprise he didn't like. Listen well, Duane, and you'll be hearing a little African accent in coyote's song at night."

Scales snorted. "Mister coyote's in for some fine international cuisine then. You hear about the herd of Persian ibex they released down in the Florida Mountains, tough little goats with beards that hang down to the goddamned ground? They're finding those fuck-ing things down in Mexico and over in Texas already. And then there's those Barbary sheep spreading all over the place, chasing out the mule deer. It's goddamned looney-toons nuts here in the land of enchantment. I read where some asshole from the state fish and game office said they figured they had some empty niches in the ecosystem they could fill so they imported all that shit. What kind of fucking minds are at work here, Paco? Empty niches in the fucking ecosystem? And all those rancher assholes are pissed off because the government wants to reintroduce Mexican wolves at White Sands. So now we've got all those redneck welfare ranching motherfuckers screaming their asses off about wolves eating their little cows that they graze for free on government land already, in wilderness areas where they're breaking the fucking law by putting in stock tanks with bulldozers. Can you really believe all that shit? Hell, I'll buy a hundred head of their piece-of-shit cows to feed the goddamned wolves. Personally. You hear about that Navajo guy who did a head-on with a fucking buffalo? Totaled his pickup and the buffalo, too. Right on this road, back toward Springerville a ways. Fucking buffalo, man. Just like Jane Fonda and that guy she's married to want to raise. You heard about that shit? I heard that guy say what environmentalists him and Jane were because sometimes they took several dumps a night without flushing. Fucking major-league environmentalists."

Paco Ortega glanced at his passenger and then back at the road, his sunglasses glinting and his long black hair shifting across the faded blue of his Levi's jacket. When he spoke, his voice was high-pitched and soft. "I've told you not to sample the product, Duane. You know it's not good for you."

"Fuck you, Ortega. I'm no fucking junkie. I just think about shit. This is important shit, man. The future of the whole motherfucking planet is what I'm talking about here." Scales's eyes narrowed to black slits and his brown face darkened against the soft landscape outside the window. Ortega looked at him and then at a gray dove that slashed across the road in front of them.

"I just don't see how you fucking Indians can stand all this crap," Scales went on, his voice like stirred gravel. "Every place you look, man, you see what white motherfuckers like me've done to you. If I was Indian, I'd start a fucking war every day."

"Duane, you would start a war every day no matter who you were. If you could get away with it." Ortega smiled. "I admire your environmentalism, but did you ever stop to think that perhaps the war you talk about is already going on and you're part of it? Maybe you're kind of like those Indian scouts who led Custer to the Little Bighorn. And another thing, Duane. I've always wondered why you call yourself white, since you're browner than I am."

Scales shifted and hunched his shoulders, absentmindedly using two fingers to scratch inside the neck of his black leather jacket. "I got a lot of Black Irish blood, and Cajun. My whole family's dark. That's why I like to work with you motherfuckers. I feel the white man's burden. Indian scout my ass. You could say I'm nothing but a bleeding fucking heart liberal who hates what the white man's done to his goddamn red brother." His face cracked into a yellow-stained smile. "The noble brown-skinned red man. Looks like those Apaches may still decide to bury a bunch of fucking plutonium on their rez. That's all we fucking need."

"The world needs more dedicated environmentalists like you, Duane," Ortega answered, his sunglasses steady on the dipping road ahead and his voice almost a whisper. "You have only the interests of mother earth at heart, don't you? Profit means nothing to a man of your integrity. But let me tell you something . . . white man." He uttered the last words faintly, so that Scales had to listen hard to make them out.

"I know about history, Duane. For example, I know that right over there in Acoma," he nodded toward the northwest, "the Spanish cut off the right foot of every adult male and made slaves out of the women and children. And that's not a drop in the bucket. Back east there was a British general named Amherst who came up with a plan to pass out smallpox-infested blankets to Indians. Those blankets killed thousands and thousands of people, especially the children and babies and old ones, and in gratitude the white people named a town and university after him. I can still hear all of those children crying, Duane, all of those Indian babies. They killed ninety percent of the Indian people who once lived on this continent. They called that genocide when the Nazis did it, but the Nazis weren't nearly as good at it as the Americans. Today they use alcohol and toxic waste instead of blankets."

"Knock off the boring lecture shit," Duane responded. "I've been to college already. It's simple. Everybody's killed everybody for as long as anybody's been around. You think what those Mongol motherfuckers did when they wiped whole towns from the face of the fucking earth was any better? Cut everybody's throats?

Those guys were probably your fucking ancestors. Maybe those Aztecs down south playing ball with their neighbors' heads were more civilized? And those old Jews in the Bible putting whole fucking populations to the sword because God told them to? Fuck that crap. The big eat the little and the biggest eat the most. I read that in a book."

Ortega shrugged. "I see our perspectives are different. But the truth is that from my point of view, Duane, you and I are evening the score a little bit. In fact," he smiled thinly, "I like to think of you as my faithful companion, my very own evil Lone Ranger."

"Lone Ranger my ass." Scales grimaced. "Jesus Christ, you're even more fucking depressing than me. Let's just find that money, Kemo Sabe, waste those fuckers who have it, and get out of here."

"Again, Duane, you're showing typical white man impatience. That's because like all white people, even brown-skinned ones, you exist within what you conceive of as entropic linear time. You need to think about time differently, Duane, about the way everything exists in the great continuum, everything related to everything else in the unending cycle of time. You have to stop believing in the terrible European lies of fragmentation and progress, and— this is important, Duane—you must avoid drugs. Drugs will kill you. Maybe I should tell you a story."

"Fuck you. You start another one of those goddamned coyote stories and I'm getting out of this truck right now."

"That's how we teach the young people."

They watched an eighteen-wheeler loaded with cattle go past toward the west.

"Just think of me as your elder, Duane."

"Just think of me as the guy who'll shove that stick shift up your ass if you start telling stories again, Ortega. Let's just get the fucking money and get out of here. This country gives me the willies."

"That's why you're so valuable to me. Your impatience and belief in a kind of teleology make you result-oriented. A man of action." Ortega pulled a red bandanna out of his back pocket and wiped his forehead before readjusting his glasses with one hand. On both sides of the road the high plains had given way to low juniper and piñon hills fractured by deep arroyos. To the south an escarpment rose like a blue-black wall, and behind that wall higher mountains climbed toward the washed-out sky. Periodically, lightning continued to flick silently through the whiffs of cloud over the mountains.

"Just because I don't believe in fucking Indian time," Scales answered. "Two o'clock means five o'clock, today means maybe tomorrow, maybe the next goddamned week. Always mañana, worse than the fucking Mexicans. You people can't even function in the modern world. You may have the right attitude toward the environment, but you're goddamned primitive."

"This is the funny part," Paco Ortega added without looking at his passenger. "The men who have the money are Indian, too." He turned for an instant to see what effect the information might have.

"No shit? What kind?"

"Cherokee."

"No shit? Real Cherokees? The same ones Ben and Rudy were sent after? You have any idea what happened to Ben and Rudy?"

Ortega shook his head.

"This is getting too fucking weird. I mean, first Arturo disappears and then those guys. You think these Cherokees got 'em?"

A car passed in the opposite direction, and Ortega seemed to study it before he said, "I think we should be careful."

"Careful of some fake Indians who think they got rich all of a sudden?"

Ortega shook his head. "Rudy said these two are real half-breed Cherokees. Actual Indian Cherokees. One of them has a full-blood grandfather living with him."

"There ain't no such thing. What do you think happened to Arturo?"

Ortega's face was expressionless. "That's something I want to find out."

"Let me see if I got this straight. Arturo made the drop thirty miles short of where it was supposed to be, and then the plane just fucking disappeared?"

Paco was silent for a long moment. With his right hand he adjusted the sunglasses and then the hat, pulling the brim lower over his forehead. "No one knows what happened to Arturo. Somebody found the plane on a strip outside of Springerville. The pilot, I don't think you knew him, was still in the plane."

"Crash?"

"Someone shot him." Ortega took a deep breath and let it out slowly.

"But they can't trace that to us."

Ortega shook his head. "No danger of that. Ben and Rudy tracked the signal device down here, but it stopped sending before they could get to it. And here's the most unusual thing."

He removed the sunglasses, pushed the hat up again, and used the bandanna to wipe the pale circles around his eyes before putting the glasses back on and resetting the hat. "They saw a big explosion in the sky, and the newspaper said the police found a helicopter that had crashed in the area."

Scales chewed on his lower lip for a moment and watched the road. Finally he said, "You think Arturo arranged to drop the cash early so whoever was in the chopper could pick it up?"

"Arturo wouldn't do that."

"You say that because he's your sister's kid or because you really believe it? Well let me see if I can get this straight. Somebody dropped the cash too soon, and somehow these Cherokee fuckers found it, right? But they sure as hell didn't fly the plane to Arizona and shoot the pilot or make Arturo disappear. There's something you ain't saying, *pendejo*. I've known you long enough to tell. You don't think Arturo was working with these Cherokee cowboys? I think you're right about that. Arturo wouldn't double-cross us. So . . ."

"I've already told you more than you need to know, Duane. That's my money, and you work for me. That should be clear enough. You know that Rudy was very thorough. He and Ben saw an old Land Cruiser coming from near where the helicopter exploded, and they found a fender that fell off the Land Cruiser. The fender had bullet holes in it. They went into Magdalena, asked some questions, and found out one of the Cherokees owned the only Land Cruiser in the county. People said the two have ranches next to each other and are always together, like brothers, so I told Rudy to find the Cherokees. He also said the Cherokees were buddies with some biker down here who does penny-ante drugs. And that's the last I heard from them."

"Something doesn't feel right about this. I smell some kind of kinky shit here, Ortega. You sent two of my friends down here who haven't come back." Scales turned in the seat to stare hard at the driver. "You fuck up in this thing because of some fucking game you're playing that I don't know about, and I'll make sure it's your ass as well as mine."

Ortega shook his head. "You and I both know that you don't have friends, Duane, but I believe your threat and that's one of the reasons I like you. You are not servile, yet you serve. However, your senses may be accurate in this case. I'll tell you what I think you need to know, just like I always have, and that's all. But there are things happening down here that don't make sense, things I can't explain, feelings that aren't familiar."

Ortega turned to look fully at Scales. "We may be dealing with mystical forces that we don't even comprehend, Duane." The corners of his mouth creased in the faintest suggestion of a smile.

"Forces my fucking ass. That redskin hooey shit may work on people like Rudy and Ben, but you can drop the bullshit with me."

"Well, Duane, as far as I know there's only one wild card in this game, and I've marked it well. Nonetheless, we'd better be very careful. There's only you and me, Duane. No one else even knows this money exists, except whoever has it now."

"You sure as fuck better have marked it well, whatever the hell kind of Indian bullshit you're talking about. I'm not ready to get my nuts shot off because of Paco Ortega's goddamn mind games."

The road dropped from beneath the truck as they plunged off a ridge toward a small town in the distance.

"Pie Town," Scales said, pointing. "They used to sell pies there."

"Would you like to stop for some pie in Pie Town, Duane?"

"They stopped making pies here fifty years ago. Fucking cowboys ate all their pies. They used to drive a shitload of cows through this pass from Arizona. Cow pies. All those goddamned Mormon ranching motherfuckers. Nobody there but a bunch of fucking corpses today."

Ortega shook his head. "Do you think about death, Duane?"

"Hell no. I've got enough to think about."

"You should, since death is your business."

Scales reached inside his coat and pulled out a nine-millimeter Glock, the barrel pointed at Ortega's chest. He jacked a cartridge into the chamber and, reversing the pistol, shoved the gun handle-first toward his companion.

"You want to know what I think of death? Go ahead. Blow my fucking head off right now. All it'll take is a little pressure on that trigger and my brains'll be all over this piece-of-shit truck. Go ahead, do it."

He motioned with the gun. "Come on, boss. I don't give a rat's ass."

Ortega shook his head slowly. "Duane," he said softly. "Life itself is valuable. It has to be because it's really our only commodity of exchange, isn't it? Think about it, Duane. If a life, even yours, were so valueless, what would this little war of mine mean, what would the last five hundred or five million years mean?"

"You're so full of shit, Ortega. I need a beer."

Ortega shook his head. "I read that a single ounce of alcohol kills thirty thousand neurons in your brain. It's poison."

"But it only kills the weak ones." Scales grinned. "You think those guys knocked off Rudy and Ben, don't you? That's what's with this death crap. Well, the way I see it is nobody knows diddly-squat about death, so what's to think about? You ice some mother-fucker or he ices you, and whatever either one of you were doing you don't do anymore. It's very simple. Everybody just goes on like before, except one of you ain't there anymore. And nobody gives a shit because there's about a quadzillion more just like you out there to worry about. It's like all those poor assholes the fucking government was shooting full of plutonium without telling them. You think those government scientists thought human life was precious? Hell, if everybody on the whole fucking planet just turned around and whacked the guy next to him tomorrow, there'd still be way the hell too many assholes alive, and the environment would be way the fuck better off. Human beings are a fucking infestation. That's why all those new weird diseases are coming out of the jungle and rain forest. That ebola virus and all that shit. We're a fucking plague that mother earth's finally doing something about."

"My people know quite a lot about death," Ortega replied. "We have stories that tell us."

"Don't get off on any of your fucking stories. All *your people* got is a bunch of fairy tales you made up to make yourselves feel good, just like everybody else. The fact is that none of us live very long. I mean think about one of these goddamned trees, or just about any fucking thing out there." He motioned out the pickup window. "Some of those trees are a few hundred years old, right? And the goddamned rocks they're growing out of are a billion maybe. A human being lives more than a hundred years and everybody starts jumping up and down and saying it's some kind of goddamn miracle like that broad in France that's just turned a hundred and twenty so everybody's jumping up and down and giving her medals. Fuck it. It ain't nothing. Let's say we find these guys, get our cash back, and terminate their asses. Or maybe, and this ain't no way going to happen, but maybe they terminate our asses instead. Big deal either way, right? I mean neither one of us is going to live more than twenty or thirty more years anyway if we're real lucky, and that ain't nothing, not even a fucking grain of dirt under one of those rocks out there. It just don't matter is what I'm saying. And whatever the hell else happens after that I just ain't going to fucking worry about.

"You want to think about death, go to the fucking Atomic Energy Museum in Albuquerque. They've got those two bombs they dropped on Japan in there, and by each one is a little sign that tells how many people they killed. All of it in the simple past tense. The fucking bomb was dropped and x-number of fucking people got cooked. A done deal. And then all around those two little black motherfuckers they have a whole fucking arsenal of colorful missile shit with names like Thor and signs that say what *could* happen or *would* happen or *might* happen if they ever used that shit. That's what they've turned this world into." He fell silent and picked at his front teeth with his thumbnail.

"You are both an environmentalist and a skeptic, Duane," Ortega replied. "But you should have children and grandchildren so you could understand time."

"I hate children. But I'll tell you what I understand. I understand that you ought to junk this piece of shit you're driving. This goddamned seat feels like it's stuffed with tin cans. I don't see why you didn't drive the Range Rover."

"Listen to that motor. It sings like a bird, doesn't it? Use your head, Duane. What are people in rural New Mexico going to notice first, a seventy-nine Ford pickup that looks just like every other pickup in the county or a shiny new seventy-thousand-dollar Range Rover?"

"This whole fucking thing's about to disintegrate in the middle of the road. What the hell do you do with all that cash, Ortega? I mean, you dress like a fucking wetback shoe salesman, you drive a fifteen-year-old pile of garbage and buy a million-dollar Range Rover for your flunkies, and you live in a mud fucking house in the middle of nowhere."

Ortega concentrated on the road. "Well, the sad truth is, Duane, that the Range Rover disappeared along with the ones you called your friends. But you of all people should realize anyway that success is not measured in material gain. Think about it. I live in the community where my family has lived for as long as anyone remembers. You could say forever. I know my relations, all of them. I know the stories that tell me where my people came from, where we are, and where we're going. How many people in America can say that? Isn't that a kind of wealth most of the world yearns for? People know me as a simple man who raises a few sheep, a little corn, and some chiles and who makes a few dollars in Albuquerque real estate. I belong where I am. I bought the Range Rover because it's good for picking up drops in difficult places, because it's an essential piece of equipment, but suppose I started driving a fancy car like that at home or began to wear expensive clothes like you do, or suppose I decided to move away from the pueblo and build one of those big, expensive houses in Santa Fe like yours. What would people think?"

"They'd think drugs. But what's the point then? If you can't spend the fucking money, it ain't worth anything. Why do it?"

"Remember those smallpox blankets they passed out to the Indians? It's very simple. I'm giving those blankets back, Duane. Drugs will destroy this country. I'm returning the gift."

"That's sick, man. Fucking twisted."

Ortega turned and raised the sunglasses so that his brown eyes showed flat and depthless. "Of course it is."

"So how are we going to find these assholes?"

Ortega seemed to think for a moment. "We could ask around town, but I'd prefer not to do that if we can avoid it. Rudy managed to tell me where their biker friend lives. I think he can be persuaded to guide us."

"What the hell do you do with all that cash anyway?"

Ortega looked at Duane and shook his head.

# 26

"I don't guess there's any reason to open that door."

Arturo studied the barn door for a moment. "No, I think you are right," he replied as Siquani took aim at the gaping hole in the barn and, with his bony hands evenly divided on the steering wheel, kept the Land Cruiser on a straight path.

"Maybe you should push the brake a little."

Siquani lifted his foot from the accelerator to jab it down on the brake pedal, but the sole of his tennis shoe slipped off the edge of the pedal into the space between brake and accelerator. He jerked his foot back, but it remained where it was.

"My foot is stuck," he said.

Arturo looked at the approaching barn and then down at Siquani's shoe. "Maybe you'd better turn off the key," he said.

Siquani grasped at the ignition switch just as the Land Cruiser reached the door and passed slowly through the hole with absolute precision, knocking only a few shards of wood from the jagged edges. As the old man fumbled for the key, the Land Cruiser struck the front range of the crumbling hay bales, causing him to bounce gently off the steering wheel and back into the deep bucket seat. The tires gripped and tore determinedly at the bales, creating a sudden ramp of composting straw and proceeding to climb, pulling down and apart more bales until the upper reaches of the stack tilted, swayed, and rumbled down in a moldering avalanche of breaking bales.

The Land Cruiser drove deeper into the hay until the wheels

seemed to congest and the engine began to lug, chortle, and finally fall silent.

In near darkness backed by the slanting light of the hole they had made in the barn door, Siquani and Arturo sat like astronauts in the seats of the steeply tilted Land Cruiser, staring at the black bulk of hay covering the windshield.

"You did well, Grandfather," Arturo said at last. "In your first lesson you drove a very difficult machine into the mountains and back again to the spot from which your journey began. Not many men could do that."

Siquani pulled the lever on the door and leaned with the corner of his thin shoulder. Slowly the door opened, dropping moldy straw into the Land Cruiser. The old man looked down through the space between open door and seat.

"It's okay," he said as he swung both legs out and onto the running board. Delicately, he lowered himself into a sitting position on the hay slope and then pushed his way the few feet to the level floor of the barn.

"Be careful when you open that door," Arturo said. He stood at the back of the Land Cruiser, studying the rear doors.

Siquani looked seriously at the specter of Arturo Cruz for a moment. "You remind me of a wife I had one time," he said as he stood on tiptoe to reach the door handle and pull down. "She was always warning me, too."

The door swung open, and the body of Arturo Cruz tumbled out, a small round bundle wrapped in the knotted sheet.

"How're we going to get you up to that spring?" Siquani asked.

Arturo smiled. "I was thinking of that," he said. "I believe the answer is right here." He pointed at a beat-up wheelbarrow near the wall.

Arturo stood in the silvery light with his arms folded across his chest. "I sure wish I could help you," he said.

Siquani stopped with the shovel half raised and then sat back

on the edge of the hole he was digging, with his feet nearly touching the bottom. "You done said that about helping me a hundred
times." He studied the silhouette of his friend. "I can't see you as
good as before," he said. "You ever think, Arturo, about the way
a man tries to make a story of his life?"

"Patterns," Arturo replied softly. "I think a man must make a
pattern of his life so he won't go crazy. I think the crazy ones never
see things in balance. I was crazy for a long time, and then when
I fell from the sky I saw everything clearly. I saw the earth then,
the way the eagle sees, and I could tell everything was part of
everything else, you know, everything in balance like the old people always said. It's hard to see that when you're down there in
the middle of everything."

"We got to pay attention, Arturo. Us Cherokees believe a
human being's power is in his eyes and his thinking. Red Man's
been walking over this land lately, and his boys have been talking,
Tso:suwa and So:suwa, the Thunder Boys. I have been hearing
them every day. They're warning us, I think, and they've come to
help. I think my grandson is like you were; he has not opened his
eyes yet. I feel responsible."

"The old ones say we're responsible for everything," Arturo
replied as Siquani returned to digging. "And now I understand that.
But I don't think it means we can change everything, like you said
before. We just have to watch, like you said just now. That's also
what I learned when I was falling. We have to be conscious, the
way the eagle is conscious of every shadow and breath below him
on the earth. It's good that you found a white sheet. The shape
the way you've tied it is like one of those clouds." He gestured
with a hand toward the scattering of gray clouds. "I've been wondering why I wasn't doing what I was supposed to. Even a spirit
must make a pattern, I think."

"I believe it's deep enough." Siquani climbed out of the hole.
"It ain't like we got to bury you in a long hole." He glanced at
the small, round bundle of the sheet.

Arturo stared down critically at the three-foot-deep pit. "We
can place rocks over my grave," he said.

A hundred yards away, the thin spring trickled out of its wall to the brackish water of the pool. Already, in the dawn sky directly overhead seven buzzards circled evenly. The sun began to rise in a diffuse glow of red-gold over the far eastern hills, and with the coming sun the sweet smell of morning spread across the landscape.

Gently, Siquani lowered the sheet into the grave. He removed a pouch from his pants pocket and opened it, sprinkling something from the pouch around the edges of the hole.

Glancing toward Arturo, the old man said, "Now you got the power of two peoples with you."

Arturo took a step backward, saying nothing, his erect form dark against the reddening clouds. Siquani watched as a raven landed silently on a nearby juniper and cocked its head toward them, and then the old man began to shovel earth and rocks back into the hole.

When the grave was mounded with earth, Siquani bent to pick up small rocks and place them carefully until the mound was covered. As he straightened and turned toward Arturo, the raven erupted from the juniper and flapped upward into the risen sun, becoming for an instant a single arc of red flame before disappearing into the eastern sky.

When the raven was gone, the old man looked toward the spot where Arturo Cruz had stood, but the ghost had disappeared. Turning in a full circle, Siquani found that he was alone on the sloping earth. Overhead, the buzzards broke their circle and began to drift eastward in the path of the raven, out over the flat of the ranch house until they were tiny dots and then nothing at all.

"The Red Raven is with you, Arturo," the old man said aloud in a kind of chant. "Your path is toward the Sunland. The Red Man walks with you."

He went to the edge of the stagnant pool, stepping unevenly in the dried tracks of deer, antelope, and wild cattle. At the edge of the water, he removed his shoes and then his clothes. When he was naked, he bent to take a small willow fork from inside his piled jacket and waded into the still water. In the middle of the pool, he squatted and settled to his haunches, the cold, pungent water rising to his chest. He began to sing, first in Cherokee and then English. *"Ne!"* he chanted. "Now a cloud is coming. *Ne!* Now water is coming." And then he lowered himself slowly backward until only the hand with the willow fork was visible, the sun laying a red swath across the water and illuminating the shaking branch.

A red path appeared before him, and he stepped onto the path and began to dance, a kind of stomp dance that seemed to shake the earth and bring bright red leaves falling from the treeless sky. He reached to catch a spinning leaf, and the palm of his hand filled with blood. Amidst the leaf storm a tiny deer appeared on the trail ahead, scarcely six inches high, its antlers tall and its eyes a burning red. *Follow me,* the deer said, *we must hurry.* The earth grew still, the air emptied, and Siquani broke from his dance into a shuffling run, following the little deer up a swelling rise that looked out across a gray, barren ground. In the midst of swarming shadows, the People were moving toward a darkened sun, the trail of broken-backed wagons and walking people so long he could see neither beginning nor end. Mourning cries rose from the mass of old and young, men and women, in a single, woven song, and the fog hovered like smoke from a hundred campfires. As he wove his way among them, the People began to fall, mothers curling around the shriveled forms of children, husbands lying beside wives. The ground beneath his moccasins was cold and hard, and he saw a woman's hair frozen in ice as she strove to rise from the blue earth, the captive hair pulling her face tight so that it was bone that beseeched him as he passed. He topped another rise and saw the little deer far ahead, silhouetted against a blade of red sky. Across the empty landscape came a sound from long before, and he knew it was the dance of the bones.

He rose from the water and moved with shuffling steps to the muddy edge. A wind seemed to sing through the shrunken marrow of his body, his entrails a dried knot and his heart a stone in the rattle of his thin chest. He stood for a long moment at the edge of the tepid pool, his eyes closed, listening. From the west came a husk of sound, like the rustling of cornstalks. The rustling grew to a murmur of two voices whispering, and the whisper gathered and deepened. His withered body tensed and his skin tightened. And then the sky splintered and broke with a crash of thunder.

The hand-painted, turquoise double-wide balanced on a low hill amidst scrub oaks and piñons a mile outside of the town. A pickup truck and a pair of Harleys sat on the hard-packed dirt in front of the steps, and a half dozen red and white chickens scratched amidst crushed beer cans in the shade of the trailer.

Moving silently, Scales slid around one end of the trailer and up the trailer steps, a pistol in his right hand. Ortega emerged from the other end of the trailer and placed himself beside the steps. When Ortega nodded, Scales edged the screen door open and placed a hand upon the inner door handle. With a sudden motion, he twisted the handle and shoved, plunging into the trailer with the opening door.

Mouse Meléndez and Gordo sat at the kitchen table, cards and poker chips laid out in front of them. Both of them saw the gun first and froze in place.

"That's good, motherfuckers," Scales said. "Don't even think about twitching."

Ortega came in behind Scales, his short, stocky body moving around Scales in a fluid motion. He nodded to the two at the table. "Please forgive our failure to knock, gentlemen," he said softly. "I'm sure you understand."

"Who are you?" Mouse replied.

"People who require information you can supply, Mr. Meléndez."

Gordo glared from Scales to Ortega, his huge chest swelling with each breath and his black eyes narrowed. On the table his scarred hands held five cards fanned out evenly, the muscles of his forearms corded beneath their tattoos. Cardboard from a Cheerios box covered a broken windowpane behind him, silver duct tape filling the space between paper and metal frame.

"What?" Mouse said.

Ortega removed the sunglasses, holding them in front of his chest, his eyes squinting. "I'm told that you can take me to the ranch of a man named Billy Keene."

"Never heard of the man. How about you, Gordo? You ever heard of him?"

Gordo shook his head, his long black beard sweeping the table edge. "Never heard of him."

"Not only are you both lying sacks of shit," Scales said, the gun held level at Mouse's chest, "but this fucking trailer smells like shit. Don't you ever take out your garbage? I'll bet you don't even have a goddamned septic system."

"Shut up, Duane." Ortega pulled the bandanna from his back pocket and began to wipe the lenses of his sunglasses. In the fluorescent trailer light, the white around his eyes took on a pale, yellowish sheen. "I hate to invade your lives this way, and I wish I could do this whole thing more delicately, gentlemen. But I'm afraid we're pressed for time. So I would appreciate it if you would just agree to serve as our native guides, so to speak."

"I told you we never heard of the man," Mouse replied.

Ortega looked at Scales and then nodded toward Gordo. Scales shifted the gun and fired. Gordo lurched backward, spilling from the chair into a heap halfway beneath the table before Scales fired a second time. Behind where the large man had sat, the wall was patterned in a spray of red.

Mouse stared open-mouthed at the wall. Finally he said, "I can show you where he lives."

"Good." Ortega beckoned with a finger. "We'll take your pickup, if you don't mind. And rest assured that we will certainly kill you if anything awkward happens. In that case we'll just have to find Mr. Keene's house all by ourselves, which shouldn't be impossible."

Ortega pushed the door open and left the trailer. Scales motioned with the gun and then went out behind Mouse.

In the pickup, Mouse sat between the two of them, with Ortega behind the wheel and Scales holding the gun at Mouse's side.

Ortega surveyed the sky through the driver's-side window. "It looks like it might rain soon. I hope you keep your truck in good repair," he said. "I would hate to break down between here and wherever it is we're going."

"It'll run," Mouse choked out.

At the end of the driveway, Ortega stopped the pickup and looked at Mouse. "Turn right," Mouse said. "He lives out that way."

"You sure are fucking white for a guy named Meléndez." As he spoke, Scales stared hard at Mouse's face. "You don't even talk like a Mexican."

Ortega smiled. "Duane is jealous," he said. "He feels that he himself is too brown for a white man." Keeping his vision on the road, he added, "You have to stop being so essentialist, Duane. I think Mr. Meléndez is what people call a coyote. He's a mongrel like most of us, but in Mr. Meléndez's case it's the white part that is genetically dominant. It's a question of phenotype, I believe. Mixed-breeds come in all colors. Identity, of course, is a question not of color but culture."

"I'm Spanish," Mouse muttered. "My family came up here with Oñate in the sixteenth century."

"Oh?" Ortega's soft voice rose with interest. "So your illustrious ancestors were the ones who massacred the people of Acoma. You must be proud of your family."

Ortega stared straight ahead, where a flatbed loaded with hay was moving slowly in their lane. "I ain't proud of a frigging thing," he said. "I'm just trying to make a living, and history ain't my fault."

"I like that phrase, 'make a living,' " Ortega replied. "It implies that if we don't make or earn that living, we die. There's a fundamental honesty in such a phrase, an honesty missing in so much of the English language, and I've always admired the incredibly many ways people conceive of to make their livings. However, I think you're wrong about history, Mr. Meléndez. History is precisely your fault and everyone's fault." Ortega pulled out and passed the hay truck with a loud acceleration. When they were back in their lane again, he continued. "That's what's wrong with this country. It's the American dream, isn't it, to commit every kind of filthy thing it takes to get ahead and then pretend it never happened?

"You see, I studied American history in college. The history books call Wounded Knee the last major Indian battle of the Plains. Does bayoneting women and smashing babies' heads against rocks constitute a battle? How can a man do that and then go home to his own children? The answer has to be in the way Americans conceive of themselves, and I think it's because everything in the psyche of this country tells people that they can just put the past behind them, that they aren't responsible for yesterday."

Scales whistled a single long note and poked the gun into Mouse's ribs. "You should never get him started on this kind of shit," he said. "I've seen him go on all fucking day."

"My point," Ortega continued, "is that you're exactly wrong. We *are* responsible. History only exists right now, in this instant; it's not something we can leave behind. And," he turned to look at Mouse, "I believe it's my job to rectify that situation. You might say that's how I make my living."

"What Paco means," Scales said, "is that he's out to destroy all you motherfuckers by giving you exactly what you want." He grinned and opened up the pickup's glove compartment. "I'll bet you got some kind of shit in here right now. Your kind of pissant pusher always has a stash right where the fucking highway patrol can find it."

Scales rifled the compartment, pulling out scraps of paper, a broken pair of sunglasses, a little envelope of fuses, throwing everything on the floor until his hand finally emerged with a small dark plastic box which he held up between thumb and forefinger.

"Now what could this be?" he said, grinning.

With his thumb he pushed the top of the box back to reveal a very small amount of white powder. "Must be baking soda," he said. "You mind if I taste it?"

"Don't mess with that stuff, Scales," Ortega hissed, but Scales had set the plastic box on the open door of the glove compartment and was sticking a dampened finger into the powder. With a big smile he tasted the tip of the finger, and then he abruptly lifted the little box to his nose and inhaled loudly. When he set the box down, his eyes were closed and his upper lip and nose were covered with the powder. With eyes still closed, he muttered through clenched teeth, "Don't even move, fuckhead. One of these hollow points would make a real mess." He opened his eyes, his teeth unclenching, and added, "Besides, my boss is in the direct line of fire, and that would break my fucking heart right in fucking two."

"It's just a few miles farther," Mouse said, his words barely audible.

Ortega accelerated, and the pickup roared. "Remember, Duane. We have to talk to this Cherokee. He has to tell us where it is before you kill him. Don't mess this up."

"Don't worry," Scales answered. "I'm sharp as a fucking tack. Right, Meléndez? Your truck needs a new fucking muffler and a ring job, you know that, asshole? You probably put out as much pollution with this piece of shit as a goddamned city bus."

# 28

"What do we do now?" As he spoke, Billy watched a stream of light spill from the sun and run down over the dam of the eastern mountains to the Rio Grande Valley. For the past two hours clouds had been moving in from the west, colliding with one another and thickening across the brightening sky.

Will, too, watched the light that seemed to rise from the distant valley like the waters of a new lake. "Well, I guess I might as well drop you at home and go on over to see if maybe he's at my house for some reason. He used to walk over there all the time, remember?"

"Twenty years ago."

"If there's no sign of him there, we ought to take separate directions maybe and start searching the roads. That Land Cruiser isn't going to make a lot of speed, wherever it went."

"Hell, they could've gone in ten directions from here."

Will lifted one hand from the steering wheel to adjust his hat. "You have a better idea?"

Billy said nothing as Will pulled through the ranch gate. But when the trailers came into sight, he said, "My truck's gone."

Will accelerated so that his old pickup rattled violently on the ruts of the dirt road. When they stopped in front of Billy's trailer, both men climbed out quickly. Billy went into the trailer and emerged seconds later.

"Odessa's gone," he said.

"She leave a note or anything?"

Billy shook his head and stood for a moment with his hands in his pants pockets. "It isn't like her."

"Maybe she went to town for something."

Billy nodded, looking at the ground. "Yeah. She probably needed Kotex or something. She'll be back in a little while. Why don't you go on home and see if there's any sign of Grampa there. As soon as Odessa gets back with the pickup I'll give you a call."

Will climbed back into the truck and drove too fast back to the paved road, bouncing across the cattle guard at the gate so that the pickup shocks slammed against themselves like stones.

There was no sign of anyone at his house, with even the barn and corral empty of buzzards, and for an instant he panicked until he remembered that he'd put Jace's car in the barn.

Jace sat at the kitchen table, wearing an old denim shirt and jeans and holding a cup of black coffee in both hands. On the floor, halfway beneath the table, Maggie wriggled a hello, the cast scraping as she made a feeble gesture that indicated she would get up if it weren't so difficult.

"Is everything okay?" Jace asked as he took off his jacket and hat and dropped both onto one of the kitchen chairs.

She stood up and walked around the table. When she reached him, she put her arms around him and leaned her head into his chest.

He let his own arms fall awkwardly over her shoulders, smelling the freshness of her hair and feeling a rush of heat from her body.

"Grampa Siquani's missing," he replied.

Jace kept her cheek against his chest. "Missing? For how long?"

"Since this morning, I guess."

She disengaged herself from him and took a step backward so that she could see his face.

"He probably went for a walk," she said. "He used to go up into the hills to pray all the time, as I recall. Nobody ever seemed to worry about him."

He stood with his arms at his sides, watching her. "You're probably right. He'll probably come walking back home in a little while."

She reached out to place a hand on his shoulder, saying quietly, "Would you put your arms around me, Will? Please?"

He stood motionless for a moment and then let his arms encircle her lightly. She pressed herself against him, her voice muffled in the flannel of his shirt.

"Twenty years is so long, Will."

He pulled her more tightly against him, feeling as though his arms were pulling and pushing at the same time. The house had changed in his short absence, as though her return had altered not just the temperature but the quality of light and weight of the old adobe. He felt abruptly like a patient coming out of anesthesia, blood flooding into cells long dry and dead, nerve endings blossoming from winter branches. Suddenly the barrenness of his life lay close upon him.

Jace reached a hand up to his face. His eyes closed, and he stood apart from himself, wondering. He felt her lips lightly graze his, and then he was following her toward the big bedroom.

She opened the door and led him into the room, and he found himself stunned by light. The window was open, the curtains gone and mottled, cloud-broken August sunlight pooling upon the wooden floor and the newly clean comforter. Walls and bookshelves were free of dust and webs, and the whole room seemed bright with new life.

Jace unbuttoned her shirt and dropped it on the floor, and he was surprised to see her breasts free beneath the shirt. She removed her Levi's and socks and stepped close, her body turning a deep gold against the light from the window as she reached to unbutton his shirt.

When they were both naked, she turned down the comforter and, holding on to his hand, slid between the clean white sheets. She lay on top of him, kissing his cheek and mouth and then moving down to his chest and belly, her tongue tracing the contours of his nipples and rib cage and down to the angle of his groin until she took him in her mouth for a long moment before beginning her search upward again, finishing with her mouth on his, her tongue tracing the outline of his lips as her hand reached down to guide him inside of her. Outside, a faint sound of thunder came from the west.

He looked up into her eyes as she moved very softly upon him, and the years of their lives together came back to him. He felt his hands tracing the almost forgotten outlines of her breasts and his fingers slipping over her distant, smooth shoulders and down her back. Her mouth bent to his chest and she teased his nipples with teeth and tongue, and then she leaned and rolled to one side so that abruptly he was on top and her hands were pulling him more deeply inside her, her eyes closed and mouth set in a tight smile.

He sank into her, his arms slipping beneath her shoulders and hugging her chest tightly to his own with his face buried in her neck. He felt himself straining for her center until she began to shudder with a faint and distantly familiar cry, and then he drove more deeply into her as his entire body seemed to empty itself in a flood that grew until he was echoing and hollow and they lay together in a kind of dormancy without sound or motion.

A vague rumbling of thunder stirred them at the same time, and she slid out of the embrace of his arms and sat on the edge of the bed.

"I have to get back," she said.

He watched the curve of her back, the soft points of her spine as it swept up from buttocks to smooth neck. "For God's sake, Jace," he said. "Now?"

She turned toward him, her face set and serious-looking. "It feels like a storm's coming, and I want to get back before it hits."

When he said nothing, she added, "I don't know what I'm going to do, Will. I have to go back and sort things out."

"You can't sort things out here?"

She shook her head and reached for her clothes on the floor.

"So you're just going back."

She slipped the shirt on over her bare breasts and buttoned it and stepped into the Levi's. As she tucked the shirt in, he said, "You're forgetting some things." Her black panties lay across the palm of his hand.

"It's okay," she replied as she pulled her socks on and then pushed her feet down into the boots. "I'm sorry, Will. I can't think this close to you. It's like you put out some kind of force field."

When she was dressed, she reached out a hand to touch his cheek and when he didn't respond she went quickly out of the room. Will sat on the edge of the bed with his elbows on his knees, watching her disappear. "Goddamn you, Jace," he said. "Goddammit."

## 29

From a distance, Odessa saw Mouse's pickup turn into the ranch gate from the west with three men crowded into the cab. She swung Billy's truck to the side of the road and locked the antilock brakes, sending the pickup into a short slide and spilling the bag of groceries beside her onto the floor. As she watched, the truck crawled to a stop in front of Billy's trailer. Blurry motions suggested men moving from the truck toward the trailer door. Absentmindedly, she noticed that one of the cans of beer had sprung a leak and was foaming onto the paper grocery bag.

Inside the trailer, Billy leaned on the edge of the sink in the tiny kitchen, his forehead resting in the cupped palms of both hands. His head ached from the drinking of the night before, and his stomach felt knotted and sour from a lack of food. He opened the cupboard beside the sink and took out a bottle of aspirin, popping three into his mouth and then bending to drink from the faucet. Reaching farther into the cupboard, he found a can of corned beef hash. He opened the can and forked the hash into a skillet, and when the burner was lit beneath the skillet he went back to the bed and sat once again with his face in his open hands.

Siquani's absence and Odessa's disappearance with the Dodge had blurred together into a whirlpool inside his head that sucked every thought and feeling into itself, sending out waves of black panic. "Corpse money," he said aloud. "Will was right." When someone knocked on the trailer door, he sprang to his feet and jerked the door open in one motion to see Mouse Meléndez standing with a strange expression on his face.

"Mouse?" he said as they looked at one another in disbelief.

"I'm sorry, Billy," Mouse said, and then Billy saw the other two, one on each side of Mouse just at the periphery of his vision. And the next thing he saw was the gun pointed at his midsection.

"Mr. Meléndez was kind enough to show us the way to your, uh, ranch."

Billy shifted his eyes from the gun to the man who had spoken. Much shorter than the other, the speaker had long straight black hair under a black, wide-brimmed hat, a round, dark face, and eyes hidden behind heavy sunglasses. His mouth was set in a relaxed and friendly looking smile.

"Perhaps you could invite us into your home so that we could talk in a more comfortable environment," the man added.

"Let's go, asshole." The bigger man motioned with the pistol and stepped forward to grasp the edge of the door, the gun still leveled at Billy's stomach.

Billy backed away as Mouse and the two men stepped into the little trailer.

"I think something might be burning," Paco Ortega said. "Would you see to that, Mr. Meléndez?"

Mouse went to the stove and stared at the burning hash in confusion for a moment before he turned the burner off.

"Thank you. Corned beef hash, isn't it? My mother used to cook corned beef hash with eggs. It's a wonderful combination."

"Cholesterol city," Scales said, looking distastefully at the skillet. "Don't you care about your health?"

"Who the hell are you?" Billy said.

"Do you mind if I sit down?" Ortega pulled a chair out from the table and sat, motioning toward Billy as he did so.

Billy sat on the edge of the bed, his elbows on his knees, watching the man who was talking. Mouse stood by the refrigerator, a tragic expression on his broad face. "I'm sorry, Billy," he said. "They . . ."

The gun lashed out and Mouse collapsed against the refrigerator door, sliding to his knees with both hands on his forehead. Blood ran between his fingers and down both wrists.

"You sonofabitch," Billy said, starting to his feet.

"Careful, Billy. Duane, as you can clearly see, is both primitive and brutal. That was pointless, Duane."

Scales turned toward Ortega. "What'd you tell him my fucking name for?" He looked back at Billy and then did a quick survey of the trailer. "Sportsman, huh? Look at all this fucking shit." Keeping the gun pointed at Billy, he reached to lift a fly from a fishing vest hanging on the closet door, taking the tiny artificial insect delicately between his fingers for a close look. "You even smash the barb down. That's humane, man." He looked back at Ortega. "I like this guy. Fucking barbs rip the shit out of a trout's mouth, so he smashes the barbs down. Not as good as barbless hooks, but not bad." He grinned at Billy, holding the pistol level. "He still shouldn't have told you my fucking name."

Ortega held an open palm up. "You worry too much, Duane. Billy Keene will soon be our friend." He looked at Billy. "You know why we are here, of course. All you have to do is return what belongs to us, provide us with information about a missing friend, too, perhaps, and then we'll go back where we came from with no hard feelings." He smiled. "After all, you only did what any rational person would have. Money fell into your lap and you kept it. People shot at you and you shot back. Who wouldn't do the same? But." He removed the sunglasses and wiped his forehead and eyes with the red bandanna before replacing the glasses. "But the money is integral to our own long-range planning, and we must have it. If it weren't absolutely essential, believe me, I would be happy to leave it with you."

"He doesn't give a rat's ass about money," Scales said, jerking the pistol in the direction of Ortega. "But I do."

Billy considered simply pulling the bag of money out from under the bed. But even if he did, they'd have to know where the rest was and they'd go to Will's house next.

He looked at Ortega. "You're going to kill me no matter what I say."

Ortega shook his head. "I don't think that is absolutely necessary. However . . ." He looked at Scales and then nodded toward Mouse, who had risen to his feet and stood leaning against the refrigerator, his face lined with blood.

Scales slid the pistol toward Mouse and fired twice, the bullets striking Mouse in the chest so that his body seemed to flatten and rise for a moment before it folded and collapsed. On the floor Mouse's legs scrabbled for purchase, and his powerful arms gathered beneath him to push upward when a third shot struck him in the back and he convulsed for a moment and went limp.

Billy leapt from the bed, his left hand shoving Scales's gun arm aside and his right fist smashing into the big man's sternum. The air exploded from Scales's chest, and the gun clattered to the floor, and then the back of Billy's head seemed to explode into darkness.

When he could see again, he found himself staring up at the trailer's ceiling. His head pulsed with a deep pain, and he heard a voice saying, "Why don't you help Billy onto the bed, Duane."

Billy felt himself lifted and dropped onto the bed, and then the room came into focus. The man in the sunglasses still sat at the table, and the other one stood as before, the gun pointed at Billy. Mouse's body lay in a fetal position next to the table, a stream of blood already congealing between the body and the door. Two holes in the white front of the refrigerator were ringed with blood.

"Very impressive attempt, Billy," Ortega said. "But," he lifted a long-barreled revolver from beneath the table and laid it in front of himself, "you should remember that everyone in this business is armed. And you should be grateful for that fairly light tap, especially since I've finally figured out what's going on here." He looked at Duane. "Did you feel it when we drove in here, Duane? Just before we reached this trailer? It's all around us."

"I don't fucking know what you're talking about," Scales answered.

"I'm not quite sure either, Duane, but I have a feeling we will both know very soon." He turned his attention to Billy. "It's funny," he said, "but I believe I actually felt it way up north, before Duane and I even started down here. But it's unusual, unfamiliar."

"You know what the fuck he's talking about, Billy-boy?" Duane said, motioning with the gun.

Billy touched the back of his head and was surprised to find no blood. His ears still rang, and the throbbing reverberated the length of his body. He shook his head.

"You don't feel like someone who knows medicine, Billy, no offense meant. So I wonder who it is? Could it be your friend, the one whose ranch borders yours, or maybe the old grandfather I heard about?"

He looked from Billy to Duane. "Be awake, Duane," he said. "Something's going on here that you probably don't feel and I am sure I don't understand. But there is a force here that I had not foreseen. Stay alert."

Ortega switched his attention back to Billy. "I really don't think it has to be necessary to kill you, but Mouse there is just an illustration of what's possible. Now, although I am doing this with a heavy heart, and I think I can anticipate your answers, I'm going to ask you two questions. The first concerns someone who is important to me, a young man who was accompanying the missing cash. The second, obviously, is the whereabouts of the money itself. If you prefer not to answer either question, or if for some very strange reason you really don't know the answers, Duane is going to kill you. I give you my word, however, that once we know about my nephew and we have the money we'll just go away and if things go well you will never hear from us again. It's clear you have a degree of power on your side. And in some important ways, you and I are on the same side in this war."

"Power?" Duane said, looking around the trailer. "What the fuck are you talking about, Ortega?"

Ortega continued as if he hadn't heard. "You will have to take care of Mr. Meléndez, without informing the authorities, but that shouldn't be too much of a problem for you. And believe me when I say I deeply regret such collateral damage."

Billy watched the man for a moment, letting the face come into clear focus before he spoke. "What'd you do with my grandfather?" he said flatly.

"Your grandfather, the old Cherokee grandfather I heard about?"

"Until I know where he is, you won't know where the money is."

Ortega looked genuinely confused. "Do you know anything about his grandfather, Duane? I think it would be in our interest to know this."

"Fuck no."

Ortega shrugged. "I sincerely wish we could help you. I have the greatest respect for elders, but I'm afraid we know nothing about your grandfather. You say he disappeared? Like my nephew?"

Billy recalled the black form of the man falling from the sky, the way the arms seemed to reach like wings as the body turned and descended upon him. And he saw again the body tree as they had walked away from it. Will had been right. Will had always been right.

"Go to hell," Billy replied.

"Kill him," Ortega said flatly, but before the order was complete the small kitchen window shattered and Duane was hurled against the trailer door. Ortega sprang to his feet and was lifting the pistol from the table when a second shot ripped into the small room and he seemed to jump backward, knocking over the chair and smashing against the wall.

Billy was still on the bed, staring at the bodies of both men and the blood-spattered wall, when the door opened, causing Scales's body to fall halfway out of the trailer.

With the thirty-ought-six held in front of her, Odessa stepped over the body and looked quickly about the small room, studying Ortega for a long moment before turning to Billy.

"I saw it all through the window," she said breathlessly. "They were going to kill you. Are you okay?"

Billy rose stiffly from the edge of the bed, his eyes closed and his face drawn with pain. He nodded almost imperceptibly as Odessa laid the rifle across the table and then put her arms carefully around his shoulders, her face against his chest.

"Who are they?" she said.

"Drug smugglers," he replied. "I should have told you before. There's a bag beneath the bed. See if you can pull it out."

Odessa knelt beside the bed and dragged the gunnysack into view.

"Open it," Billy said.

With an expression of disgust, Odessa lifted the bag, dumping the bundles of cash onto the floor. For a long moment she looked at the money before she stood up and stepped backward.

"Will and I found it," Billy said. "It's a long story."

Odessa lifted the rifle from the table and swung the barrel toward Billy. "I know the story," she said. "Where's the rest of it?"

Billy stared at her, his eyes moving from her face to the rifle and back to her eyes. "What?" he said.

"The rest of the money, Billy. What did you and Will do with it?"

"You know . . . ?"

"I'm sorry, Billy. I really do like you. You're basically a nice guy, and you're a great fuck. But the money's mine, and I want all of it."

"You?" he said.

"Yes, me. I was the one who pushed that fool out of the plane with the money, and I was the one who arranged for the helicopter to pick up the suitcase before these two could get to it." She shook her head. "Who could have ever imagined that two locals would just happen to be out there in the middle of nowhere when the suitcase landed? And that those locals could shoot down a helicopter."

She smiled. "I have to admit you and Will make an impressive pair. And it's all working out for the best, anyway. Paco Ortega," she nodded at the body, "was one of the biggest importers in the Southwest. He was the only one I was ever afraid of, because he didn't care about the money. Money makes people irrational. It makes them overlook important details, act too impulsively, but Paco never lost control. He was always cool."

"I was in love with you," Billy said, looking from Odessa to the body of Paco Ortega sprawled beside the upset chair.

"I wanted you to be in love with me, Billy. Love is like money; it makes people careless. And like money, it can be an excellent tool if used wisely." Her mouth formed a thin smile. "Paco was in love with me, too."

"Him?"

"That's right. Paco Ortega was my lover before you, Billy, and I believe that's why he's lying there right now. Paco never would have tried to take care of this problem himself unless he suspected that his own true love might be involved in the mess. He would have sent Duane Scales down here immediately, and Duane as you know is ruthless. You see, I did somewhat of a disappearing act at the same time that Paco's suitcase full of money fell to earth half an hour too soon. I was supposed to be visiting friends in California, but I'm afraid Paco must have suspected me and didn't want to tell Scales because he knew Scales would be violent. He probably thought you would lead him to me and that he could convince me to give it all back so everything would be fine again. Paco was an idealist, his only flaw besides me. But this is all really fortuitous, Billy, because there's no one left now who even knows this money exists. Except you and me and Will. There's no trail to it at all, thanks to the two of you. So where did Will hide the other half?"

Billy's hand shot out and grasped the barrel, jerking the rifle upward. The explosion threw him onto the blood-splattered bed where he lay facedown.

Odessa let the rifle dangle as she looked at his back. The bullet had exited high between the shoulders, leaving a ragged hole in the Levi's jacket where a red stain was quickly spreading. She laid the rifle on the table and reached to trace the contour of Billy's ear with one finger. "I'm really sorry," she said. "I'm really, really sorry."

Moving quickly, she scooped the money back into the bag and went out of the trailer, stepping carefully over the body of Duane Scales. In a moment she came back in and reached under the pillow for Billy's pistol before leaving the trailer once more.

## 30

Siquani listened to the Thunder Boys moving across the western mountains. They were running, leaping from peak to peak, striking fire from the granite that flared off into the blackening sky. Their voices boomed a protective warning at him, and he felt the bones of his spine harden and lift his shoulders and back until he stood as straight as a tall pine. Clouds rushed from the four corners to collide and form a lowering ceiling, and lightning began to whip across the sky and strike at the earth.

The rain came at first in sparse, heavy droplets that lashed his head and shoulders like small stones, and then the tempo increased until the whole world seemed filled with pellets of water that struck the earth and bounced a few inches before falling to an infinity of tiny streams. Siquani bowed his head beneath the pummeling, hugging his arms to his chest and feeling the water running in countless falls from the highlands of his body. Death had come out of the west and was pounding the resilient earth, and with it the Thunder Boys had come, too, carrying new life. Out of the earth, ancient bones began to emerge, washed with harsh rain from the edges and sides of arroyos.

"Billy," Siquani said, the sound of his voice erased in the crashing cloudburst. Slowly he began to walk down the hill, continuing past the wheelbarrow with his eyes fixed upon the earth where water gathered and surged in every crack and fissure, joining and swelling toward the plains and the farther valley. As he walked, the rain redoubled its assault until the surface of the earth seemed to be a single flow that lifted and moved him as it beat down the grasses and carved free the roots of piñon and cedar.

# 31

Odessa shoved the gunnysack behind the pickup seat and jumped in, pulling the door closed just as the cloudburst struck the windshield and hood. She laid the gun on the seat beside her and flipped the wiper switch to high speed before backing the truck around.

On the highway the rain struck the asphalt and leapt back toward the sky. She strained to see through the flood on the windshield, the cross-motion of falling and rising rain leaving her dizzy and disoriented. When she turned into the long driveway to Will's ranch house, the Dodge fishtailed across the cattleguard before the rear wheels grabbed and shot the pickup forward.

She pulled up in front of the adobe, sliding the pistol beneath the seat before she jumped out and ran to the door. Knocking twice, she pushed the door open, shouting, "Will? Is anybody here?"

Will emerged from the kitchen, his flannel shirt untucked from his jeans and his wool socks silent on the wooden floor.

"Odessa?" he said, looking at her as if he wasn't sure.

"Will," she said, running to him and throwing her arms around him.

He stood stiff and awkward, his arms half raised, as she began to sob into his chest. "What's wrong?" he said finally.

Odessa pushed herself away from him, choking her words out through a terrified voice. "They killed Billy," she said.

"What? Billy?" He took two quick steps to the gun cabinet, opening it and jerking the deer rifle out.

As he headed for the door, Odessa said, "No, Will, wait. I think they might be coming here."

He stopped and turned back to her, looking dazed. "Who?" he said.

"Two men came to the trailer looking for money they said Billy had. They made Mouse show them where Billy lived. When Billy wouldn't tell them where the other half of their money was, they killed Billy and Mouse. I got away when they shot Billy."

Will sat down on the couch. "Siquani?" he asked. "Was Grampa Siquani there?"

Odessa shook her head. "I didn't see him."

"Jesus Christ," Will said softly. "Billy."

In the doorway between the living room and kitchen, Maggie appeared, leaning awkwardly on the cast and growling, the hackles of her shoulders raised and her massive canines bared. "I'm scared," Odessa said.

Will looked up at her as though seeing her for the first time. "You think they followed you here?"

She shook her head. "No. I got to the highway before anybody left the trailer. But they know your name. They'll find out where you live."

He nodded, watching Maggie still growling in the doorway. Behind the huge dog he saw the squat silhouette of Molly peering through Maggie's legs. Absentmindedly he thought that it must have been the rain that had driven the shy pig into the house with a stranger and that the back door must be open.

"You and Billy were involved in something," Odessa said.

Again, Will nodded. He rose to his feet and went to the gun cabinet. Taking out a box of shells, he shoved several into the ought-six before leaning the rifle against the wall. Next he took out the thirty-thirty and filled the magazine in it, leaning it beside the bigger rifle. Finally, he lifted an ancient twenty-gauge shotgun from the cabinet, looked at it, and put it back.

"I came here looking for you and Billy," Odessa said from behind him. "I met your wife."

He turned to face her. "My ex-wife."

"She said you were still married."

He nodded. "Technically."

"She was nice. Is she still here?"

He looked at her strangely. "She's gone back to Albuquerque." Without saying more, he went into the kitchen and down the hallway, the dog and pig following. At the back of the house, he closed the door and dropped a heavy oak bar into brackets across the massive door before going into the big bedroom.

Rain was bouncing off the sill of the open window and glancing into the room. The floor near the window glistened with water. The summer heat and rain combined to make the room feel like a sauna.

He pulled the heavy outside shutters closed and slid an iron bar into place and then closed and latched the two halves of the window and hooked them. As he left the bedroom Maggie trailed after him, but the pig slipped away, heading for the smaller back room.

In the living room, Odessa was standing in the same place, apparently still in the same position, and he realized for the first time that she was soaked, her hair hanging straight and heavy and her clothes dark with water.

"You need to dry off," he said. "I think you could probably wear some of Jace's clothes. I'll show you." He turned and retraced his steps to the bedroom, Odessa following close behind and Maggie retreating in hostility to a corner of the kitchen.

Inside the bedroom, he pointed to the chest of drawers and then went to the closet, throwing open the door. "Take whatever you want," he said before he turned and left the room.

When he was gone, Odessa looked around. The room was different. The dust and cobwebs were gone, and the bed, though unmade, was clean. She stripped off her wet clothes, standing the boots carefully beside the bed and hanging pants, shirt, and underwear over a straight-backed chair. Freed of the clothes, she stretched luxuriously and then went to the door, opening it just enough to put her head out.

"Will," she half shouted, and when he answered, she said, "Do you have a towel I could use to dry off?"

In a moment he appeared outside the door, carefully not looking at the crack in the door where her hand reached out for the towel. "Thank you," she said as she closed the door and stepped back into the warm dampness of the room.

She ran the surprisingly soft towel over her body, starting with her calves and carefully drying every part until she finished with her hair. As she laid the towel over the end of the bed, she noticed something shiny and black, and bent farther to lift up a pair of bikini panties.

Holding the underwear to the light from the window, she smiled and then bent to slip them on, pulling them up over her hips with her eyes closed and the smile still on her face. She stepped in front of the full-length mirror and turned to one side and then the other. The small, centered triangle of shiny black rose to thin bands over each of her lean hips, and she turned fully around to look over her shoulder at the narrow vee in the back. She ran a finger beneath one side of the panties from front to back, arching her shoulders slightly and smiling. A flimsy black bra lay on a chair near the bed, and she looked at it for a moment before going to the closet to sort through the dresses, blouses, and skirts there, marveling at what Jace Striker had left behind. Will's wife had either wanted a completely new life, or she had wanted to be sure her claim to this one was unbroken.

She found a white cotton Mexican dress with red flowers embroidered along the buttons down the front and held it up over her breasts. When she slipped the dress on, it came halfway down her thighs, the rolled sleeves reaching to her elbows. She buttoned it almost to the top, exposing a vee of dark flesh that shone invitingly in the mirror. Her black hair hung straight over the shoulders of the white dress, leaving a damp pattern where it touched the material. The cotton dress felt cool and exciting, sensitively brushing against her erect nipples as she walked to the bedroom door. Outside, the rain hammered on the roof and walls, and the house seemed ready to break open with the thunder that exploded again and again right overhead.

Will stood at the living room window, watching the rain-blurred road that led to the highway. When she entered the room, he spoke without looking around.

"The doors and windows are locked. Nobody could get in without busting in, and we'd hear them. Besides, Maggie would . . ." He turned as he spoke, and his face seemed to freeze.

"I hope this is okay," Odessa said, her expression open and questioning.

Involuntarily, his eyes moved from her bare feet and the long muscles of her legs up the lightly embroidered dress to her mouth and dark eyes framed by the intensely black hair. He breathed deeply. "Sure," he said at last. "It's fine."

"You were about to say that Maggie will warn us if someone tries to break in."

He nodded.

"It might take them a couple of days to find out where you live," she added.

"Tomorrow I'll get the sheriff. Billy and I let this thing go too far."

"Why don't you call the sheriff right now?"

"The storm's knocked the phone out. We'll be okay in here till morning. You know how to use a rifle?"

She nodded. "My father taught me."

"There's a twelve-gauge in the back bedroom, and that twenty-gauge in there still works." He motioned toward the gun cabinet. "Plus those two. Could you eat dinner?"

"I'm not hungry, but I'd like to cook something for you. You look like hell, and maybe it would help take my mind off the horrible things that've happened."

"Well," he replied, "I have some corn in the garden, but it's not ready. I don't know what's . . ."

She turned and he watched her walk into the kitchen, her body moving inside the white dress with the smooth motion of a stream, or something he couldn't quite name.

As he took the smaller pump shotgun out of the cabinet and slipped shells into the magazine, he heard cabinets opening and pots rattling in the kitchen.

"Too bad it's so warm in here. A fire would be nice," she called from the other room.

He looked at the fireplace, where he'd installed a stove-insert ten years earlier, and at the stack of split piñon and juniper that had sat along the wall next to it for months. Without replying, he began to build a fire in the insert, crumpling newspaper and laying kindling in a precise pattern before adding split cedar. In a few minutes a small fire was blazing up over larger pieces of pine, the smell of the cedar kindling sweet on the damp air.

He stood looking out the window, the thirty-thirty cradled in one arm. The creek had changed already from a trough of dry earth, stone, and desiccated weeds to a gleaming brown snake that thrashed from bank to bank as it rushed beneath the wooden bridge two hundred yards away. A flash flood, people called such things, gully washers. He thought of Billy's trailer and what must be there. The place inside him where Billy had always been had become a dark hole that held him like a whirlpool. Had they killed Grampa

Siquani, too? In his mind he saw an image of the old man, bent against lines of black rain, moving resolutely. The picture reminded him of something powerful and familiar, of people he had known walking like that, or himself, or perhaps something he'd dreamed years before. But he felt that the old man was alive and moving somewhere in the storm.

The rain darkened the long day quickly, drumming without alteration throughout the afternoon and evening, breaking open with the extraordinary thunder that seemed to hover around the house, smashing against the thick adobe and dancing like bones on the flat roof. When Odessa called him he went into the kitchen and saw her standing before a table he didn't recognize. Against a burgundy tablecloth, two wineglasses held a shimmering black liquid, and before each glass were white plates with crescents of gold and green.

"I hope you don't mind," she said. "I found the plates and glasses up there." She looked at the cabinet above the refrigerator. "The wine, too. And I'm afraid I used the last of your eggs for the omelets." She sat down and picked up the wineglass, cupping the bowl of the glass between spread fingers and raising her eyes toward him.

He leaned the rifle against the wall and stared first at the table and then at Odessa in his wife's dress. Jace had bought the dress on a trip to Nogales just after they were married. She'd worn it once or twice and then left it in the closet. Within the white cotton of the dress, Odessa's flesh was a luminescent brown, as though she held light just beneath the surface of her skin. The overhead bulb cast a faint, bloodred crescent through the wineglass onto her breast.

"I'd forgotten I had that wine," he said. His knee began to ache abruptly, as though it had just become aware of the rain outside, and he pulled out the chair opposite her and sat down, straightening the stiff leg beneath the table.

"Even in the worst times, we should toast life and strength." She smiled a half-smile as she lifted her glass in his direction.

He hesitated, his fingers on the stem of his glass. Finally he shook his head. "Wait," he said. He stood up and walked to the sink, tilting the glass and pouring half of the wine onto the darkly stained basin, watching the liquid follow the water marks as it disappeared.

"I understand," she said, lifting the glass to her mouth and downing half the wine in one drink. "For Billy." She went to a cupboard and lifted out a half-gallon of cheap burgundy. "Cooking wine, I suspect?" she said as she refilled her glass and then walked around the table to stand beside him.

He felt her hip against his shoulder as she leaned to fill his glass, her muscles hard and warm through the white cotton. And when she was seated once again, the big wine bottle on the counter behind her, he lifted his glass and held it toward her until she carefully touched hers to his.

He took a drink and felt his face crease with the bitter wine. "This is pretty bad wine, isn't it?" he said.

She smiled and took a sip. "Awful," she responded. "Really awful." She took a longer sip and set the glass down.

"I don't know how long I've had it."

"Well," she lifted a forkful of the omelet and held it halfway to her mouth. "A month longer and you'd have pretty good vinegar." She swallowed the omelet and lifted the wineglass, holding the glass to her lips for a long time and watching him before she drank. When she set it down half of the wine was gone.

"You're the most isolated man I've ever seen," she said.

He forked a bit of omelet into his mouth and chewed slowly for a moment before answering. "I live alone."

"No. It's more than that." She seemed to study his face. "I know what it is," she said at last. "I think you're like me."

He shook his head and drank more of the wine.

"There's a core that even you can't reach, isn't there? Some place inside that echoes now and then, so that you know something's there but you also know you'll never see it or really feel it. You look in the mirror, and there's nothing there. Right?"

"I didn't think you were a romantic, Odessa. But the answer

is no. Wrong. What you see is what you get. Not much, huh? I'm simple. Billy was complex."

She finished the second glass of wine and turned to lift the bottle from the counter and refill her glass. When she held the bottle toward him, he shook his head.

"One of us had better stay awake," he said.

She set the bottle on the table and lifted her glass, smiling over the top of it. "Don't worry," she said. "I'll stay awake. I've been trying to get drunk all my life, and I've never been able to. I've always envied people who could."

"I hope you don't have a delicate stomach. That wine'll do a job on a person."

"Like a coyote," she replied, the smile returning after another swallow of wine. "Sometimes I feel like there's nothing in the world I couldn't devour."

"Coyote's appetite gets him poisoned sometimes. Some ranchers around these parts still put out bait. I hate that. I really hate it."

"You haven't complimented my cooking yet." She was looking at him steadily, her skin seeming to glow, and he heard a log collapse in the fireplace.

He looked down at his plate, surprised to find that he'd eaten the whole omelet. "It must have been delicious," he said.

"You must have been hungry." She took another bite. "Living alone makes a person hungry." She smiled. "Eating your own creations gets old, doesn't it?"

He washed the dishes while she sat at the table swirling a remnant of wine inside her glass and watching him. When he had put the dishes away, he picked up the rifle. "Thank you," he said, and then he went to stand at the front window again, watching the evening spread upward from the creek, darkness splashing over the heavy planks of the old bridge and rising toward the house as the rain kept up its pounding. The thunder had moved eastward, existing now as remote echoes like corrugated tin whipping in a wind.

"You shouldn't be in front of the window like that, with the firelight behind you," she said from behind him. "You'll stand out against these white walls."

"You're right. I was thinking of Billy." He stepped to the side, away from the window, and turned toward her. "Thanks again for dinner. I've been living by myself for so long I don't even know how to act around somebody else."

"Jace doesn't cook for you, ever?"

He shook his head. "Jace doesn't come here."

"Today?"

"Today was the first time in months, and it'll probably be the last for a year."

"You sound like you miss her."

He sat down on the couch, the rifle leaning against his leg, and rubbed a big hand over his jaw before speaking. "I guess I do. I didn't even know how much until today. And now Billy."

"Maybe Jace'll be back sooner than you think."

He shook his head, saying nothing.

She sat down on the rug in front of the couch, her legs tucked beneath her. "I'm really scared, Will," she said. "I'm really scared."

He looked at the dark square of the window and listened to the wind now hurling rain against the house. "Maggie'll hear anybody trying to get in," he said, "even if you and I don't. And Molly's in the back of the house somewhere; she doesn't miss anything." He stood up and unfolded heavy shutters across the inside of the window, hooking them in place at top and bottom. The storm became a dull thrashing through the thick wooden shutters.

"Molly the pig?" she said.

He nodded and picked up the rifle again in the darkened room. "She's afraid of her own shadow. Any strange noise in the house and she squeals like a pig." He smiled thinly at her.

"You sound tired," she said.

"Yeah. I'm about to turn in. You can sleep in the big room, the one you changed in."

"What will you do, sleep on that couch?"

"No. I sleep in one of the back rooms usually." He looked

around him. "The doors are bolted and the windows locked. This old adobe has inch-and-a-half-thick shutters. It was made for Indian raids, I think. Nobody can get in. Not even white people. And here." He held the rifle toward her. "Keep this by the bed. I have a twelve-gauge in the back room."

She took the rifle and watched him disappear through the doorway before she headed toward the bedroom.

A scream followed by panicked squeals awakened him from a dream of water. An ocean of fresh water was rising around him and his wife and children isolated on a single hilltop. The sounds of dancing came from across the water, and he was straining to hear more when the scream cut through the dream and sent him to his feet in nothing but boxer shorts. Wedged halfway beneath the bed, Molly was crying in little grunts, and Maggie stood straddle-legged looking out of the door of the room, growling.

He reached for the shotgun and, pushing the dog aside, ran toward the big bedroom. When he shoved the door open and flipped the light switch, Odessa was sitting up in the bed, the sheet held up to her neck with both hands and a terrified look on her face.

As she seemed to recognize him, the terror disappeared, and he could see tears running over her cheeks. "I was dreaming," she said. "I'm sorry."

"You sure it was just a dream that scared you?" He took another step into the room and glanced around. Behind him Maggie continued to growl.

"Yes. It was horrible."

"I'll be back in a second," he replied.

When he had made a quick tour of the house, checking both doors and all the windows, he returned to find her in the same position, the rifle leaning against the chest of drawers near the bed and Maggie standing beside the bed, fangs bared and growling.

"Maggie," he said, but the dog ignored him.

"She doesn't like me," Odessa whispered.

He grabbed the dog's collar and lifted her backward, turning her in a gentle half-circle and then leading her to the bedroom door. At the door he said, "Go to bed, girl," and the dog walked slowly away toward the back room, the cast making a splintery sound on the wooden floor.

"Maggie's a funny dog," he said when he turned back around. "She's used to sleeping in here. She's probably mad as hell that you took her bed."

"I'm scared, Will," she replied. She began to cry, her sobs barely audible, and he leaned the shotgun against the wall and sat on the edge of the bed.

"It'll be okay," he said, reaching to touch her arm with the tips of his fingers. "Tomorrow morning we'll go into town and get the sheriff. It's drug money. I have the other half hidden out back."

"Could you stay here with me," she said softly. "Please?" She leaned forward, releasing the sheet with one hand to grasp his upper arm. The sheet fell away from her shoulder, exposing one breast, but she didn't seem to notice as she leaned her forehead against his chest. "I'm scared," she added, her voice breaking in a sob she fought to control. "They'll kill us."

He stroked the back of her head, letting his hand slide down the long slope of her hair. "It's okay," he said. Very carefully he gripped her arm and extricated himself from her embrace. "I'll stay in here."

He stood up and picked up the shotgun, pulling the door partway shut before turning out the light and going to sit in the straight-backed chair with the gun across his lap.

"Why don't you lie down?" In the complete dark of the shuttered room and closed house her voice seemed directionless, floating from all four corners and hovering in the air.

He sat for a few minutes without replying. The thunder rumbled far to the east, two voices whispering back and forth as though in urgent conversation, and the rain swept in deliberate waves across the roof, growing less intense with each wave. The hard chair cut into his shoulder blades and hips, and finally he rose and walked delicately through the blackness, finding the end of the bed with his legs and maneuvering around to the far side of the headboard. Feeling the cool adobe wall, he leaned the shotgun between it and the wooden headboard and, probing in the dark, turned down the comforter and slid between the sheets.

He lay there, realizing only after several minutes that his eyes were still open. When he forced them closed, the darkness remained the same, the only difference the pattern of sounds that came to him with the rain, muted thunder, and, from across the bed, the choked and faintly audible sobbing Odessa was trying to suppress.

He thought of Billy, and then of Grampa Siquani. This time he saw the two of them side by side, faces bowed before the black rain, walking determinedly eastward. The sun was rising over the flat landscape, sending a red path through the streaking rain toward the two walkers.

He became aware that he was dreaming when his right side grew warm and he woke to feel Odessa's body touching his. Her arm lay across his chest.

"I'm terrified, Will," she whispered. "I felt all alone in the dark over there. I didn't think I would wake you."

Silently he let his breath escape. Her bare skin was hot against his arm and leg, an almost painful electrical current flowing from her deep into his core. "He was always there," he whispered back. "From the first time I can remember, Billy was there."

She moved more tightly against him. "Maybe that's why I needed to touch you, Will. It's as though Billy's still alive in you." Her voice caught, and he felt dampness where her face touched his bare arm.

"It'll be okay," he said, and he shifted the arm she leaned against and turned to his side, so that his arm now lay under her and her head rested on his chest. As if acting of its own volition, his free hand stroked her shoulder and arm, and with the action he became suddenly aware of the focused heat of her breast against him.

"Maybe we could get the sheriff tonight," she said.

"With this storm we can't be sure how the roads are. We could get stuck and be sitting ducks in the dark out there. The rain'll be gone by morning, I think."

His senses were filled with her, a sharp, musty fragrance that seemed to warm even the air he breathed. The nipple pressing against his upper arm had grown hard.

Her hand slid like fire across his stomach. And then, with a subtle shift, she was above him, her mouth moving gently across his forehead and down his cheeks. As her lips brushed his own with a faint touch, he breathed in the dizzying richness of her breath, a scent of warm earth and cedar and something deeper still. Her hand reached down for him, and he had a feeling of being pulled into the liquid earth itself.

As she moved over him, he heard the soft undulations of rain upon the house and sensed the dark motions of the sky that poured like a flood out of the west. He imagined lightning that walked with violence across the land. For the first time he realized that the blades of lightning didn't stop at rock and tree but must reach down deep into the flesh of the earth and lay a pattern there. His hands reached for her shoulders and slid down the tight muscles of her back, pulling her closer. And as she thrust more violently against him, raising herself until he almost escaped and then plunging him deeper still, he felt suddenly that he was locked in a struggle with some kind of enemy. She hates me, he thought as he felt the fluid of his body gathering and rushing upward. Her teeth sank into his shoulder and he heard his own scream as he poured himself into her, her hips locked on his own as though she were afraid something might escape.

And when it was over he felt her above him, her muscles tensed, her face poised in the dark to watch him. His groin and legs were wet, as though a hot salt water had been splashed over them, and his shoulder burned with pain.

In one motion she lifted herself from him, leaving him feeling cold and vulnerable as he heard her move in the dark. He lay still, his arms at his sides, listening to her feet whisper on the floor, until the room was suddenly flooded with light.

Odessa stood at the foot of the bed, the thirty-thirty held in front of her and her body gleaming in the light from the overhead bulb. As his eyes began to focus, he could see droplets of water on her breasts and on the flat surface of her belly, her pubic hair and thighs dark and beaded with liquid.

"Where's the rest of the money?" she said. "I have Billy's half. Now I want the rest."

He looked at her in silence, noticing the way her dark hair lay across her shoulders and touched the outside of each breast, and the surprising cords of muscle on her shoulders and arms. Her eyes were black, her open lips set in a thin smile. His shoulder throbbed, and he thought of that mouth on his, the white teeth sunk into his flesh. Outside the house now the rain was silent, the thunder gone to some other place.

"You killed Billy," he said.

"Correct," she replied. "It was just the money. I liked Billy and I like you, but I spent a long time planning this, and you and Billy screwed it up. Do you want to tell me exactly where you hid it? I'm sure I can find it myself, but you could make it easier. Though I don't see why you'd do that since you know I'm going to kill you, too."

He watched her, saying nothing.

"You deserve everything that's happening to you, you know. This land was the home of my ancestors. They never pretended to own it, but their bones are in the earth you call yours. You and Billy aren't supposed to be here. You're no better than the whites. You let them push you off your own land in the east and march you into the homes of other Indian people in that so-called Territory, and you became just like them. You let them fuck your women and create half-breeds like you. Westering, it's called by white historians. That's what your families did. You came here and became part of the whole pattern. You live on top of my people's bones now."

"So it's not just the money," he replied.

"I have a Ph.D. in genocide," she said. "When I was young and innocent I thought I could get a white education and fight back. But I was stupid. Now," she steadied the rifle, "I'm going to have the American dream. Almost a million dollars. It's not that much really, but I'm taking it all south. I can live fairly well in South America with a million dollars. I'll be a rich, brown-skinned Yankee in the middle of all those poor Indians."

"You'll have to find it for yourself," he said. "Maybe you'll dig up some of your ancestors' bones while you're at it."

"I liked you better than Billy," she said. "You're stronger than he was. And I'll confess that I'm going to enjoy driving away from this place with a million dollars and part of you still inside of me, an amazing amount of you really. It's too bad men can never know what that's like."

Maggie erupted into the room with a thundering snarl, bracing her feet and confronting Odessa with fangs bared. The rifle exploded, and Will felt his body hammered as he was thrown sideways out of the bed. He landed on his back and reached for the stock of the shotgun beside the bed, swinging the gun with one hand and firing. The shotgun's blast struck Odessa in the chest as she worked the lever of the rifle still aimed at him.

Will heard Maggie struggle for purchase and then clatter out of the room. He listened to the sounds of the cast retreating, his ears ringing with the noise of the twelve-gauge, and then he let the shotgun fall to the floor and pulled himself up onto the bed. His left side flamed with pain, and blood poured down his side and leg. Spotting Odessa's damp white T-shirt hanging on the foot of the bed, he wadded it up and clamped it against his side with his arm. He took a step toward Odessa and passed out.

# 32

He awoke to light. It poured through the open window and flared from the tall mirror to flood the room. He closed his eyes again and opened them gradually until the objects of the room came into focus. For a moment he wondered where he was, and he struggled to put events in order. The hospital room had been dark, so he wasn't there any longer. His left arm lay awkwardly alongside the bandage over his ribs, but the pain in his side was a fraction of what he remembered. He was home.

The door of the room pushed slowly open, but no one was there. Then he saw the head and shoulders of Maggie moving smoothly toward the bed.

"Hey, girl," he said as she nuzzled his arm. "No more cast."

"I took her in to have it removed this morning while you were sleeping." Jace stood in the open doorway, smiling at him. "Harrison said she'd be a little tender for a while." She walked to the bed. "How do you feel?"

He sat up, feeling as though one side of his body had been tightened. "Great," he said, recalling his first awakening in the hospital and the sight of Jace's face then.

"They said your recovery was remarkable. The infection in your shoulder was almost worse than the gunshot."

"Infection?"

She watched him silently for a moment. "They said it looked like a bite of some kind. There'll be a small scar, but it won't be your first, will it? Ready for breakfast?"

He nodded. "Sounds wonderful. I guess I'm hungry."

"Good. Nate called this morning and asked if you'd come down to the sheriff's office when you feel up to it, maybe in a few days, to answer some questions. He said they found her fingerprints on the rifle that killed Billy and the others. I don't think he should be telling me so much, from a legal perspective."

He watched her gray eyes as she spoke, remembering Odessa the night of the storm. She sat on the edge of the bed and rested her hand on his leg.

"He said she and Billy must have been involved in some kind of drug deal together. They found a bag with nearly half a million dollars in Billy's pickup, and they say it was Billy's rifle that killed the man in the helicopter as well as two of the others in Billy's trailer. They also found Billy's Land Cruiser in the barn with bullet holes they say were made by the gun they found at the crash site.

"I don't believe it," she added. "Do you? Billy wouldn't have hurt anyone."

He shook his head. "No," he said. "What about Grampa Siquani?"

"He's okay. It was Grampa who discovered Billy and called the sheriff. That's how they found you so quickly."

She paused on the verge of more, and he waited. When she didn't continue, he said, "What is it?"

"Grampa Siquani told me he might be going home."

"What does he mean, 'going home'?"

"I don't know; maybe he'll tell you. But he's giving you the other half of the ranch. He had me make out the forms."

She picked up his hand. "By the way, I quit my job. While you were helpless, I moved home."

"What about . . . ?"

Before he could finish, she shook her head. "I wanted to come home. There was an opening in the public defender's office in Socorro, and there's someone in my firm who has pull. He owed me a favor, and I got the job."

"It's a long drive," he said.

"Forty minutes. Just a bad day in Albuquerque traffic. I'm going down there this morning to sign the papers. It's a good thing I got a job so fast, considering the mortgage payments on Billy's ranch we're going to have to make."

"Did you think that maybe we should talk about it?"

She shook her head. "I thought we decided the last time I was here."

"Well, I never had to decide." He hesitated. "But there's something I need to tell you."

Placing her hand on his lips, she said, "No. It's a complex world, Will. We have to live with our secrets."

She bent and kissed him lightly. "Forever, and I mean that. I'll bring your breakfast in here."

"No. I'd rather eat in the kitchen. I'm ready to get out of bed."

"Both Si and Holly will be here tonight. They're coming together from El Paso. They were both up while you were in the hospital, but you weren't awake. And by the way, Holly's pregnant. You're about to become Grampa Striker."

"One more thing," he said as she was about to vanish through the doorway. "Sell that damned Jeep Cherokee."

She paused and looked over her shoulder. "I don't want to know, Will. Why she shot you, or what she was doing here like that. Nate figures she just didn't want to leave anyone who could identify her. He's too much of a gentleman to mention the rest. I believe he thinks he can make that story work."

He closed his eyes and opened them again slowly. "What do you think?"

She looked directly at him. "I think he's right. They have the criminals, the gun, and the money. They'll be satisfied."

"And we have?"

She smiled thinly. "The rest of our lives."

# 33

Will stood outside the front door with Maggie behind him and watched Jace drive toward the highway. The day was huge and brittle with the light of early fall, the New Mexico sky a luminous blue. The creek ran two feet deep and clear beneath the little bridge, its delicate splashings carrying easily on the still air.

"The spring must be running," he said aloud, and then he saw the old man emerge from the juniper thicket beside the corral, a dozen crows scattering above him to land on the ridge of the barn.

Siquani walked slowly up to the house, a hat pulled low over his braids, and his hands shoved deep in his pants pockets.

"You're better, Grandson," the old man said when he was close. He placed a hand on Will's good shoulder.

"I was worried about you, Grampa," Will answered. "I've been worried."

"I had to help Billy find the path. He's very young, and for the young especially it can be a time of confusion. They been piling up things to hide it for all these years now. But our world is still here, Willum. Sometimes we forget because we got to look so hard to see it, and people get tired and forget how to look. But the animals know; they don't forget. We got to listen. I think maybe it's time to go home, Willum."

"Back to Oklahoma?"

Siquani shook his head in the negative. "You still got that house pig?"

Will nodded. "Jace exiled her to the barn. She's out back right now, I think, trying to figure out how to get to the corn. Jace and I would like you to live with us. To stay with us here on the ranch."

The old man looked eastward for a moment and then back at Will, shaking his head faintly. "I don't know. I been gone a long time; maybe I watched enough. This is a funny place to end up."

"We'd like you to live here with us." Will looked at the ground. "You know, Grampa, I feel like I'll have to learn how to live all over again. Billy was always there. There wasn't ever a time."

Siquani looked deeply into Will's eyes. "You got a lot of work here, Grandson. Billy is okay now. And this earth is full of death, but you can feel the life, too. The water has come back." He looked toward the creek. "Arturo is buried up by the spring now."

"Arturo?"

"The one in the tree."

"How'd you—"

"We cut that tree down. It was time for him to go. I think maybe him and Billy together went and brought the water home again. I was going to leave this morning, too, but them coyotes kept singing. Them coyotes and crows been having a big celebration all night and done wore me out. You got any strong coffee?"

Will nodded. "You won't find stronger, Grampa. And the corn is ripe. We'll have it for dinner tonight. Seven of the biggest ears you've ever seen."

The old man grinned widely and once more reached to touch Will's shoulder.

An hour later Will looked down at the old man asleep on the cot in the back room. The blue wool blanket rose and fell minutely with each breath. After a moment, he left the room, continuing out the back door of the house.

A thread of white cloud lay along the top of the Magdalena Mountains in the west. A hundred yards from the house, the creek ran in a shallow, steady current. Obviously something had brought the spring back to life, maybe the aquifer filling up with the heavy rain, or maybe a fault slipping somewhere in the earth to release water that had been long trapped. There was no way to know, but the creek that hadn't run much in a hundred years was running fast and clear toward the southeast. He closed his eyes and listened to the water slipping toward the distant Rio Grande. The earth around him felt heavy and dark, populated by the dead, piñon and grass seeds falling to burrow and sprout in flesh, tree roots reaching and twining through the eyes of the dead, stitching them to the ageless earth. How could a person live and walk upon such earth? he wondered. He felt a desire to flee, to find a place where nothing was buried, where the surface of the earth bared all secrets.

He went to the corral, putting a boot up on the splintered boards and leaning with folded arms against the top rail. Where a cornice of shadow spilled over the barn roof, the two ancient bulls stood shoulder to shoulder. Heads drooping close to the muddy earth and tattered hides marked with rain, the bulls seemed already part of the land. As for the heifers out on the range, they could continue to run wild until their time was over. With no bull around, the little herd would disappear in one generation, feeding coyotes and foxes somewhere up in the draws of the Magdalenas. The D-6 he'd sell to Nate's father-in-law.

As he walked toward the well, he watched the thickening trail of clouds in the west where a fine gray web of rain curved toward the mountains, the kind of rain that would dissipate before it touched the earth. He thought of how the higher canyons would feel beneath such clouds, of the way shadows would lie along the rock outcroppings and the fragrance of pine and cedar would lace the damp air. With the clouds already beginning to spread and deepen, there would be thunder up in the mountains by midday, and lightning would make its way down the crest toward the ranch.

The boards of the hatch cover were dark with rain, and water spread through the stunted grasses around the well. With the hand of his good arm, he grasped one edge of the cover to lift, and the board began to crumble in his grasp. When he moved around the well to grip the firmer ends of the planks and lift, he was startled by the lack of resistance.

He pushed the cover over backward, and it splashed upside down in the inch-deep water with no sign of the duffel bag. The nails had pulled out of the sodden wood, releasing the rope. He looked from the cover to the well itself. Water brimmed out of the hole, brilliantly clear. He sloshed closer to the edge and peered into the well. The water, lit by the eastern sun, seemed to reach forever toward the center of the earth, darkening from blue to black in the depths.

A breeze slid through the low grass and moved upon the water, bringing the scent of sage and cedar down from the hills. Thunder muttered in the mountains behind him as he bent closer, and out of the corner of one eye he saw a delicate branch of lightning slip from sky to earth. As he stared into the water, the reflection of a man rose and hovered just below the rippling surface, the image wavering and breaking apart before merging once more. He knelt in the cold water, and in the deepening well a crowd of faces began to rush upward only to shatter and flutter downward and then rise again with the motion of leaves in a fall wind.